Praise for *Lucky*:

'Betrayal, blackmail, a marriage on hold, *Lucky* has all the ingredients of a page-turning thriller or a top-notch noir crime novel and yet Edwards is also writing towards conversations about race and everyday social injustice too. Read *Lucky* because it embraces the concerns of our everyday humanity in a post-Brexit, post-pandemic world of debt and insecurity. Her protagonist, Etta, is driven by the forces of a world on the edge'
MONIQUE ROFFEY,
author of *The Mermaid of Black Conch*

'A brilliant portrayal of one woman's descent into the world of online gambling – I felt every spin of the wheel; the highs of adrenaline followed by stomach-churning nausea'
NIKKI SMITH, author of *All In Her Head*

'Addictive! I have been consumed by Etta's poignant and chaotic world, a tale of gambling and friendship and food and chances and love'
AMANDA REYNOLDS, author of *Close to Me*

'Tense beyond belief but impossible to put down. Dark, absorbing and brilliantly terrifying'
LOUISE HARE, author of *This Lovely City*

Lucky

Also by the author

Darling

Lucky

Rachel Edwards

4th ESTATE • *London*

4th Estate
An imprint of HarperCollins*Publishers*
1 London Bridge Street
London SE1 9GF

www.4thEstate.co.uk

HarperCollins*Publishers*
1st Floor, Watermarque Building, Ringsend Road
Dublin 4, Ireland

First published in Great Britain in 2021 by 4th Estate

1

A catalogue record for this book is available from the British Library

ISBN 978-0-00-836456-4 (hardback)
ISBN 978-0-00-836457-1 (trade paperback)

This novel is entirely a work of fiction.
The names, characters and incidents portrayed in it are the
work of the author's imagination. Any resemblance to actual persons,
living or dead, events or localities is entirely coincidental.

Set in Minion and Optima
emojis © Shutterstock

Printed and bound in CPI Group (UK) Ltd, Croydon

MIX
Paper from
responsible sources
FSC™ C007454

This book is produced from independently certified FSC paper
to ensure responsible forest management

Find out more about HarperCollins and the environment at
www.harpercollins.co.uk/green

To my parents, Patricia and Okon,
for taking a chance on the United Kingdom,
and each other

Fortune is painted blind, with a muffler afore her eyes, to signify to you that Fortune is blind; and she is painted also with a wheel, to signify to you, which is the moral of it, that she is turning, and inconstant, and mutability, and variation; and her foot, look you, is fixed upon a spherical stone, which rolls, and rolls, and rolls.

Henry V, Act 3 Scene VI. William Shakespeare

She electrifies the room. Her swallowed fear, her femaleness, the accounts that must soon be drawn from her – fugitive truths flushed out from the dark into the glare of the strip lights. Her difference. They all feel it, even the second policeman standing at the door.

She knows she is having an effect. Will it help her? Ordinarily, she has the advantage, a physical impact few choose to ignore. Still, her voice cannot grow bold enough, her phrasing stalls.

She does not like the one questioning her. He has tried to cow her with power talk – no lawyer on the way? – and a drip-drip of innuendo. Where are you from, originally? Your first home, your parents, your past. Her roots feel more foreign than ever in this crushing white room, before these most authorised of Englishmen. When she thinks of the sacrifices that have been made, the paths that have brought her here ... Where are you from? He does not get to ask that question. But of course, he does.

She is under arrest.

The policeman by the door clears his throat, a fist up against his dark beard. The blond man rises and moves away so his colleague can approach the desk. This other man, PC Howard, who she had assumed to be a junior officer, sits down in the vacated seat, taking his time about taking up space, telling her – with his amused stare, and the entitled set of his arms and chest, stretching back, now leaning close – he is in charge.

'How?' he asks.

'How what?' she says.

'How the hell have you got here?'

She looks up. The losses, and the risks, and the lies; the terrible fun, and the wrong men, and the surprising choices, and the victories; the boundaries breached and the many rivers of cash crossed; the unknowable connections, pathways and turns, a constellation spreading backwards to infinity; all that has brought her to this point.

'Just lucky, I guess.'

PART I

Chapter One

SUNDAY, 1 APRIL 2018

Today, Easter Sunday, was going to blow their lives wide open. She felt the pressure building, sweet, acidulous and fizzing like fine French wine: the moment she had been waiting for, ready to pop.

'Did you hear me, Etta? Come down here to me, my love.'

This had to be it, at last. They had already exchanged ostentatious chocolate eggs and now she thought about it, Ola had, for some days, seemed on edge, over-excited, secretive. She scooped the contents of their laundry basket up into her arms and edged downstairs, peering over the clothes heap, the musk of him right under her nose.

'Etta!' Ola called again.

'I'm here, what is it?'

'Abeg! Oya, come down, woman!'

'Ah! Abeg! Oga, I dey come now!'

Each one's laughter reached the other.

'Come down please, my dearest dear. Please. Come through to the sitting room for a minute. I want to talk to you.'

Yes, a pressing matter. A joyful matter.

A snatch of Ola's melodic mumbling, his 'happy' tune, drifted through the door. *Hm-mm, do-di-do.*

Etta had felt a stirring, then that old horse-kick of hope. Could this be it, this time? Now, as she stood clutching soiled cotton? It would be their 'anniversary' in two weeks' time. The upcoming sham celebration had slammed into her thoughts over and over in recent days: *All that fake rubbish again. Nonsense!* But now . . .

The lounge, vacuumed that morning, was ideal for planned kneeling, better than a cold restaurant floor. He just might.

'I'm coming!' She dumped their dirty clothes against the newel post.

Ola looked up at her from the sofa and gave his trademark dazzle. The impact of his bone-white teeth bared from the dark sateen of his face never failed to impress her. She did not smile back with equal confidence. Instead she sat down next to him and adopted the expression of someone you could ask anything at all; someone who was more than ready to swallow any doubts and acquiesce.

'I've decided, Etta. We need something to look forward to.'

This was it. 'OK.'

'I thought we might start to think ahead, make a few plans.'

'Go on.'

'I wanted to ask you.'

'Yes?'

'Well, it's just . . . OK. Where would you like to go most, if we could go away?'

That throb, right at the base of her throat.

'The Maldives. It's supposed to be gorgeous. But that's a . . .' *honeymoon* '. . . dream. No way we can afford it.'

'Heh.'

'But . . .' *Say it, Ola.* 'Why?'

'I think we should think about going there.'

'When?'

'Soon enough, God willing. We're still saving, of course, so it would not be this year, maybe not next year either. But you know . . . Someday. We need goals to keep us on track, heh?'

Etta rose from the sofa, holding her arms out before her, as if they still carried stained laundry.

'That's it?' she asked.

'Heh?'

'Is *that* all you wanted to say: we'll go to the Maldives "someday"? Well, if we're just making lists, let's also go to Hawaii, someday, and Antarctica before it melts, someday, and go to hell, someday—'

'Etta! What's up with you?'

'I thought you meant real *plans*, Ola, proper plans, not just more silly talk. Tcha!' She sucked her teeth with virtuoso flair.

'Ah, I understand.' He leaned forward so his elbows rested on his knees, looked grave. 'Etta, we've been through this a thousand times. We need to have a deposit for a house saved up before we can even think about getting married.'

'But Ola, we've got savings!'

'Not nearly enough.'

'But—'

'Etta. We've talked about this. We need at least thirty thousand before we can even think about it, otherwise the mortgage repayments would cut us like a knife.'

'We'd manage, Ola.'

'We'd be broke, I'm telling you. Payments too big, income too small. QED.'

'Don't give me all your QED, Ola. We would get by. We could make up the money later.'

'Ah! Listen to me o. Why are you trying to make me feel bad?'

'I'm not! But not everything can hang on money.'

'Wah? Everything hangs on money. Ah! If only you understood. On a monthly basis we are battered, Etta. Ba. *Turd*. If we marry without the funds, it will only get worse.'

'But Ola, it's you who doesn't understand!'

'Eh? Abeg! May you no dey vex me! I always understand. I am a great big tower of understanding. Tcha!'

'Always, these excuses! I thought . . .'

'What? What did you think now?'

'Nothing,' said Etta, standing. Ivory chiffon floated way out of sight, confetti went down the drain. 'Not a bloody thing. I've got to get this washing on.'

'Ah! And now you're bloodying me and everything. I'm going out!'

He jumped up and walked away.

'Go, go!'

The door closed just short of a slam.

Off he stormed, into the badlands of Rilton, their nondescript home town, where he was more likely to die of boredom or be brought down by crimes against fashion than come to any real harm.

'Bloody, bloody hell,' said Etta.

It was all 'someday' with that man. The contentment with which he browsed the future, lazy and optimistic, as if he owned the deeds to endless acres of time in which their lives might unfold. It was breaking something in her, something more than mere patience. It messed her up, caused her insides to ferment. What was passion without *urgency*?

She shoved the clothes into the asthmatic washing machine then returned to the lounge and switched the TV on, too angry to focus on a programme but too angry to sit in silence.

Easter surprise? Try April Fool. However, she needed to chill, dial it down a touch. They would marry, she was sure of it. Their parents' traditions carried a certain weight and, between them, they were three quarters Nigerian, after all. She simply had to sort out the financial shortfall.

Etta knew that their savings stood at around £22,000. But they needed more, faster. What could she do? How could she get the money? She had tried everything. She had looked for work-from-home opportunities, a second job to expand their income. She had surfed and scrolled, finding not one money-spinner that was feasible, legal, or practicable without funnelling her life savings into some fellow Nigerian's bank account. (At least they all now said they were Nigerian, but that could easily just be a stereotype smokescreen or a double-bluff by others with sinister motives.)

She had soon given up. It had proven too depressing: so very many people must have bitten to make it worth these stateless hustlers dangling their syphilitic bait. She had blown out the homeworkers' schemes, the get-rich-quick schemes and every other scheme that had landed in her inbox, cosmetically enhanced to resemble an 'opportunity'.

An ad came on, jarring her from her thoughts. This ad, and so many like it, punctuated her day: air-punching carnivals of largely slender Caucasian females, with always one markedly unglamorous black woman widening her eyes like a cartoon as she presumably won that week's fried chicken money.

'Deposit £10 today and get £50 more to play with!'

Pink-and-white ads, produced by pink-and-white ad execs to please boards of pink-and-white overlords; ads effervescing with acceptable pink-and-white women; each of them happier than their well-made-up faces could take.

Despite her distaste, their elation was galvanising. Could this be the answer? She had already made the calculations: £200 per week, that was all. Put by £200 per week and she and

Ola would be settled in their first home by the middle of next year. Their roots would then grow together, spreading under the foundations of their home, until they could not grow apart (not even if they fell into negative equity after Brexit); their life would exemplify the quote that someone, someday, would read at their wedding. One life from which adventures, security, babies and as-yet-unthought-of advantages would spring. Real life, at last.

She was right to start culturing this creamy future: romance died unless you fed it often, with your mind. Ola would never spend his house savings and, during these long unmarried months it had somehow become his money to manage, no matter that she had put in the majority of their savings. Leave it to him and bang went the dress that would break Instagram, the chocolate cupcake tower and the meadow flower confetti.

Etta tapped on her phone. Into her upturned hands fell a windfall of websites: Vixen Bingo, Leggsy Heaven, Celebration Bingo, Winners.com, Bingo Chat, Heavenly Bingo, Clickety Click, 24/7 Bingo, Happy Jackpots . . . She licked her lips; she needed a bigger screen and some privacy. She went upstairs to where her laptop waited, in the spare room.

She clicked and scrolled.

Cozee Bingo, with its brassy homepage and swollen prize pools, had a certain tarty appeal; you hunched closer to breathe in its heady blend of over familiarity and otherness. Cozee was stacked with an eye-catching Welcome Bonus, doubled today as an Easter Special; the homepage danced with white rabbits and beribboned eggs, Christ's resurrection celebrated with capitalist gusto. The site did look welcoming for a certain strain of true believer (God Helps Those Who Help Themselves), or the sort of people who had wet dreams about Las Vegas fountains. Etta stared at the hot pink styling and flashing graphics. Was she really going to go there?

She stared into the screen as it pumped out its jingles and its dancing lights, as mad-bright as the gleam in her eye. The laptop was speaking to her and to her alone:

Come and play.

Come play.

Come.

Etta looked down at her hands on the keyboard. This was it. At last, the answer.

What if you could consider this sort of gambling to be low-rent and embarrassing, if you could see through all the snazzy tricks and *do it anyway*? You could study the odds, research, insulate against losses, cogitate, calculate, speculate, win. Had to be worth a try. Each win would inflate their savings and confirm her cleverness, someday, to her grateful husband. How Ola would praise her foresight! Her slaying of snobbery to gain the spoils. Her impeccable judgement. Her devotion. Even if it all went tits up, this would simply be *her* mistake. He'd had his. He'd had Zagreb.

Joining took seconds. Etta was assured that she could register any normal debit card, so she chose the one tied to her personal account, not their joint household funds. Other banking methods were cited as acceptable, many of which she had never heard of. You had to admire the democratic principle: everyone deserved a chance to win, even if they lived off luncheon vouchers and benefits cheques.

Cozee asked you to choose a username, essential for using the chat rooms which appeared in boxes on the main screen, bottom right. There, members typed in their feelings as they played; boasting, begging, bargaining with fate, wishing each other luck. That side of Cozee held no interest for her, but anonymity was non-negotiable. If anyone were to discover her scrabbling around in the underbelly of online entertainment, no Netflix this . . . No. This was a whole world you were joining; your familiar-other place. You signed up, they protected you, and no one need ever know.

She clicked 'Join Now!'

From here on, she only needed luck. There seemed to be plenty to go around on Cozee: banners shrieked '£10,000 Full House Special!' and 'New Games, Bigger Prizes!' and '54,716 jackpot winners this year!' All going to plan – *abracadabra!* – Etta's winnings would fly through the air with the greatest of ease and into her overdraft, turning red to black. *Ta-da!*

She would win.

She would conjure up success.

She would work like an alchemist, in secret and alone.

At least now they had a bloody chance.

●

A minute after she had signed up, an email appeared:

Welcome to Cozee Bingo! You are now free to enjoy our fantastic range of premium bingo games and slots whenever the mood takes you. To make you feel at home we are giving you a special Newbie Bonus of £50. Excited yet?

Bingo. Premium. Newbie Bonus. It ought to feel naff, but no, her mind opened wide to the seduction. She *was* excited yet.

The *chuk* of the key in the front door. 'Hey!'

Ola was back.

'Hey!'

'I'm sorry about earlier!' he called up the stairs. 'Can I come up? Friend or foe?'

The balance in the top-right corner read £50.00. The Newbie Bonus was real. Virtual lights danced around the edges of the Cozee world, promising heaven-knew-what treats.

'Friend!' Etta called, laughter ringing in her voice.

Before she could partake of the knowledge of angels, she x-d the screen.

●

'What?' asked Ola.

'What?' she said.

'You're smiling to yourself, Etta.'

'Was I? No.'

She shook her head and felt her curls quivering from root to tip. Thanks to her, a sweet five-o was chilling upstairs while they ate dinner, ready to be put to use. Cool. The free £50 from Cozee was her cash-hunting trap, a money lasso which would draw down the moon.

Honeymoon. Maldives! Sorted.

Ola tapped out a knowing rhythm onto the back of her hand.

'Ah-ah, do not try to play the fool with me. I know you, Etta. That's the smile that comes when you're looking forward to an "Olala Special".'

Etta tipped back her head and made the expected noises of outrage and delight. Ola would often tease her into a better mood; it was how he won all their arguments. But, tonight, she laughed loud and fast, hoping he might hear the lie in her haste.

The £50 bonus might expire that evening. Would it? She should have checked; a rookie error.

She wound down the hilarity and squirmed, a passable impression of pleasure.

'Yes!' Ola slapped a hand on the table, forked up more rice and the special Easter stew she had prepared. 'I knew it. I know you.'

'He-he, you got me! My oxytocin's soaring, babes, my endorphins are going wild.'

'Oxytocin? You do listen to me after all!'

'Now and then. When it suits me.'

'Ha! Troublesome woman. Learn from your husband.'

She ratcheted up the Riltonness of her accent:

'Would if I had one, babes.'

'Ha! Yes, trouble.'

They smiled at each other. But Etta could no longer taste the meat; she did not care that Ola had unconsciously started to chivvy up his thighs with frenetic micro-bounces. A £50 bonus was not nothing. It held value, possibility, weight, so much that the ceiling beyond the doorway, the one directly below the spare room, was pressing down upon her peace of mind. She needed to play.

Etta scraped up her stew and, with a cool eye, watched Ola eat. Fork, rice, stew, plantain, lift, lips, chew. Fork, rice and stew, lips, chew. Fork, chew, taking for-bloody-ever.

'You enjoying that?' she asked.

'Of course. Another spoonful of it, please, my love.'

She swallowed down her mistake and served him two of the smaller cubes of beef.

What was her problem? Most days, she thrilled as he ate her food; she would watch his mouth as if together, quite as one, they tasted the smack of stewed tomatoes, the bullish meat, the Maggi seasoning if eating Nigerian, or allspice on more

Jamaican nights, or indeed garlic, or wine; his enjoyment flavoured her evening, ordinarily.

She dredged up a smile, the tingle of pepper playing over her lips and tongue.

'This stew sweet o,' said Ola. 'Happy Easter, my love.'

Etta retreated inside a slow blink as – *uh* – he helped himself to a third ladleful. He rested one hand on her arm and dug into his food with the other; gave a glutinous sniff.

'Good bite, this one. Good spice.'

Etta blinked faster. Mischief: the spice of all action. She rubbed one finger on her eye.

'*Ah!* Oh, shi—'

'What is it?' asked Ola, fork down.

'Just . . . stupidity! My eye, I forgot to scrub off the chilli and now it's . . . *ow*.'

Weeping, but only at the brilliance of her performance, Etta rose from her seat. 'You carry on eating, my love, I'm going to sort myself out. Sorry. I might have to take a shower, or something. See you in bed.'

'OK, as long as you're all right.' Fork up, lips.

'Take your time.'

'See you, then.' Rice, stew.

April Fools back atcha, she thought.

A hot lie; untruths soaring up the Scoville scale because, upstairs, Cozee was calling. In the spare room, bingo beckoned.

Etta powered up. First, the games with £1,000 prizes; she bought a modest six tickets out of a possible thirty-six each time. The games started, numbers popped up onscreen and checked themselves off the digital cards; the games played on and petered out. No wins, scarcely enough of a thrill to quicken a newbie pulse. There had to be more to it.

A game bigging itself up as an 'Easter Eggstravaganza' was starting in four minutes. It offered a larger prize, a £2,000 pot. She should 'max out', judging by the other players' chat scrolling fast in the box onscreen:

Ron1964: You gonna max out? £2k!!!
dreamcatcher: I'm maxing 4 this one.
CathLovesBingo: Maaaaax!

Etta maxed out. This allotted her all thirty-six tickets, six strips of virtual bingo cards that would automatically check off their own numbers as they were called.

Ten seconds to go . . . 4 . . . 3 . . . 2 . . . 1. The game began. A moment of watching revealed that the tickets, being the most one could buy, had to rearrange themselves in a mesmerising dance, so that the leading card would always sit highest on the screen. When just one number remained – 27 – until Full House, it would flash and a heartbeat thud would start up loud on the screen.

27.

27?

27! 27! 27! 27!

42.

No win this time, but Etta, a girl who had always loved to shake it with a Shaku Shaku or old-school bogle, was thrilled by the jig, the flash, the whole gaudy onscreen jive.

Again!

The bingo schedule listed a £5,000 Midnight Eggstra Special, over three hours away. Silly not to. But Ola would soon have forked up the last of his stew and she only had two eyes in her head which she could pretend to wash free of chilli.

Best buy and run; the cards would go ahead and dance themselves out unwatched.

There, his dense tread on the stairs.

Etta tensed; breaths came heavier. *Hurry.* A full £5K, the
joy of waking up to that! Three clicks. *Done, done* – hope was
born – *and done.*

Just in time: the guttural cry sounded from their bedroom.

'Woman! Must you keep me waiting?'

'I'm coming, Ola!' she called.

Such sober complaisance seemed suspect, even to her own
ears, but as it was too late to make their usual jokes, she went
to him without a smile.

●

After he had kissed the smarting out of her unharmed eyes
with his still-spicy mouth, kissed fire onto her lips, traced
the geography of her sides and stomach, and lost himself in
the wheaten hills of her body – they switched on *News at Ten*
and stared at their television screen, slipping from satiety into
numb dismay. The migrants were back at the top of the bill for
the first time in many revolutions of the rolling news. There
was a report about bussing migrants to borders, where they
were being penned into new improved camps. The incomers
were cycling and walking long stretches, storming through
and surging over impotent barricades. Coming on, coming
here; in ever-closer union as Europe itself was pulled apart.

There came the obligatory close-up of the death-trap boat,
rammed full of exhausted Africans; these people looked
stunned, scarred, scared. They showed the same boat shot
every single time – how could they not? – and Etta was sad-
dened to note that the image had become near banal in its

atrocity; while at some level it destroyed her, she could not deny it was now a touch less shocking, that it battered the heart less forcefully than the first time they had seen just what people would do to get to Europe.

Desensitisation, thought Etta.

'Poor bloody things,' muttered Ola as he swung his legs out of the bed, preparing to brush his teeth. 'They keep on coming.'

●

After brushing her own teeth, Etta turned out the bathroom light. She was walking back into their bedroom when the fat bulldog next door started barking, loud and angry. Someone had to be outside.

'Ola?'

'Nnh.'

He rolled onto his side, taking most of the duvet with him. That man could fall asleep in seconds.

The dog barked again, faster, more furious.

Etta could not be more awake. She went downstairs to check the door was locked, boldly turning on lights as she went.

She reached the front door. Through the glass panel she could see that the security light was on.

Someone was out there.

She pulled at the front door. Locked. But even rattling the lock herself unnerved her; she glanced back over her shoulder. Could someone see in with all these lights on?

The dog was still going mad: a warning shout every half-second or so.

The barking echoed through the night. Etta tried to block out the sound of her own breathing and her thumping heart to listen in the half-second spaces.

She leaned closer to the door, not daring to look outside, not daring to turn away.

That was when she heard the padding, pounding noise on the pavement.

The sound of someone running away.

Chapter Two

The next morning, Etta sat at the mirror, smoothing coconut oil balm onto her curls until they shone, a dark aura radiating from the horizon of her forehead. She had been too on edge the day before. Nervy, a bit extra, listening for bumps in the night. Today would go better.

As soon as the shower pump kicked in and Ola released his exaggerated sigh, she saw her chance to satisfy hope. She rose, wrapped her dressing gown tighter around her and went to log on to her Cozee account. Steady, holding down the slightest swell of anticipation, poker-faced, she typed and clicked. Her account balance flashed up . . .

£175.00

A *win*! A decent win. More than she made in a whole day at FrameTech, when you took tax, NI and a terrible pension into account.

She was winning, already. Cozee could work out for her. For them. It could *work*.

They were still £8,000 short of a house deposit, but now – at last! – she could see a way through. A fast, fun, money-spinning way through. A *chance*. If she went in harder, only ever maxing out, and if she stuck at it, 'processing' their funds in a controlled fashion so that they came out, mostly, as more money; if she didn't get too emotional, or carried away, then living their real life – at long bloody last! – would be her reward.

Etta would win them their future.

•

As soon as Ola went out for his Easter Monday newspaper, she went back to the laptop and maxed out on tickets for that day's One O'Clock Rock, then logged out. She got as far as the door before turning around and logging back in. *Buy, click, buy, click, buy.* Tickets for all the big bingo games on the hour, every hour, up until 10 p.m. She had to win. She logged back out and went downstairs.

The whole pre-booking system for bingo games was a brilliant idea. Not only could she play bingo without running a gauntlet of grannies; without the decades-old stench of dead fags; without chips mashed into nasty carpet strewn with neon dabbers. She could, thanks to pre-booking, play bingo while she washed up the glasses, planned that evening's effort-free dinner – those sausages in the freezer, maybe, or leftover stew – and got dressed. On a normal working day, she could play bingo while at work and she could still be playing bingo when she returned home, ate the effort-free dinner with Ola and washed up the glasses again. She could play bingo while she played bingo. She could play bingo while she was not playing bingo. It was the most brilliant idea.

Etta felt a deep pull of excitement. She was starting to see why lesser minds might get addicted. No doubt that could be a danger. For those who had nothing else to do – no lover to roll with, no career to speak of, no flights abroad to look forward to, no baby baskets and school runs to dream about – you had to sympathise.

Nonetheless, she ought to tread carefully. Should Ola find out about her new hobby, after going *berserk* African stylee, he might, with a lot of effort, be talked down, persuaded that this secret fun constituted an ironic stroll through the cultural slum of bingo alley, but Etta could by no means rely on that. Gambling would never marry with his idea of her. It was sacrilegious, stupid and wrong.

See me see trouble. Which kind wahala be this? What kind of woman would set herself against both God and common sense?

You're better than that! he would say.

Oneness, united? We are locked, he would say, *into our own highly personalised neurophysiological experiences, both the genesis and the expression of our own miraculous universe of brain cells. QED: it's existentially flawed!* he would say.

Think about what it's doing to your brain! Food for thought, he would say.

Bloody waste of our damn money! he would say.

How he would detest her online world and all who inhabited it, each of them sitting around in their unowned accommodation, gawking at two fat ladies flashing pink . . .

It was pointless, however, to over-think her boyfriend's prejudices. He was a man who housed enough of his own contradictions, not least his strange ability to nibble at sustaining crumbs of faith while in pursuit of scientific truths.

Time to get real. Time to change their luck.

•

On Tuesday morning, Etta went into work. She hurried through the anodyne business park; head down, she made her way into the grey monolith that housed a number of insipid ventures. The FrameTech office, on the second floor, welcomed her with its proprietary blend of familiarity, uptightness and lack of interest.

'Hi Etta. Y'alright today?' Winston, her manager and the only other black employee, was eyeing her with amusement that stopped just short of a wink.

'Fine, thank you. Sorry.'

Jean, senior to both of them, sallow overseer of Accounts, cast a glance in Etta's direction that felt anything but neighbourly, even though she lived right opposite her and Ola. Dana bared pointy teeth, already bored, primed to hunt down weaker colleagues and suck the gossip from them. John, the MD, sat in his large glass-fronted office, and did not look away from his screen. In the slightly smaller glass-fronted office next to him was Robert, Head of Finance, and her departmental manager. He looked up at the clock on the wall.

Etta was twelve minutes late into her seat and the whiff of employee inadequacy clung to her like body odour all morning.

At lunchtime, she was refreshed by seeing Joyce's name flash up on her phone.

Government has got it in for Mum big time, can't believe it. Seriously? Been calming her down all over Easter. Need your help! xx

Etta replied straight away:

Of course I'll help. At work, speak later xx

She would ring Joyce that evening when she got back from the office, away from unsympathetic ears. Friends mattered, Joyce more than most. Government harassment? Etta would get up stand up for the Jacksons' rights the minute she had got through eight hours of corporate servitude at Frame-Tech.

Twenty minutes before the end of her working day (four hours highlighting spreadsheets that no one would read; lunch in the park; three hours and ten minutes reading a spreadsheet she did not understand), her extension rang.

'Hello, it's Reception. I've got a Joyce Jackson here to see you.'

Etta made her surprise chime like delight.

'Ah yes! Thanks, Angeline. I'll be down in a tick.'

Joyce was standing in reception, or rather she was pacing erratically – four steps, turn, three steps, turn. In her DMs and slim-fit jeans, and with her multi-directional twists of hair, she was a Jamaican Nemesis stomping all over the glass-fronted heart of suburban commerce. The security guard, white, broad-chested and hairless beneath his cap, looked itchy. Etta made a show of opening her arms wide and smiling.

'Joyce!' she contained her in a hug and steered her into yet more glass, the visitors' room off the main reception. 'What's up?'

Joyce was shaking her head, as if to dislodge a painful idea trapped beneath the hair twists.

'Please, Etta, you've got to help me. They want to deport her.'

'I will help, Joyce, I promise. Calm down.'

'Can you believe they could do this to her? What's wrong with them?'

'No, I can't. There must be some sort of mistake.'

Joyce wasn't listening. 'How can they threaten a woman who's going to be seventy-six next month?'

'It's terrible—'

'It's outrageous! She's scared to go to sleep because she's worried they might come knocking in the night and cart her off to Yarl's Wood.'

'God, that is beyond out of order.'

'It's beyond beyond, the outest of order, right? Deport her, why? Where to exactly in Jamaica, tell me that? Her corner of Negril must be one massive hotel resort by now. She's been here for fifty years.'

'I know, Joyce, it's madness.'

'All my aunts and uncles are dead or over here, anyway.' She raised her voice. 'What the hell's she supposed to do on her Jack Jones in Jamaica?'

The security guard looked over.

'Shhh!' said Etta.

'Shit, sorry.'

The guard walked closer to the transparent walls, putting extra effort into the evenness and efficiency of his own pacing.

'Not like I can go out there with her,' said Joyce, her voice rising in the nasal crescendo of a woman who had shed tears and now needed to shout. 'My kids are in schools here. We've not got the money. Oh, Jesus . . .'

'We need to contact them, calmly,' said Etta. 'We'll explain the situation so that any reasonable person could understand it, OK?'

'Yeah. Yeah, that would be good. But, you know, my dyslexic brain and all this stress . . . Your First Welcome thingy, you know all this immigration stuff. You'll write them for me?'

'Course. I've pretty much finished up here. I'll grab my bag, let's go to yours.'

•

As they neared Joyce's house, the ordinary terrace on this decent street, Etta's sense of purpose burgeoned. What they were doing to Cynthia Jackson was wrong. Reprehensible. Beyond beyond. Immoral as hell. She knew how to put a letter together and – the United Kingdom being a just country, one built on fair play – she trusted that would sort it.

'Mum, we're back!' Joyce shouted through the front door as she opened it.

'Hello, Mrs Jackson,' said Etta.

In the front room, Cynthia Jackson was sitting in an orange armchair that appeared to be slowly digesting her; the old lady had to have shrunk since Etta's last visit; she may not even have moved. She raised watery eyes to the guest. The TV was blaring out the wrap-up to a holiday property show. Joyce rested her hand on her mother's shoulder.

'Mum's not been the same since they started up with this nonsense. Have you, Mum?'

Mrs Jackson spoke: 'It's not fair.'

'No, it's not,' said Joyce.

'I was just thinking that,' said Etta at the same time.

The woman turned back to the TV to watch the credits roll.

'We'll go in the kitchen, Mum.'

Joyce nodded towards the door and Etta followed her out.

'She's not even going out into her garden these days. You know how much she loves her flowers. It's really getting to her.' Joyce shut them into the kitchen. 'Come. Here, take a look at this bollocks.'

She handed her a letter that had been sitting on the breakfast bar. Etta read.

'It does sound ominous. I wonder whether—'

'Thing is, when Mum came over, she thought that was it. Forever. Far as she was concerned, she was *English*, never mind British. They all grew up thinking the Queen was theirs too, they had this massive photo of her on the schoolroom wall and everything. Back in the day, the UK government said to them, come on over, help us out, we need you nurses and whatnot. Work hard and we'll look after you, you're one of us. Next thing? Fuckers are telling the old folk that they got it all wrong, telling our older ones, the first generation – real pioneers, you know? adventurers – that they never were proper members of the club like they thought they were, not like the people born here, and to show papers or get the hell out and it's just . . .'

Joyce walked to the window. Etta followed and placed both hands on her shoulders from behind. Joyce was not crying, she was shaking.

'Thank you, Etta,' said Joyce. 'I'm sorry.'

'What for? Hardly your fault.'

'Mum is just so *hurt*. It kills me to see it.'

'I'm sorry.'

'She's ashamed. Like she's done something wrong.'

'It's horrible,' said Etta. 'Why did they have to bother her after all this time? This whole thing is such a ridiculous lottery, isn't it?'

'Is that what it is?' Joyce turned to face her with a mouth that could have been sucking on a bad tamarind ball. 'Mum just thought it was her home.'

●

Etta took the long way back from the Jackson house. She went along Firth Road, then turned left onto Aspen Street.

Etta slowed as she neared the right white gate. The house wasn't even all that, probably, not to most people. But 31 Aspen Street still soothed her. Aside from the exercise and the chance to clear her head, this street was the reason she chose to walk to and from work rather than drive. Ola had no idea how often she strolled past it, just to feel her pulse slow and her spirits rise higher, above the car exhaust fumes and into the sunwashed air, or the dusk. If this house, this to-die-for dull house, in this great-crap town, could speak, concrete wisdoms would surely pour from its foundations: *Strive. Hope. Anything's possible.*

It was vital to dream. What did she think she was doing with herself these days? Scraping a living on a business park, in warehouse-style offices designed to depress: all those high utilitarian ceilings and low aspirations; at least it depressed the hell out of the auxiliary staff like her, the ones without titles and side offices. This was her tribe: the hot-deskers. The quirky-coffee-cup obsessives and parking-space fetishists. When you were stuck in the margins of suburban life (suburbia already being, to Etta, the margins of Life), and when success yawned daily in your face, you needed distractions. You needed a 31 Aspen Street and memories of forays into the wider world, and Cozee Bingo: bright bursts of light from the past and present to shine promise onto your future.

Etta hurried on. Tonight, 'Spring Wins' kicked off: three hours of back-to-back games with jackpots ranging from £1,000 to £10,000. A genuine opportunity. Moreover, it was the beginning of the month, her salary was in the bank. Funds to process!

She stopped dead.

Damn.

All of her salary had gone into their joint account, as usual. She had signed up to gamble only with money coming from her personal account, so that no joint statements would ever shout 'Cozee!' She needed to move money. But should she transfer one great lump sum across to her personal account now, it would stink up Ola's senses higher than a catch of cray-fish left out in the West African sun.

Unless.

She turned back on herself and took several turns, left-left-right-left, right into the heart of town, hurrying towards the high street where, without pausing long enough for a better idea to occur, she plunged the purple card into the cashpoint's mouth. Just £100. Then £80. Then £120.

Etta crossed the road with £300 in notes smooth in her hand and went to the other bank, the one where she kept her personal account, which by now held little more than a tenner. She would feed this personal account with cash, taken out in innocuous amounts, these little sums that might slip under the radar, or be explained away as a hairdo, or market shop, even though withdrawn in one day. It was for his own good, a temporary deception; not for long, not too much. Just *funds*, now and then, to tide her over.

As she walked back towards Sycamore Road, through the all-day waft of bacon from Teddy's Café towards home, she tried on successive emotions: triumph, dismay, glee, alarm, guilt. She ought to feel horrible. But then again, *Zagreb*. Ola took risks, he had risked screwing everything up. So why shouldn't she?

As she neared the house, she saw that Jean over the road had beaten her home: her houndstooth-clad shoulders and that lethargic hair were hunching towards the front door. Poor cow, had to be a tough gig with that ancient mother. As far as she knew, Jean had never married or left her mum's side, had spent fifty-five years as a devoted daughter and little else. And apparently the mum had dementia. The two old ladies shared a crepuscular companionship, the inside of their house bathed in a semi-permanent twilight. They were no doubt saving on light bills.

Etta watched Jean fiddle in her bag for keys.

Etta had always thought of the concept of spinsterdom as a misogynistic, anti-feminist construct, until she had come across Jean. Dana fancied herself an authority on the whole FrameTech team and sang it this way: Jean had reached an age when she felt free to spit her sourness with impunity; something in her had turned bitter, like a lime past sucking. Not her femininity or her fertility, nothing so sexist: her humanity. She knew herself to be dull, deadened, and that knowledge now curdled in her soul, lime in milk, adulterating all her thoughts and deeds. Still, Jean knew how to work a badass spreadsheet and could take out a whole row of colleagues with one well-aimed decimal point.

As Jean turned to push the door shut, Etta waved. Jean paused, recessed in her doorway, a shadow within a shadow. She shut the door without waving back.

●

Etta turned to enter her own empty house, poured a glass of red, went to the spare room and glanced at Ola's papers – *chemical flood . . . chain reaction from cell to cell* – then pushed them aside for the interesting stuff: she maxed out on as many bingo games as she could for the next three hours.

The first game started up almost before she had made the psychic shift from worker to player. She did not win, but she did receive the consolation of two pregasmic seconds: the heartbeat sound, the flash. So damn close; worth it.

No life-changing wins yet, but she did not require a mountain of money; a hillock would do. All good things . . . *She who waits.* A stutter of her heart: the letter. She would write Mrs

Jackson's reply to the government now and post it off first thing. Had to be done. She pulled the Home Office letter out of her bag and scanned it again. There was an email address, better still.

The Cozee page winked myriad pixels at her, a seduction in pink and gold. She blinked at Cozee. It winked and winked.

She minimised the page and opened a blank email:

Dear Home Office,
    I am writing to you because of my friend, Joyc—

[DELETE]

Dear Home Office,
    I am writing to you on behalf of my mother, Cynthia Jackson, to whom you sent a letter (Ref: HOCMJ1092846). You have requested that she sends proof of residency to your department without explaining why she needs to prove she has the right to stay in the UK. Could you please clarify? I can assure you that my mother had all the correct paperwork when she entered the UK in 1966, as your own records must show.
    Thanks for your help in clearing up this misunderstanding.
    Yours,
        Joyce Jackson
On behalf of Cynthia Jackson

Short, fair, to the point. She hit send.

Within seconds an acknowledgement had popped up in her inbox, reassuring her that her email had been received and would be dealt with. She shrugged and lifted her shoulders as if they had indeed been lightened: duty done.

Ola was interval-training at the gym, as he did most Tuesday evenings, enjoying some energy-boosting fun.

Time to play.

Though eager, Etta was no fool. She could see the mechanics that worked under the slick skin of the Cozee money machine. Of course, their corporate multimillions took some making. Of course, they banked on attracting people with low incomes and high hopes. She had read the scrolling, misspelled chat. Sexykezzas and Luckyjezzas and Shazza69s would deposit the £5 minimum, buy a couple of tickets for each of the cheapest games, eke it out over woeful hours of pathetic odds, lose, lose, lose . . . *plz come on 3444444* . . . Not her. She had more funds than most on the site, it would seem. She could play the bigger money rooms, max out on every worthwhile game, up the odds by . . . quite a lot. Winning, as someone rich had once said, was for winners.

She had no choice. She could not face any more anniversaries like the one all set to wind her up at the end of next week. The romantic scenario was static and stale: he would take her out to an unambitious Rilton restaurant, and he would roar and joke and not understand a bloody thing, and fail to propose to her in front of a hundred strangers eating off the same set dinner menu, and she would be forced to choke down disappointment for dessert.

It would be the last time. They needed money to marry.

They had far more to lose than cash.

•

At 4.13 a.m., the security light outside their front door came on. Etta did not know whether it had woken her, or whether she had been staring into the dark, and seen it. Ola was still sleeping.

She rose and padded to the bedroom window, which overlooked the path. No pounding feet, no barking dog. Nothing below, although she would not be able to see someone right on their doorstep, hidden as they would be by the porch. Not breaking the silence of the night with her breath, she waited for the light to go out. A movement across the road caught her eye: a bending body wrapped in a flannel robe, reaching into the wheelie bin by their front wall. Was that Jean, or the mother? The dark and cold did unkind things to faces, Etta could not tell. Was she taking something in or pulling it out? At some point the old woman succeeded, or maybe gave up, and walked back along her path to her house. From where she stood Etta could see that their front door was open and the head of another woman with limp white hair – Jean, or her mother – was nodding at the first to come inside. Both of them up at quarter past four. The door closed, the security light died at last and everything sank back to shades of pewter.

Etta drew back from the curtains and lowered herself into bed.

Risk I

PLITVIČE – AUGUST 2015

She is waiting for her piece of good fortune. Leaning up against the wall, at the entrance where they bring in the cabbages, the beef and the crates of beer, hoping to catch the manager before he has given all the work away. It comes so easily to the others, the locals first, always, but surely it has to be her turn at last. She is a woman to whom things ought to come more easily. One day soon. This she trusts when she studies her dark curling hair and the taut face that does not reflect its troubles back at her in the mirror; she trusts it with every glance returned, whether in her cheap long-handled glass or in the street.

It is more a question of when. She is young enough – still, just – to believe. She had travelled here, so far from home, first off to visit the famous lakes. Now look at her, running low on money so soon, a foreigner, alone in Croatia. When will she be given her allotment of luck? Would it simply be slopped into her life's dish like a portion of the fishy brudet these people so adored? Or would it fall from the sky like one of their endless goddamn downpours? When, already?

There is a man in front of her with grey hair. His shoulders slope, ruining the lines of a cheap leather jacket; he does not turn to chat as she stands behind him. She hopes he's a kitchen man, a porter or dishwasher, maybe. She needs to finally get onto the restaurant floor: the promise of tips gleams silver bright; hope rustles in her ear like a clutch of notes.

A door opens. It sways, slows, then falls closed again with no one coming out.

All this queueing, this waiting. She needs to enlist help. She is a stranger, after all, miles away from where she was born. Everyone knows that she has come here for a job, that she is alone and hoping on foreign soil. At least, she has had work for three days, cleaning up in this same fish restaurant. It is a good one, well-reviewed online: she knows it, as does the man ahead of her in the queue. Work has panned out these past few days, thanks to some locals who do not mind her, pointing her in the direction of that dirty office, this café where they pay in cash, but she has yet to stumble upon her particular piece of luck. If she gets another shift tonight, that will be something.

The man ahead gives a snort of impatience; spits at the base of the wall.

She will know her true luck when it comes: it will not be scuffing along in a restaurant's back alley. It will be outsized and as showy as her smile, and it will know her in return.

Her luck will come. There is a beauty and a pain that weaves through it all: the searching. There are lessons to take away from the daily condescensions and disappointments and the failure of favours to materialise and the bad ideas at the bottom of deep glasses which leave rings on tables she must wipe. There is rich knowledge to be gained from living life under a hostile gaze, a gaze that only softens upon catching the generosity of her lip and her meanness of thigh. But that softening is a powerful force. It gives her hope.

For now, she will watch and wait for a sign. When it is time, she will make her move.

Now he comes out: the manager.

'One more!' He looks at the man's grey hair. 'We need a waiter.'

She should stay quiet, blend in, wipe and scrub unnoticed. The kitchen team are a blur of shadows and everyone likes it that way. She has none of the right documents. Speaking up to serve would mean trouble, one way or another.

One cool surge of courage and she straightens up from the wall, and edges out, hip first, from the queue so she can be fully seen.

'I'm the most experienced waitress I know in town,' she says, which is no lie.

The man looks, the gaze heats and softens, but still his eyes dart right to query the man before him.

'Potwash,' says the grey head, already turning back the way it had come.

'There you go,' she says, walking past both men into the kitchen entrance.

To get lucky, you have to take risks.

Chapter Three

SATURDAY, 14 APRIL 2018

This evening could only end in disaster and disdain. He was going to hate her. Why the bloody hell had she done it?

They should not be here.

The Royal Delhi seethed with commitment: couples celebrating, couples arguing, couples ignoring each other. The pair on the nearest table were doing all three in swift succession and out of sync, although the blue-green flourish of matching neck tattoo did suggest a rough stab at living in harmony.

Outside, it was raining harder than Etta could remember it ever doing before; any romantic spirit had been dampened on the run from the car; she was drenched in shame. She speared more lamb as if it might save her, all appetite murdered, the guilt hard to swallow.

'Great, isn't it?' said Ola, reaching for the sag aloo, fibrous in its copper bowl.

Her forehead dipped. 'Mm.'

'I was just thinking,' he went on. 'A bit suspicious how they always call it "having an Indian", isn't it?'

She raised her fingers in front of her lips, humiliated by the act of chewing. 'What do you mean?'

'Well,' Ola put down his knife and fork and cupped both hands, weighing the gravity of his point. 'You know, as if they're actually possessing some poor bastard Krishna or Dev. Colonial throwback, am I not right?'

Etta stabbed another piece of meat she could not stomach.

'Maybe,' she said. 'But they say, "having a Chinese" too.'

'This is true. But not having a Greek. Never having a Swiss. QED.'

Etta clamped her lips tight; the sigh escaped, despite her. He knew full well that 'having an Indian' or indeed a cuppa or a fag, did not automatically suggest violent conquest or hark back to the Empire (if you left aside all those tea and tobacco plantations). Moreover, Ola knew she knew this. Like a man in a stuck lift, he was jabbing at all her buttons in the hope that one might work, but she was not up for it, not tonight. 'To have' was just a bloody handy verb.

'Pass me those poppadoms, my sweetness, I am taking this vindaloo *down*.'

Would he not stop? Desperation had an overpowering smell, something between them was dying; you could detect the rot high above the scent of cumin, turmeric and coriander. Her deception stank. Her man, an optimist, sensed they were a touch out of whack, so for the rest of the evening he would be sure to throw out pseudo-political notions and Nigerian wisdoms, quibble and pump himself up larger than life, arse around and only hack her off more. Almost tolerable, if you played along.

'Vindaloo? Ah, yes,' she said. No other option. 'Your basic 1980s masculinity crisis on a plate.'

'Yeah, but with chutneys *to die for*.' He paused, expecting a laugh that did not come. 'Anyhow, it'll clear up this damn cold in the absence of any pepper soup.'

'I told you, Ola, I would happily have made you pepper soup.' Nothing to pay for, no menu, no fuss.

'Heh? I know.' He leaned forward. 'But it's our anniversary!'

A wince that Etta could not hide. Ola misread it.

'I know. Sorry sorry o. Last year it was that place. Ah! Where was it now?'

'Le Mijoté.'

'Yes! All Frenchy-Frenchy, Michelin star and whatnot . . . But you love Indian, right?'

'Of course.' She meant to stop there, but the stringy meat had lodged between her molars and with one bite it had all become too much. 'And you love my pepper soup!'

'OK,' Ola put his fork down. 'What is going on?'

'What?'

'You're in a funny mood this evening, Teetee. Everything OK?'

'Yes.'

'I know you didn't fancy coming out, but we are here now. Relax.'

She had always reared back from his command to relax; whenever he used it, at the most critical of times, it was never a word designed for her.

'I am relaxed.'

Etta gave up on the lamb, swilled with water and forked up as much pilau rice as a relaxed person might opt to ingest. She was not up for it, no. It was not their anniversary, because they were not married. She had made that same point for the past two years on each fourteenth of bloody April, yet Ola still seemed keen to disregard it. Boyfriend–girlfriend 'anniversary' meals when you were thirty-four and thirty-five did not constitute a great night out. Because one of you might want a little more from life before her ovaries dried up and the other one of you was a selfish bastard.

Etta felt black laughter bubbling up. She choked it back with a gulp of bhindi bhaji. A bitter aftertaste: for a second, she had forgotten that now she was the bastard.

Only she knew that the crash was coming.

'See, smiling now, that's better!' said Ola, organising the metal dishes around their table; he was now a man wholly in charge of his dinner destiny. 'Come, chop! Please, my sweetness, pass me the mango chutney.'

Etta chewed her way towards the end of the enforced celebration, growing sick with nerves. Would dinner be done if she accepted that last morsel of naan, a swipe of vindaloo? No, because then he ordered kulfi – 'Two spoons, please. It's our anniversary!' – and when had they ever had pudding after a curry, let alone one at £9.50 a pop? Following that, coffees; the chocolate mints on the saucer, foiled in gold but still failing to dazzle, and then, only then, could the bill come.

The Indian finally had, Ola waved his card at the waiter.

'Thanks very much. Deh. Li. Shoss!'

He inhaled deep to demonstrate a newfound olfactory clarity.

'Pleasure, sir.'

Etta's chest felt as if it were bound tightly by constricting facts; venomous, snaking truths which might slither from between her ribs at any second.

Her hands were shaking, straining to pull at the reins of the evening before it galloped away from them altogether.

Not possible. This problem was no nest of vipers, or runaway horse. Though wild and intractable, it was a simple maths problem. But she would have to ride it.

Ola was punching the right numbers into the machine, humming a snatch of his signature melody, the one that signified contentment. He never knew when he was doing it.

'No, I swear: amazing curry, that one. We will come again.'

'Thank you, sir.'

'Sah?' He laughed. 'No need, and anyway it's doctor, not sah.'

The waiter blinked; it could have been a wink.

'What's your name?'

'Me? I'm Krish.'

'Aha!' Ola all but winked at Etta.

She dug a thumbnail into a flap of tablecloth. The waiter had a lazy eye that could not blink or, it would seem, look away from her.

Still Ola went on. 'Just to check, Krish – do you get the tip?'

'I'm sorry—'

'What?'

'Your card has been declined.' The whole time giving Etta that one-eyed stare.

'What? No. Really? Let me—'

'We should try again. This machine can misbehave, sir.'

'OK then . . .' Ola punched in the numbers once more, no longer emitting the jaunty tune.

The waiter waited; his dry smile turned upside down. 'Declined, I'm sorry.'

'What?'

'I'm sorry, one moment, sir.'

He went off to seek the advice of a colleague. Ola glared down at his folded hands, as if they were at fault. The couple to their right had given up on speaking; the couple to the left had paused their ping-pong game of flirtation and recrimination. Both pairings, still on mains, were eating with unconvincing concentration, studying their plates as if they might be great artworks of protein and sauce.

Etta lifted her own bowed head: she had to speak.

'Ola, I wanted to . . . I just—'

'What? Ah now, here he comes.'

The waiter was swerving through the tables with his new machine, and his deference, and his watchful eye.

'Here we go, sir.'

Right,' said Ola.

He pressed his PIN into the keypad, dead slow, as if administering the last rites to his manhood.

'Actually, Krish, it could have been blocked because, you know, we're new to this place. It's not stolen, ha!'

The waiter gave him a lopsided look. A gentle understanding suffused his features. The neck-tattoo man smirked at his neck-tattoo girlfriend. All of it, intolerable. Etta felt the blood rising and coughed to divert attention from her flushed cheeks.

An interminable pause. The seconds unfolded and draped over them, as ruined as their napkins.

'Ah.' Their waiter bowed his head, the shame all his. 'Declined, sir.'

Ola puffed up his chest, taking on oxygen for the fight . . . then he exhaled and fixed – *there* – that larger-than-life smile on his face:

'Any good at washing up, Etts?' Volume up, a more anglicised accent. 'Your Olly's got no lolly!'

'Wait, Ola, I must have a—'

'No, do not trouble yourself, I have other cards. But, heh? It is strange, we *have* money in our account. Never mind. Here, take this.'

Ola pulled out a credit card, took the machine as if he had been kept waiting and jabbed at the keys once more. He did not ask again about the tip.

Etta looked on. She counted the smattering of flecks in the skin which cloaked the wide contours of her lover's face.

It called to mind a natural resource, processed by man: a polished, flawed African hardwood.

At last, the machine whirred and stuck out a tongue of receipt.

'All fine, sir.'

'Heh.' Ola sucked his teeth. 'Good-good, all done now. Actually, I'll take the voided one too.'

Temper still heated his stare as he took his own sweet time, folding the receipts in quarters, putting them into his wallet.

The waiter's good eye spotted some urgent business on the far side of the room; he hurried away.

Etta parted her lips, inhaled.

He got there first:

'I know, Etta, and I'm sorry. Wetin happen? That has to be a sacking offence!'

There, again, a sunburst lighting up his voice, so the next tables could not fail to appreciate the joyful Nollywood denouement:

'I am a rational, organised human being, heh? A doc-tor,' he visibly relaxed, having reiterated this to their fellow diners. 'But I have had so many more work drinks and things lately. This *olodo* has been too busy to check the balance!'

A stab of regret somewhere under her ribs. Good with money, though, Ola? Rubbish; another one of those cute nonsenses that oiled their wheels. If he were, he would realise that he had not overspent. If he had any talent in the finance department, he would never have taken out that five grand, four years before, straight after their early days' amorousness broke the bed and his car collapsed of exhaustion. There would have been a buffer, or bumper: some give. He would already have hit his precious £30,000 mark which, he had decreed, would allow them to 'move on to marriage', that most romantic of relocations.

Tonight's failings though, were down to her. Etta lowered her gaze from the grin that was fast collapsing opposite her and sipped the grit from her cup. Finally, it was done.

'Not your fault, Ola, you've been busy with your research. Come on, can we go now?'

They walked out. Rain was still coming down hard; he jogged ahead, planning to drive his car up to the door for her. Upset by this chivalry, distracted, she stepped in a waterlogged pothole; as the car pulled up, she lurched forward, leaving the left foot of her heels standing empty in the silt. She thrust her toes back into the sodden shoe.

Ola leaned across to push open the passenger door. 'Come on, quick, get in.'

They moved off, Ola blasting the windscreen with the fan. Beside him, Etta shifted, the snakes troubling her chest. Theft was theft. A lie of omission was still a lie. And surely it could be nothing less than a sin to let the man you loved wander blind into an ambush.

The short journey home was slow, wet torture.

As they dripped into the hallway, Etta shrugged off her coat and moved towards the stairs. Ola placed one hand on her shoulder, used the other to stroke a cluster of curls above her neck, then bent to kiss the fine hairs at her nape.

'Ah, woman. What a night!'

'Rainy,' said Etta.

'Horrendous. Let's go up.'

'OK,' she said, aching for the top step. 'I just have to check on something first, an email. I'll see you in bed.'

Etta moved upstairs and turned not left but right, into the spare room. She shut the door and drew the curtains. Her laptop was off but open, on the desk; Ola's was next to it, closed. He was rarely in there in the evenings these days, although his pages of research often spread themselves out across their desk. The mess didn't matter: no one had stayed in there for months, not even her mother. Not even them: she had once suggested making love in the redundant bed, just for a change, and Ola had laughed loud and hard, thinking she was joking. She had laughed along and never raised it again. The spare room/study's remit was dual but narrow: it knew its place.

She tried to power up her computer, but no industrious click and buzz came: she had somehow let the battery drain dead. She plugged it in and waited.

'Etta!' An urgent cry.

She rushed to their bedroom. Ola, in boxers, was holding his phone high.

'I thought I had not spent that much! Did you take the £120 from the joint account last week? Here on my app: £120 on 3rd April. And £80. Look, there's even £100 missing. No wonder I could not pay at the restaurant! Ah, this must be bloody thieves! Are we being defrauded?'

Etta fixed her stare past his shoulder, to her side of the bed. There was a smear of lipstick on her pillow. *Messy woman.*

'We did not take out all this money,' he went on. 'What is that, £300 that they just—'

'Actually, Ola,' she began. As he looked her in the eye, her voice died.

'Yes. What, Etta?'

It had to be now.

'It was me. I needed to get cash out a few times but forgot to tell you.'

'Eh? What did you spend all that on? What about the budget?'

'I know, Ola. But I went to the food market to get some things, you know, the stuff we can't get at the supermarket, the okra, the plantain. Garri. I stocked up a bit.'

'Yes, but—'

'Then there was my hair. I had a conditioning treatment, ready for our . . . anniversary. Not that you noticed.'

That felt bad: not just the fabrication, but blaming him for this imaginary neglect. It also felt better than it should.

'So: hair and food. That's it?'

Etta clenched a hand at her side; and crossed her fingers within the folds of her skirt, a child protecting them from her lies.

'Oh! I know, now. I forgot: Dana at work wanted me to lend her some money for petrol so . . .'

'So, what, you're the cashpoint for all your friends now?'

'Ola . . .'

'I don't know why you suddenly think we're rich—'

'I don't, Ola, honestly.'

'Spending like water. Why, Etta?'

'I know; I should've held back, or at least remembered to speak to you about it. Sorry o.'

'Yes. Well. We will not have any more spending money for little things this month . . . but mystery solved, heh?'

'I really am sorry, Ola.' In that moment, she meant it.

'Hnh.'

Ola wandered past her, into the bathroom. He came straight out again and walked over to wrap her in a firm hug. Then he returned to the bathroom.

Absolved, Etta slipped back to the spare room.

She shut the door behind her, eyes closed; here again. When she opened her eyes three drops of blood were sinking into the carpet. They must have fallen from her. Nosebleed.

She tugged a handkerchief from her handbag, raised the cloth to her nose and rested her head on all she had: the off-white gloss of a rented door.

This was a warning: she could never again use their joint account. She would have to find alternative sources of funds although, with any luck, she would not need them.

When the flow appeared to have stopped, she turned to the desk. Her laptop was charging, waiting for her. She huffed out the stale taint of the air stagnating in her lungs and tried to breathe in hope. She released the bands from her hair; pulled, pouffed and patted until it resumed the normal dimensions of her black curly afro. Then, she powered up.

●

On Sunday evening, she took a long shower, washing from her mind the sticky residue of that day's wins and losses. Also, the grit of irritation: her mum's habitual loving pressure, applied via phone after lunch. In her widowed years, her mum was exhibiting a Darwinistic drive to push Etta over the line, to married woman. When a Jamaican mother had her heart set on grandkids, she usually buck up on dem sooner or later.

Etta opened her mouth under the stream and let the hot water ease her body, though her mind felt tight, ready to crack. She shampooed and thrust her crown under the stream; tension was pummelled from her soaked skull.

Perhaps she *should* get knocked up. Lord knows fatherhood might put a rocket up Ola's arse. He had, in their earliest days, made a big deal about wanting 'four-plus' children, like he was angling to hook her in for good. He was no babyfather, see? No player. *Four-plus.* It had long been their in-joke, their motto, their kid-filled castle in the air, although Ola had not mentioned it in quite a while. Thank heavens – Joyce had told her, with some relish, what a baby could do to a body. Two would probably do her, max.

The water worked its magic, smoothing out the knots of both muscles and mind. No, she should not gripe, mums were so often right—

'Damn.'

She had forgotten to chase Joyce's email. Since going to her friend's house and watching her stress right out as they cursed the government – fit to bust, all but spitting plantain chips – she had been meaning to follow up on the email she had written on behalf of Cynthia Jackson. It had now been almost two weeks. There had been an automated acknowledgement, but no reply had come back.

'You not heard nuttin?' Joyce had asked.

'No, sorry. I'll get on to them. Has to be a backlog of cases. Or my email could have been destroyed as spam.'

'I'll give them goddamn spam, my mum's a wreck!'

The water coursed down Etta's back, good and steaming. The original email must have been too weak, lacking fire-power. She would call somebody, tomorrow.

She stepped out from the shower and towelled herself hard. She scurried a finger across the mirror; stared with respect at her cheek and its half-inch scar, in the form of almost a full V or broad tick, below her left eye.

Based on years of feedback, she could not pretend that her face was anything less than appealing. Her scar tissue was an aesthetic anomaly, caused by an infantile fall from a stool. It was only remarkable – a vivid slash across the smooth dun expanse of her childhood – because her earliest years had been *nice*: safe and warm and bright.

She scrubbed the rough towel across her cheek. Granny would say to her:

'Scar unlucky. That skin *lucky*.'

She did not buy that her lighter skin presaged a radiant destiny. Not like her mum's schoolfriend, Auntie Agnes, who had wrecked her face with bleaching creams. Etta shivered in the cooling steam. All these women, treating their skin like dirt; scouring their faces, whitewashing an eroded sense of self. She hated it, all of it; wished every last inch of skin-bias and racism dead.

She was clean, dried off, ready to attack the working week with a fresh attitude. A last glance at the mirror brought comfort; unlike most, she could face the world pre-scarred, stick almost a full V-sign up to the perception of perfection, and life was all the better for it.

●

The next day was Monday. Mondays meant meetings and meetings were the worst.

The clock on the wall said 12.45 p.m., but the meeting showed no sign of ending.

'Excellent point, Jean,' said John, the lanky white male MD. 'Robert, could you walk us through how that would work?'

Robert, Head of Finance, also white and male, but bald and as stocky as the MD was tall, crawled them through each cost-cutting detail until 12.51 p.m. He passed the baton back to his neighbour, Jean, who spoke for three more minutes.

'And so,' concluded Jean, the white female middle manager, 'all our departments will benefit in the longer term. Winston, could your team manage it?'

Winston, the black male team leader, smiled:

'Of course. Etta, we need to prioritise this, yes?'

'Certainly,' said Etta, the black female boss of no one but her own sweet self, noting that it was 12.59 and evidently 1952.

And with that, authority had once more cascaded down the well-worn FrameTech hierarchy as naturally as water down a hill.

The minute hand moved: 1 p.m. Even the best-paid people in the room started packing up their notepads and picking up their pens.

Lunchtime, at last.

●

As the afternoon limped to a close, Winston wandered over to her desk; he tended to wander her way at quieter moments. Or busier moments. Or moments when Etta was wearing something new. They both knew, but were both attached – him to the lovely Dawn, her to his homeboy Ola; a sporadic four-way admiration established at the last two FrameTech Christmas dos – so that cancelled out tacit complications, technically. It did not matter that Winston came across as a kind, amusing man and was more built than a team leader needed to be.

'You OK there, Etta?'

'Yes,' she replied. 'All done now.'

'What would I do without you?' he asked, all teeth and eyes.

'I don't know. Maybe actually get some work done?'

'That's . . . pretty damn . . . cheeky,' smiled Winston.

'But accurate,' said Etta. 'Please God, tell me it's a sacking offence.'

'Sorry, no,' said Winston. 'You're stuck with me in this place for-*ever*. What circle of hell did you say this was?'

'Limbo, I believe, the First. But no doubt we'll sink through them all before the end of the financial year.'

'I'm holding out for the second one, personally.'

'What's that?'

'Lust.'

Etta laughed. 'Ah, bless. Been googling Dante on my account, have you? Don't worry, I haven't read him either.'

Winston looked thrown for a moment, then chuckled low.

'You're quite a handful to manage, you know that?'

'You're welcome,' said Etta.

Still smiling, Winston backed away, wandered back to his desk. He fancied himself a dormant player, too loyal to Dawn for purposeful chirpsing; he kept his approaches mild and, most days, largely professional. They were just messing with each other.

Etta's work was not quite all done, in truth, but she was. She was about to power down her PC and leave the office when she remembered and brought up one last page:

GOV.UK – Home Office

Even one day was too long for Cynthia Jackson to have suffered this sword dangling above her head, a head crowned with more wisdom than white hairs. Still no reply. There had been no cut-off date on the original letter. Was her case stuck in some bureaucratic bunker or email traffic jam? Etta dialled the number.

Voicemail. It was 5.03 p.m. and the department closed at 5 p.m. Making a mental note to try again the next day, she gathered her things and hurried home.

•

Ola's car was not in its usual space, next to hers. He ought to be out for a while yet. She glanced back and saw Jean walking up the street to the house opposite.

She dashed into her own house and went upstairs without pausing to open the post or pour a drink. The air in the spare room had its own welcome tinge of contamination: the taint of stale perfume, gin and sweat. The blood spots on the carpet had mellowed to a rust brown. No room in this hired and deficient house had felt as much her own.

At last, her coming-home treat. She turned on the laptop and logged on to the site she had been tempted to check on her phone all day. Cozee. Had she won?

For a fraction of a second it all – everything, life itself – hung in the balance. The page was not loading fast enough. She tried to wrong-foot fate. *Zilch, going to be nada* . . . No. Yes! £127.45! Her balance showed a £125 win.

Head rush. Her vision thrilled, her mind gasped, joy rocketed through her. Total and utter head rush.

Her head was fizzing. She patted a palm to her nostrils, just in case. No blood dripping this time, just a bloody decent win.

Cozee was the bomb.

Bang! A clatter from downstairs made Etta leap out of her chair, hitting her knee.

No, it was OK: the free paper being slammed through their door, that was all. She sat back down, guilt radiating from her like perspiration.

She was a disgrace. How could she go behind Ola's back like this, using what was their money, whichever account she drew it from? She knew how: by telling herself she was helping them both, when it was – no messing, now – atrocious behaviour. How could she have lied to him after the restaurant, without a stutter? She could not stop replaying mental footage of her lips letting falsehoods out against her wishes, as if she had starred in a dubbed TV drama.

The hug in those dense arms once she had 'confessed' had hurt in all the wrong places. But was she entirely to blame? Wouldn't her stories have smelled off to someone who truly loved her? Or, as she was expanding her pool of talents, perhaps she was growing into a more adept liar.

On the screen, a pink dot blinked. Someone was messaging her.

Who? She knew no one, had engaged in private with no one on the site. She clicked.

StChristopher75: Hi there.

She went to delete but stopped. Foolish to send bad karma out into the Cozee universe.

EO1984: Hello.
StChristopher75: Just saying hi as u new yes?

Etta stalled; she had not joined to make friends or attract attention. Still, manners cost nothing.

EO1984: Yes ty.

Nothing.
Twenty seconds later:

StChristopher75: 😀

Then the pink light went off. He was gone.

She inhaled deep and yawned, stretching up her arms. She needed to chill out, the rules were different here; genuine bonhomie coursed amongst the seasoned Cozeers. Etta was not used to bonhomie, living in Rilton (which sounded like the Hilton, but ought never to be confused with anything approaching leisure or even moderate luxury. It was a town of water-treaders, grafters and dossers, apart from a few roads like Aspen Street, where people lived when they knew good things were meant for them.) Unexpected approaches were doubtless all part of the benign embrace of Cozee, a good omen from that unpredictable and munificent cosmos. Indeed, Etta was blessed with a further sign: a banner flashed up to announce that Midnight Mayhem was running a special £5,000 jackpot. She clicked and clicked. There: maxed out – the tickets would play later. More than enough hope to go to bed on.

She stepped over the blood spots. Had she been a better housewife, she would have got those stains out with carpet cleaner, or bleach, or whatever it was that better housewives used.

But she was not a wife and this was not her house.

She ought to tell Ola everything. She intended to tell Ola.

But not just yet.

Until their £30,000 future was banked and they stood, side by side, on an Aspen Street or wherever else Dr and Mrs Ola Abayomi were destined to live, she would not say a thing to her man.

Not one word.

Chapter Four

Longest drought ever.

Over three weeks had passed since her 'anniversary' ambush at the Indian restaurant. They had indulged in no sex at all – not a squeeze or stroke or crafty lick – in the days since then. No blame had been vocalised, but Etta suspected that she was coming across as uptight, or guilty, or in some other manner guaranteed to quash carnal appetite.

She tried, but her optimism was flagging; things were slipping. Ola's work was one problem. He might currently hold a research post that stoked the envy of junior colleagues in the world of neuroscience, but he had been there for two years and funding was never guaranteed. His work was demanding without being permanent; he had been called away once more tonight, this time to a seminar in Birmingham and, as he had wanted a night in front of the football, he had slunk off laden with self-pity, plus a beef, mustard and tomato sandwich for the journey.

Cozee, on the other hand, was always there for her. It remained excellent company. The bingo called her back time and again, punctuating her day with excitement and opportunity, while the odd message from other players made her feel welcome within the fold. StChristopher75 was the friendliest.

Active on chat and popular among Cozeers, he tipped her off about bingo specials and had even sent her another private message the day before:

StChristopher75: How u doing, been lucky? U will be. Look out for Treasure Island Bingo Special!

She smiled at the unmistakable mark of the pre-Tinder male: that former-boy-scout enthusiasm when chatting to a woman. What would he be, in his mid-forties? No doubt a sad divorcee after a spot of flirtation. Fair enough: divorce had to be rough. Faded tats, lager habit and a greying crew cut, probably. Harmless enough. It would not be the first time she had been chatted up in the corner of a room, even if this was a virtual one. Whatever, he was fast becoming her virtual best mate at the virtual party. And he might just give her a life-changing tip.

Cozee. Just by tasting the word in her mouth, Etta experienced that old Pavlovian response; her tongue grew slick as she hungered for colour, movement, excitement.

She went to the spare room. There was time for a little play before bed. If she spent the last of the money in her personal account, all £153.21, on a quick bingo game now, plus pre-buying max tickets for later that evening – Closing Time (£250 jackpot), Midnight Madness! (£1000 jackpot), One O'Clock Rock (£100) and so on – until it all ran out, she would be giving herself a true winning chance.

Etta clicked onto the main bingo room and started to buy tickets until a buzz shook her phone. Joyce:

Hi Etta. The government sent another letter. It's still going on. What do I do?

Etta typed a quick reply:

Hi, just send me a copy. Leave it with me, I'll sort it.

Like Joyce, Etta had surmised that the problem must have gone away, what with Westminster being called out in the national papers for rubbishing the retirement dreams of a host of old black folk and trashing the trust and good relations long ago established with the Caribbean community. This trashing and rubbishing now even had a name, the Windrush Scandal, and a 'day of national shame' had been pronounced some weeks before. That minister had resigned. But now, another letter? Etta sensed she might have over-promised and under-delivered on this one, but it was not her fault the government didn't give a toss: not like it was *their* mothers, their granddads. Life had been a bit too lively of late, but she *would* sort it.

She looked down at the disarray at her elbows. She also needed to sort their shared office. All this crap, always, across the desk. Ola's research, everywhere, demanding to be read.

Instead, she played.

Bingo was not calling her to any great extent. Her gaze drifted to the left of her screen. She had noticed the trailers for the 'mini games' some time before – so-called slot games that did not take you out of the bingo area – but had felt them to be too alien to explore. Now though, with three minutes fifty-four seconds until the next bingo game began, she wanted to get to know the alien.

She clicked.

When Lucky the Leprechaun opened up, it was no bigger than Etta's palm. There were five reels to spin, each revealing a different symbol and ten possible winning lines. You could adjust the amount that you gambled per line, as well as the number of lines. Etta took all this in at a glance, but what she really saw was the rocking four-leaf clovers, the leaping rainbows, fat Lucky dancing himself sick in some Irish meadow, bright jade upon bucolic green, as the oi-tiddly-oi-toi music played over silence where the bingo calls should be. All a silly, merry cartoon. But if you brought up all five clovers, you would win the rolling jackpot which currently stood at . . . £175,673.

Etta knew this would not happen. It was highly unlikely, at the very least. But, oh, how much greater was the thrill of that first £2 spin when one, then two, plump clovers rolled into view! She won nothing, of course, but . . . She deposited the rest of her money to play on the slots.

After five more spins, she upped the total stake per spin to £5. After another minute she stopped counting the spins.

One minute thirty-two seconds until her bingo game would start. Her tickets were bought and all but forgotten as Lucky frolicked. She had spun down to £45. Then: one, two, three . . . pleeease . . . four! Four clovers!

Etta leapt; rose clean out of her seat. Before she could calculate or check the paytable, it was there, instantly in her account balance: £1,045.

A thousand pounds, in one spin. Four clovers. Plus one yellow horseshoe where the jackpot should be.

A win!

Rewarded.

Etta clutched her hands into raised fists and shifted in her seat, but she did not shout. She withdrew every last pound: Cozee knowhow had become second nature in the weeks since she had joined the site. You had to stay savvy, had to suss out how it worked. A cursory scan of the slots information told her that each game had its own RTP, or return to player, for example 95 per cent, which meant they were programmed so that over time you were meant to lose and you knew it. It was a reminder that you had to keep on your toes and stay lucky. Big time lucky. Four clovers lucky.

Etta now believed she was meant for the slots. Just as with bingo, she would pre-empt errors of judgement and wrong-foot the RTP by applying a few rules, the cardinal one being to win and withdraw the difference; win and withdraw. Order came naturally to her: she had been keeping a spreadsheet of her overall winnings and was now, thanks to Lucky the Leprechaun, £1,728 up. If you were smart about it, you could make a fortune.

Etta was on to a very good thing.

•

At around 10 p.m., the neighbour's bulldog freaked out; he barked when anyone as much as scuffed the driveway. None-theless, Etta went around the house to close windows and lock up; Ola's nightly task. She left a light on in the spare room (he'd never know) and drew back the shower curtain, peered in the man-height wardrobe, stuck a head into the cupboard under the stairs. She checked that the kitchen's back door was locked and, after a second's thought, dragged a stool up against it; at the same time, she tried to shove the weight of her experience up against her closeted fears.

She went to the front door and, as she always did when left alone to secure the house, opened the door to peek outside; an odd tic, but she would not sleep without satisfying the urge. She opened the door.

A white box stood on the front step, as tall as her knees. It looked heavy. Beyond it was just the depth of purple-black night, broken only by the glow, here and there, of street lights. Nothing else; no one near, no van in the road. This box alone, a late delivery. On the top was a blue sticker: FRAGILE. She bent into a squat to perform a strong lift, heaved and almost toppled backwards: it was light, as if empty; no, as she carried it there was the light shift of something within. Etta double-locked the front door and put on the chain. She carried the box inside and placed it on the kitchen table, tilting it to read the address label. Electronically printed, it was addressed to 'Etta' – no title, no surname, but with the correct address. They both received the odd delivery after work, but rarely so late. And why had the courier not knocked?

The package was sealed up with dun parcel tape. She opened the cutlery drawer and removed the best tool: the large knife with the red handle. She stabbed the tape and sliced the box open, tearing back at the flaps. The scent of something rotten reached her nose too late; she had already thrust her hands deep into the high-sided box and pulled out handfuls of stinking, dead flowers.

Etta reeled back, droplets of vegetal gunk slopping onto the table. She held up her hands before her. Who? Why, this bouquet of hate?

She hurried to the sink and washed the slime away under a cold torrent. Turned the water hot, soaped, rinsed with more cold. Shook and dried. Sniffed at her fingertips to see if she could still detect that too-natural stench of dead beauty; that bosky decay clinging to her skin.

She drew the blinds down on the kitchen window and picked up her phone to call Ola. It went to voicemail.

She tried to sound normal in a text:

Ola, did you send me flowers? xx

A second reading suggested a certain ingratitude; she would explain when they spoke. She poured herself a drink while staring at her phone. Nothing. As she waited, she continued to examine the box.

No card or note. At the bottom lay a glass vessel holding a stagnant inch of water. Not a proper florist's vase, more of a jar, a crack near the rim which may have been caused by the lack of packaging around it. She lifted the jar up clear of the box; the phone buzzed; an explosion, a stab of horror. Horror that *this* should have come to her door caused her hand to spasm and fail and the jar to tumble to the floor and explode into a loud and comprehensive disintegration of her night.

On the floor, everywhere, shards of glass, putrid water.

Etta stared into the mess. She read the text. Ola:

No, what flowers? Stuck at drinks do with bad reception. Will call tomorrow. xx

Unable to stomach cleaning the tiles just yet, knowing that some unwanted darkness from outside was encroaching, she drew the blind down on the kitchen window; they never did that. She took a can from the cupboard and sat it on the stool barricading the back door; an early warning system, a booby-trap of butter beans. She checked each door once more and, working hard not to crack and call Ola again, threw a tea towel over the mess.

Surely the oozing remains of flowers had to be a gift gone bad. Had it been sitting at a wrong address for days, unnoticed until it was past saving? A neighbour might have gone on holiday, come back to find the mistake and dropped it on her doorstep, all too late. But who was it from? It was not her birthday and she had received precious little good news of late, nothing bouquet-worthy. Her mum would have called the second the blooms had been due to arrive. Colleagues sent her nothing, ever. Friends, including Joyce, would have rung the bell. Who then?

Etta turned the box all around once more. There was no date stamp. It had been hand-delivered. No one sent flowers hand-packed like this, anyway, with water and in that weird jar.

No stamp or sender's name. No note. No quirky misspelled scrawl and no newspaper cut-outs: no exhortations to 'Die, bitch'. Nothing except one fetid truth: someone hated her. The noxious gift had not been handled by a delivery man, so the warning sticker was for her, and it hit home:

FRAGILE

Etta took gin from the counter, poured it high into her glass and downed one hefty hit of it, relishing the cathartic shudder. She took another sip, another to drain the glass, then refilled it with gin. No tonic. The spirit heated and numbed her whole being, down to her feet; she would go upstairs, rather than run to Joyce. Police? No, for what? The present was sinister, her unease was real, but that did not add up to a crime. In any case, there would be nothing for them to come out to see: in the morning, this rank filth – crisp petals, dank stems, broken glass, the tea towel too – would go straight into the bin. She would not dump this *nastiness* on their foot-deep attempt at a compost heap: she did not want the revolting mess rotting down over months, to pollute their tomatoes, or to nourish nascent onions, ending up months later in an unassuming stew and then inside them. She was chucking the lot, box and all. It would be gone, destroyed tomorrow. For now, though, her hands would not approach.

She left the box on the kitchen table and went upstairs, checked every room on that floor, leaving another light on in the bathroom, and then crept into to her bedroom, locked the door and checked the windows and wardrobe. Only then did she climb, fully clothed, into her bed.

●

In the morning, Etta's first thought was of money. Her second thought sliced through the first: cut, dead flowers on her doorstep.

Ugly, but stunning in its daring. The cracked jar, that vicious gift. Who knew she would be alone? Who was watching her?

Tiredness was leaching from her bones, slowing her blood. She had tried to stay up and listen for the flower-bringer, but found herself waking at gone 3 a.m., no Ola beside her, lamp still on, charging phone in her hand. She had not dared move.

Now she jumped up and opened the door wide – what a brave friend was daylight! – and ran down to the kitchen. The box was where she had left it, the detritus still on the floor. She mopped, brushed, took the waste out to the wheelie bin and ran back inside. Unbearable: the rotting smell still hung in the kitchen and the hall. She fought down a tremor of nausea. Another essence, harsher and sharper but every bit as rotten, now seemed to be hanging around the whole house. She suspected that it emanated from the spare room.

Above the stench, a screaming from within: *You deserve this, skank!*

It was not OK to help herself to their joint money as if it were all hers for the taking. This was *bad*.

Her penance was waiting: the First Welcome Project. She worked there two Thursdays a month if she could; if not, then one. She pulled that day's sackcloth out of the wardrobe: a lilac shirt, fitted jeans and plimsolls.

She would immerse herself in the lives of others. People mostly poorer, and better, than her. She would solve their problems: do all the right things, at all the right times, and slap a goddamn smile on it. She would be *useful*. Then, she would return home and cook as she had not cooked since she discovered Cozee. No microwave-thawed sausages tonight.

•

The line was out of the door of Seacole Community Hall today. Etta walked past the elderly woman folded into her sari, the pregnant teen with pink ends to her hair, the man with dreads standing still and stoic, a couple of friends in their twenties, one pouty and one underdressed, speaking Russian, the woman in a cheap suit wearing earphones . . . all the beating hearts of Rilton coming to her door.

'Hi! Everyone OK?'

She smiled as she walked past the queue into the civic centre. The new posters looked half-decent, with the First Welcome Project fresh again in purples and greens, not the bleached-out hues of the past year. Kim, a new volunteer, was a graphic designer in her day-job.

Etta was looking out for Janie, that five-foot-high maelstrom of efficiency and kindness topped with a shock of bright copper. There: she bustled out from the broom-cupboard kitchen, holding a mug.

'If it isn't Ms Etta Oladipo!'

'Janie McJanieface!'

The women wrapped arms around each other for a moment. Etta felt a warmth envelop her: a small bloom of renewal, resolve and relief.

'Five minutes, OK?' said Janie. 'Then we'll get them in. Sit!'

Etta's supervisor brought her up to speed on the past month: this new scheme to steer clients towards, and that improved leaflet to give the most needy, and this mind-blowing injustice to break to your heart and that heart-breaking case to blow your mind.

After five minutes Etta felt, as she did on her Thursdays, ready to take on the whole goddamn world just to help her fellow humans who were queueing at the door.

She was sitting at the trestle table nearest the kitchen, her usual spot.

'Hi Tunde, hi Felicia, hi Kim!'

Etta's first client was sitting on the chair opposite before she had put down her handbag. It was the teen girl with pink hair, hunched over her baby bump.

'Hi, how can I help you?' asked Etta.

'Hi,' said the girl. 'I'm in a massive mess. I'm panicking . . .'

'OK, don't worry,' said Etta. 'What's your name?'

'Cally.'

'Hi Cally. Let me pour you some water.' Etta filled a glass for her. 'Right, what's gone on?'

'Basically, Dad kicked me out 'cos I'm pregnant.'

'Right. So sorry. Where are you living now?'

'I'm staying at my mate Taz's. But she lives with her mum so . . . I can only stay a few more days . . . God!'

The girl started to cry. 'It's not like I wanted to get knocked up.'

'And where's the father?' asked Etta, feeling about a hundred years old and predicting the answer.

'I don't know. He ghosted me straight off.' The tears were coming harder now. 'It's doing my head in.'

As the girl went to scuff the tears away with the heel of her palm, Etta noticed a criss-cross of razor scars up her forearm.

The girl went on. 'Not like I ever even wanted kids. Still don't.'

Etta leaned to pass her tissues from the box she always kept close to hand.

'OK, Cally. Here's what we can do.'

Etta went through the leaflets, explained about a benefit amendment, then made a phone call as Cally texted, one hand resting on her bump.

'So yeah, great news. Spoke to Sandra over at Fitzgerald House and they have a room for you. Here's their address . . .'

Etta would not let Cally get broken, not on her watch.

The next one in the hot seat, Ray, fifty-seven, only needed help filling out a benefits form and details about the food bank. He eyed Etta with suspicion as she explained the paperwork, as if confused.

'All OK, Ray?'

'Yeah. Just wondering why a sort like you would be doing this to help. You lot have enough on your plate, don't you, being coloured and that.'

Etta did not scowl or smile. She did not correct him, did not say 'I'm black', because Ray had enough on his plate being Ray. She simply put Xs where he needed to sign the forms and pushed it over to him.

He looked down, then up again.

'Actually . . . I did read a little bit, inside, but . . .'

'Give it here,' said Etta and read the details aloud.

Ray gave her a respectful bob of his head as he left. It was something.

●

A two-minute breather before the pair of Russians came to her table. The mousy one in a playsuit stood and played on her phone while her friend with cascading black curls sat and pouted darkly at Etta.

'I must have indefinite leave to remain. Or be citizen,' she said.

'OK. What's your name?'

'Medina. *Čeliković*.'

'When did you arrive from—'

The friend muttered a place name that could have been 'Neatrinik' or 'near Trahvnik' or 'new Trivnik'.

'Sorry, I don't . . . is that in Russia?'

Both young women laughed. Etta bit her lip; never assume, this was not a FrameTech *meeting*, she needed to re-engage with her sensitivity. She let them slowly unpack the who, what and how, while she did paperwork.

'How did you get here?' she asked at one point.

'Oh God, I cannot tell you.' The friend dug the client with her elbow, said something fast in their language. 'OK! This friend, Nadia, she helped me.'

'How?' asked Etta.

The friend looked down. Medina shook her head.

'With paperwork. Just like you.'

Etta nodded, knowing not to venture further. As usual, the client answered some questions, evaded others. Etta tamped down her suspicions.

'OK, so, what do you need right now?'

'I must stay in the UK.'

'OK. Do you have family here?'

'I have a husband. Fiancé, we marry soon.'

'OK, good. Then you might well be eligible for indefinite leave to remain.'

The friend started talking fast in their language, gesticulating as if frustrated.

'OK, I know,' said the client, followed by some more foreign words. The friend walked away to sit in the waiting area.

'All OK?' asked Etta.

'She worry about me. What happens if . . . he changes his mind?'

'What do you mean? If you don't get married?'

'Yes.' She looked Etta in the eye, almost vibrating with the need to share. 'I had an illness. Cannot have babies.'

'I'm sorry.'

'Hm, yes.' Now she lowered her gaze. 'It is hard.'

'It's good that you have your fiancé's support.'

The client bit her lip, her face pale and intense, mouth twisting as if torn between laughter and tears. She burst out:

'He does not know! And he wants them, soon.'

'Ah, OK,' said Etta.

'It is why I need everything to be secure.'

Etta gave a few gentle nods to mask how dumbstruck she was by the great unfairness of life. How much fairer might the world feel if, illness aside, the situations of this client and pregnant Cally could be swapped? But as a volunteer, her job was not to decide suitable fates, it was to chip away at the unfairness, one problem at a time.

She straightened in her seat and smiled.

'OK! Let's see if you're eligible for a Form SET(M).'

'Thank you. Must stay in England. I will do anything . . . oh!'

The young woman reeled back, touching her hand to her nose. Blood trickled through her fingers.

'It's OK, relax, pinch there. No, higher,' said Etta. 'Nosebleed. I get them myself from time to time. You're fine.'

'God,' said the friend, wandering back towards the desk. 'So nasty.'

'What?' snapped the client. 'At least it's not broken.'

'True,' said Etta, pulling tissues out once again. 'OK. Take five, while I look through the eligibility requirements.'

After a good bit of digging, her client was sent away with a clutch of papers and renewed hope.

The next five clients who came in, all needing, all broke, none yet broken, were given encouragement and advice and addresses and vouchers and sympathy and cups of tea and water, and forms. It was a great result when she was able to give them a form.

No one would get broken here. Not at Seacole Community Hall. At least not on one of her Thursdays. Not on her watch.

•

By the time Ola walked into their kitchen that evening, setting down his briefcase and pulling her into a tight embrace, there was a festive feast of a *suya* starter, followed by A-grade rice and stew, with a teetering side of plantain on the table, and Etta was ready to confess all.

'Good seminar?' Etta asked as they sat down.

'Yup.'

'I'm glad you're home.'

'So am I. Oh my heavens, this food! I swear, you say you're half Jamaican but, deep down, you are all Nigerian woman!'

'Go back far enough and yeah, I probably am!'

'Hehe!' Pleased, he leaned closer. 'We should try to spend a bit more time together, Teetee. You are working too hard most evenings now. You must not let them start taking advantage of you.'

'I won't.'

'And which man is bringing flowers to my woman, heh? What nonsense is this?'

They laughed.

'There were just these flowers, at least I think they were. They were horrible, all slimy and gone bad. Must have been a raffle prize, or something else that I've forgotten about. Anyway, I chucked them.'

'Good!'

Raffle prize. Etta pressed her head into the nook where his arm met his chest and where he could not see her eyes. That devastating musk: he could not be replaced. She had to tell him.

'Ola—'

'I know, work is work, but tonight you're all mine. Come, may we chop? Then early to bed, heh?'

She smiled up at his generous black face, the light sheen of a day's effort on it. He gleamed. His attractiveness to her towered above all else, unassailable as Chappal Waddi mountain. She wanted to be his good woman once more. Perhaps no words were needed. She would lean against him until she melted into his form where he stood. She would press her lips to his chest, smooth his brow, make fresh *chin chin* for him, undo all the untruths. In that moment, he was *everything*.

'OK, darling.'

•

They went to bed sated. But in her sleep a weighty itch settled upon her, more than too much pepper and undigested rice. During the night, the shadows danced and shifted; her priorities did much the same. She had coughed her eyes open at 4.53 a.m. and crept away from the heavily sleeping Ola to go to the spare room.

Her winnings had tipped into her bank account in the night and now she could think of nothing but winning more.

Etta powered up. She reached into the top drawer for the headphones and pushed away the haunting thought: that this was more than *bad*, this was not normal behaviour. She had turned an entire room of their home into a lie. But she had no choice! How else could she bring on their sluggish nest egg; how else to transform their cash into the windfall their futures demanded?

She was not addicted, she knew that; she took strict precautions against that specific eventuality. She took breaks, held back, maintained her Cozee spreadsheet, controlled herself.

And so, she played.

Etta managed to creep from spare room to bathroom and turn on the shower minutes before Ola's alarm went off.

Chapter Five

On the last Tuesday in May, following a lazy Bank Holiday weekend, Ola had to take the train north and would not be back until late that night: a new scientific facility in Leeds required his presence. He viewed this as professional validation; she was not clear why. Etta moved around her own working sphere in a torpor of indifference, the FrameTech office a mere waiting room for an appointment with destiny. Life would spark into being when she got home.

By the afternoon, her apathy was arousing interest.

'You OK, sweetness?' asked Winston. 'Maybe you need another coffee, 'my right?'

Etta made a small coffee, then downed a large water.

Minutes later, Dana said. 'We do actually need those docs today. Jean's asked for them.'

'Joy. Thanks, Jean.'

Dana laughed. 'Can you do them by close of play?'

'Sure.'

'That's if you can raise your head from the desk. You OK, hon?'

'Fine.'

'Do you want me to get you some water? I know all that caffeine crap is tempting but most tiredness is caused by dehydration.'

Etta had made that one mid-afternoon coffee; a third of it had been left to go cold and her water glass was still on her desk.

'You see, you probably don't realise how bad caffeine is for you,' Dana went on. 'You think it gives you a boost, but it actually works against your body so that—'

'Stop whitesplaining,' she muttered, louder than planned.

'You what?' asked Dana.

'Never mind,' said Etta, simulating typing: a gunfire of adshjklrwqyisn on her screen. 'I don't need water. Thank you, though.'

Dana walked off.

Stares and sharp smiles came at her from all directions; the sickly artificial light seemed to dip further, darkening shadows across faces. Were they all watching her, monitoring her?

Jean was walking over to her from the corner where Accounts tended to huddle. As she neared, a tide of panic began rising in her chest: what work did she owe? What wrong had she done? Why was that bird-like grey head craning her way?

'Hullo,' said Jean. A lift of tufted lip, a wobble of neck as she appeared to swallow an urge to spit out something kinder. 'You don't look too good, missy . . . Feeling fragile?'

'I . . .' She tried to read the older woman's face. 'No. Thank you.'

Etta lowered her head and sipped at long-dead coffee until Jean had shuffled back to her corner. She took cold, bitter sips until the paranoia – surely what it had to be – had percolated through her mind, draining down and away, dissipating into the muscles of extremities which gave twitches of reassurance: her tapping foot, a flex of her fingers. She would be OK.

The end of the day called Etta home to the spare room.

She had been mining diamonds and rubies – £20! £55! £17! – for some unknowable length of time, until the lump of coal leapt out, leaving black smuts across her screen. Bonus over, but her account read £492. She was still winning.

Etta clicked onto My Account and changed her username from EO1984 to DestinysChild. Just for luck.

By 6 p.m., DestinysChild had lost all £492 of her winnings and deposited another £300. Twenty minutes later her Cozee account stood at £1,320. The bonus rounds, won on three or four different slots, had triggered an explosion of joy that made her eyes roll back in her head. Just mind-boggling, ridiculous luck.

Etta knew then: she was made for Cozee. And Cozee was remaking her.

•

She was still in the spare room when she heard his voice.

'I'm back!'

'Hey you!' she cried.

Ola had come home at precisely the wrong time. Chat was insisting that a new slot – Aztecarama – was offering these crazily boosted bonus rounds only until 9 p.m. and it was twenty to. Making a face that it was better he could not see, she shut down and went to greet him.

'How was it?' she asked, features readjusted.

'Actually, not too bad,' Ola replied. 'More interesting than I had expected.'

'Meet any nice people?'

'One or two, I suppose.' He picked up his bag and moved to the stairs. 'There's still dinner, right? I was going to take a shower, but I wan chop.'

'Go ahead, shower first.'

As she heard the pump kick in and the water start to stream, Etta considered sprinting upstairs. But she did not breach the boundaries of their unlovely kitchen. She continued to do nothing to the supermarket lasagne, heated long ago in the oven. She half-arsed the salad and burnt the garlic bread as the reels spun her thoughts. Aztecarama would be going batshit with bonus rounds right then, she could sense it. She would run to the spare room, if she could get away with it.

Ten minutes later (there had been time!), Ola ambled into the kitchen, wrapped only in a towel, and gathered her into another hug.

'Missed you in the shower.' He kissed her.

She met his lips while pulling away.

'Olala, are you going to eat like that? Get dressed, the plates are hot!'

'He he he, woman. Don't nag me o!'

Still laughing, he went to pull on his dressing gown. What must she do, for this evening to succeed; what must she not do, how must she look? His damp body warmed her, as ever, but she could no more engage with his muscles than juggle the cutlery she held in her hand. She had to focus.

Upon his return, she served him up the pasta.

'It is good,' he said after a few fast mouthfuls. 'Not your usual recipe though, am I right?'

His arch gaze fixed on the foil tray wedged at the top of the recycling.

She styled it out. 'Detective!'

'Ah! You know I am genius!'

'I know.'

'No really. I've cracked the angle on the Science It! piece they want me to write. I've worked out the way of explaining the action of Ecstasy on the brain in layperson's terms, found a way of explaining how MDMA triggers serotonin . . .'

Etta smiled as he went on and on. She got the gist, she usually did. But right now serious cash prizes were waiting to be taken down and all this sitting, and smiling, and admiring, and playing along while he—

'. . . brain cells made of supermarket bloody lasagne. Etta! I can tell you're not listening. Tcha!'

'I am. I was! Sorry. But give me a break about dinner, will you, please? I was expecting to have a busy evening.'

He looked at her from under lowered brows, a boy-child with a grudge.

'Next time,' she smiled. 'I'll make my extra-special one for you.'

Ola folded his work back into his pocket and sat up straighter.

'So. They have given you homework again?' he asked.

'Yes,' said Etta.

'Ah,' he said. 'Too busy for her man, these days.'

'Don't start, Ola.'

'Actually . . .' he put down his fork. 'It's true. You say I'm always away, but at least when I am back, I am *back*. These days when you're here, *you are not really here*.'

Etta flushed. 'Why are you being weird all of a sudden? Like you said, you're the one who is away all the time. Why is that anyway?'

'Oh, come on, don't—'

'I'm not joking. How do I know you're not—'

'What, woman? When I am working all the time to support our lives, what am I doing that is so wrong, Etta? Please, I dare you to tell me.'

He stared at her; she stared at her plate, wondering whether she could set free that one word which would tip their evening into a searing silence.

'How do I know,' she said, 'that it's not another Zagreb?'

Ola made a low noise at the back of his throat – *humh* – and said:

'That is unfair.'

'Yes. It was.'

'So, you are going to bring all that up again?'

'I'm not bring anything up, Ola. It lives with us the whole time, forever, like a disease.'

'Yes, like you've got a brain fever.'

'No, like we've got herpes.'

'Etta!'

'Well, how do you want me to be? I still don't understand why you did it.'

'I've told you, over and over, I did not *do* anything.'

'But you wanted to. And I can't understand it. How could you even get into that situation?'

Ola gave a heavy sigh:

'I was away from home and a bit messed up. That horrible conference. Every single person having a bad time and collecting endless business cards to remember it by. I felt isolated. I was drinking. You felt so far away.'

'But why didn't you just call me?'

Ola closed his eyes. 'As I told you, I did meet this woman. But I did not want to hurt you. I did not want to . . . to . . .'

'To what?'

'I did not want to want her!'

Etta took a step back, as if she had been slapped. That one firecracker fact exploded into the kitchen, bigger than the mechanics of the denied infidelity. Hotter and more danger-ous. She had wanted to fire his anger, but had got burnt.

'Are you happy now?' said Ola quietly. 'I wanted her.'

'So then,' said Etta. 'You made sure you got what you wanted.'

'Oh Etta,' said Ola. He rose and walked out of the kitchen. Seconds later their bedroom door closed.

He had wanted someone else.

He had not screwed her.

But he had screwed *them*.

Etta swallowed hard, but the tears fell all the same. That night two years before when he had first explained that something had nearly happened in Zagreb. They had talked through until dawn, sending increasingly conciliatory words across the chipped wooden surface. By the time sunlight had flooded the kitchen they were getting married. Someday.

Now she had brought it all up again. That cruel twist of the knife had hurt her too. She would spend the night in the spare room, making secret amends.

Etta cleaned up the kitchen and went to the spare room, taking a glass and three quarters of a bottle of Malbec with her. Ola, meanwhile, had plugged his laptop in next to hers to charge, there on the desk. He never did that, these days. It was an obvious aggression: he was pissing on her parade, reclaiming the territory and marking it like a dog. That man! He was attempting to take over the one space that had organically evolved into her own. Notionally a shared study, it was actually hers: its wardrobe housed an overspill of clothes she could not face giving to charity just yet. Her mother and late father smiled at her, draped in their wedding finery, from a landlord-approved hook on the wall. If Ola was forced to work at home, he preferred the kitchen table, its proximity to brain-sustaining snacks and drinks. He was making a loud point.

Etta was more into making money. She spun the reels, over and over, and lost another £700. That was that. Every penny she had left of her salary, taken out via her personal account was now gone. Her late dinner grumbled low in her abdomen. What point had she just made?

She needed to sleep on it, to dream up a plausible story overnight. She went to power down her laptop. The green charging light of Ola's computer winked at her.

Seconds later, she had powered his machine up and was looking for a Word doc called 'Motsdepasse'. In Ola's ordered world no prying opportunist, hacker or thieving rascal could possibly speak French.

There it was, in the Home folder. Every password that mattered to them, right there. This trusting document set out all their credit card, account details and passwords, in case a wallet should be lost, or a handbag stolen. He did try so hard to look after them. The list of accounts, licences and online registrations in alphabetical order, so orderly and proper:

Library Online Account
Licences – Cars
Licence – TV
MO Money
Mortgage
MOT

She found what she needed and took it.

Etta soon felt water rising in her eyes, beading above her brow. The night was melting; it was so hot, precociously sticky for May. Was that down to high pressure or low pressure?

Climate change, no doubt. A large part of her yearned to go through to their bedroom, lie down and rest her head on Ola's chest. To whisper the truth, every last word of it, into his sleep-bound ear. But there really could be no rest for the wicked.

So: hello Merlin's Miracles.

Shuffling up the spare bed, she propped herself up against the wall, plugged in her headphones and deposited £500. In an instant she became an Arthurian knight, on a quest to accrue money in place of glory. Whir, blur, £470, £460, £490 . . . £590! She withdrew the £90 and carried on as if starting again. Every time she went back over £500, she creamed off the difference. She found her rhythm. Then, Merlin waved his wand! Etta sat up as if her own buttocks were giddying the grey mare up the drawbridge.

OK, here we go . . .

Onscreen, three vast oak doors, complete with coarse grain and strap hinges, lay ahead. One would open onto the Holy Grail and all its riches, the others onto a medieval dung heap of self-loathing. She hovered the cursor: middle, no left, no middle. Click.

The door yawned wide to reveal a golden goblet fashioned from the old World Cup trophy and bathed in graphics of purest light. Etta gasped as a jingle started up and serious cash began effervescing up at her from the grail's very lip: £400! £250! £100! £150! £700!

This was it; this was the sweet liquor of the Cozee experience.

This was what it was to be mind-fucked by free money. You had to be assaulted by cash coming at you. Bam-bam-bam! It was a feeling like nothing else.

Winning, really winning, was intense. Done right, it was an unparalleled multi-sensory experience. Etta liked to do it right. Her earbud headphones ensured that the beguiling music, turned up to a vibrant volume, played deep into her ear canal. Her mind was macerated in pleasure. She let mock folk rock lead her into the experience, beyond mere watching; inside it. The watching, though, was spectacular. There were colours of candy and gemstones, primaries and purples; a whole Hatton Garden of brilliant-cut diamonds; brash, beautiful gold, and enough silver to make you betray your own reason. In case the emos did not bite, there was Vampire Wonderworld with its half-light of black joy and white pain. Something for everyone. The games that enticed Etta tended to be the brightest, the most delicious, those that exploded into honey-sweet kaleidoscopes as soon as you hit a bonus. Colours, then: all your favourites, hand-picked by you. Dancing, flashing, cavorting, cartwheeling, sambaing, swaying and doing the Shaku Shaku. The eye was brutalised with pleasure.

She hovered the arrow over Withdraw; £2,800 was sitting there. It was 1.57 a.m. She had already dreamed, now she just might sleep.

•

She got as far as the door. Then she turned around, sat and powered up once more.

Merlin, make my night.

You had to ride your luck while it lasted, even at 2 a.m.

A pink light was waiting for her. The message flashed onto the screen:

StChristopher75: Thought you might be up.
DestinysChild: Yes. On a mission!
StChristopher75: Good wins?

DestinysChild: Yes, ty. Merlin, almost £3k.

StChristopher75: Wdwdwd

DestinysChild: How about you?

StChristopher75: Couldn't sleep, apu.

DestinysChild: Sorry. So, 1975 . . . you drinking cocoa in your slippers right now? 😄

A ten-second hiatus. Too much?

He finally answered:

StChristopher75: Yes. Slippers are the number one accessory for all that geriatric clubbing.

DestinysChild: 😄 OK, I get it, 1975 – you're not really THAT old.

StChristopher75: Damn right.

DestinysChild: 😄 Thanks for sharing your Cozee wisdom btw.

StChristopher75: Pleasure. You newbies don't know you're born. I'm a natural winner, me 😄

DestinysChild: Glad to hear it!

StChristopher75: Stick with me, kid.

DestinysChild: Oh yes? Why should I do that?

StChristopher75: Cos I bet I'm just what u need.

DestinysChild: Bold claim.

StChristopher75: Fortune favours the brave.

DestinysChild: Brave or naughty?

StChristopher75: Both. And lucky.

DestinysChild: I'll bear that in mind.

StChristopher75: Do that. Gtg.

DestinysChild: Me too. Stay lucky.

The pink light blinked off – he was gone.

Etta laughed, without a sound and to no one, then moved the cursor away from Withdraw. Merlin liked her and a £30K target was not so much; she could end it all, tonight.

Spin, spin, spin: she crested along on desire, good intentions and a 2010 Barolo.

She was aroused. This was bliss. This was indeed Ecstasy.

More, more. Again!

Yes, she was unequivocally aroused. What to do?

Autospin: On.

Etta let her eyelids droop and settled into the rhythm of the reels. She slipped her free hand down the waistband of her knickers. Down, there, she played on.

StChristopher75 was flirting with her.

(Lucky, she thought, as she stroked.)

He had singled her out.

He had good chat, so probably good looks.

(Through her lashes: three wizard staffs on the reels: £100.)

He was brave, and lucky.

Was he naughty?

(Stroke faster for yes.)

Was he rich?

Might he save her?

Yes.

(Three wizard hats. £200!)

She would show Ola.

Yes.

She would show Ola.

Yes!

She would show . . . oh, oh! Oh!

Ecstasy . . . She floated free, outside herself.

Five minutes later, hand firmly back on the mouse, Etta was no longer blissed out. Her buzz had proven more costly than any drug-fuelled high, and it was not lasting as long. Terrible play, just now. This game was sucking her large deposit down to nothing like a Camelot courtesan on the king's honeymoon. Merlin was a bitch.

Spin, spin, spin.

£1,100, £1,080, £1,060 . . .

Too hot, too close. Merlin had to appear.

£340, £320, £300 . . .

She lost all notion of time, she lived in the fluid moment. Spinning in her ecstatic void, swept along on a cool tide of novelty and hope, warmed by limitless red wine, she soon reached her last £20 and then . . . nowhere, nothing. £0.00. All £2,800 gone.

She had been slaughtered. She was slaughtered.

Her eyes roamed the room, seeking an escape. A fly had died on her window ledge. Was that climate-change heat? Suicide?

This could not be the end. She needed more funds.

Motsdepasse.

Within seconds another £5,000 was on Cozee, waiting to be processed into wins.

Etta exhaled, long and slow. A Rubicon had been crossed, one five-grand deep. She was tempted to hate herself but instead crept downstairs through Stygian gloom and returned with another bottle of red.

Play on.

The overcooked fly trembled, spindly legs pointing upwards on the windowsill. They used to bury you in the sky, didn't they? The Z people. Zars . . . That lame RE project she had giggled over with her classmate Victoria Barnes: A for Anglican, B for Buddhist . . .

Spin, spin, spin.

Time was stuck; it was suspended. As her balance dipped, Etta had the sensation that it was herself, not the reels, revolving in the middle of the night.

Spin, spin . . .

Zoroastrians! The end of the religious alphabet. This fly was being purified as it putrefied, a comforting thought as Etta hit £0.00 once more. Zero.

It was too damn hot. It was 3.32 a.m. And Merlin's Miracles had royally screwed her over.

She padded downstairs and took the last bottle from the rack.

Try Cash King. Spinderella's Ball. Try.

Etta deposited, drank and gambled with a devotion as pure as any she had known. She was changing their lives, she would see it through. At some point, a silver light shone through the gaping curtains, two bright shafts illuminating the wine bottles in the bin.

It was 5.57 a.m. She had failed and won, won and failed all night. The worst kind of gambling. The only kind of gambling: no lie on earth could save her today. Etta shut her eyes, and out came a madwoman's sighs. She had managed to withdraw £380, which would hit her bank account in forty-eight hours. Bar that – no getting around it – she had lost all £22,000 of their house deposit.

Chapter Six

WEDNESDAY, 30 MAY 2018

Fuck.

OK.

Fuck.

OK.

Twenty-two thousand . . . *fuck.*

OK, OK.

No.

What was this, now? Who even was she? She groped in the half-dark, looking for herself, needing to see. A mirror she had never much considered, fixed to the wall by the door. She stooped to look at herself, the woman who had lost £22,000, and all she saw was scar tissue.

No.

Etta had *lost* it, but she would not lose it.

Whatever her brain was doing now, whatever was controlling the sad chemicals and consoling the stunned synapses she did not know, nor did she care to think. Her loss – this big-ass catastrophe – needed to be spilled out of her mind and spelled, in a neat black font, onto white screen; the shame shrunk and locked into the boxes of her spreadsheet.

She had squandered the money – all of it – for now, but she still had her smarts; no need to waste energy mourning the loss. So no, she would not throw her laptop across the room, or crawl into the wardrobe and cave in, or sink to the floor and wail. No. Above all else, Etta now needed to prove that she had not lost all power: she still possessed the cognitive wherewithal to rewind, delete, undo.

Before Ola awoke in their room next door, she would have thought of a solution.

Could family help, her mum? No, she had no money to spare and, even if she did, Etta would never, ever tell her what she had done. Family though . . . the cloud of an idea started to form: a distant relation, a cousin of her paternal grandfather, somewhere north of Lagos. He was hailed within family folk-lore as a man who carried as many pounds on his body as he held in the bank. Uncle Moneybags barged his way into her thoughts, a fat black saviour, but she forced him out. Total non-starter. Never even met the bloke; plus in genealogical terms he was no form of uncle, nor was he, by all accounts, all that great.

Think on.

She scrolled through the Jamaican side – the cousins, aunties, uncles and maybe-somebodies; she flicked through her whole mental address book, from colleagues to old class-mates, but not one offered more promise. As hopeless as it was urgent: she would only have the £380 she had withdrawn to her bank account and that would not clear for two days.

Think on. Think!

Loans. There were these payday loans. They said the rates were high, but that would only matter if you could not repay them. She would win again, win better. She would pay them back.

Payday loans could not be that bad. If you needed £500 and had to pay back £900 after a few weeks, then of course it was not *fair*, you bet your life it was not *reasonable*. But when you were broke and needed funds you just did whatever was *doable*.

And she would do it: an instant solution, no familial complications. Well worth the incalculable interest when you knew you could win everything back and more – £1,000, £2,000, £100,000 – in one single spin. At least you had funds to process.

Here we go:

Kwikee Loans, the PayMaster, Wonky Loans, Moolarge. com, EezeeLuker, CashGod.com . . .

Etta filled in the form of the one with the highest star review average, 4.6, decent. She assumed her credit score was perfect. The PayMaster agreed and within fifteen minutes £1,000 was in her bank account, ready to Cozee up.

She went through to their bedroom and eyed the still-sleeping Ola. She was at such a remove from his blind ignorance; they had never been so far apart, not since Zagreb. She could only try to repay, and to repair, and to – oh, the irony, the agony, the shame, the goddamn stupidity! – earn serious dollar by hiding away from him on Cozee. It was all she could do. That and phone in sick for work, quick-smart.

•

Her phone rang almost as soon as she'd hung up on Winston.

'Joyce! Hi.'

'Hi Etta, how's it going?'

'OK. I'm off work today.'

'God, wish I was. I've got to be quick: listen, I was wondering if you got that second letter? I sent it to you a few days ago.'

'Yes, Joyce. Sorry, meant to say. I got it.'

'Great. Are you still OK to write back for us?'

'Of course, of course. I'm on it, hon.'

'Aw, thanks so much, you're brilliant. Gotta go. Laters, yeah?'

'Bye.'

Etta placed her phone face down on the desk. A pixelated Hansel and Gretel blinked improbable eyes at her from her laptop, waiting for another candy-house bonus round. When that came, pear drops, chocolates, sherbet and nougat would rain down upon their orphaned heads, exploding upon impact into cash amounts, until the witch burst forth from the pantry to call time on the whole sickly bonanza. Etta was all set to gorge again.

But first, Joyce. Joyce had forwarded her the second letter which had arrived only the day before. It was the uglier twin of the first letter: 200-odd words that spelled out an officious lack of concern that the writers – the committee, or cabal – were too arrogant to disguise. Worse, it was designed to shake you up, just as it shakes you up when your life partner tells you, without remorse or regret, that they want to split up, that they're kicking you out of the house and that oh, by the way, you were never actually married.

Etta would write again to the government. And call them too, if necessary.

The fairytale siblings blinked again.

Maybe she could do it after she hit a bonus round.

She kept spinning. Moments later, as if her laptop could read her thoughts, a tinny trumpet sounded, a gnarled witch threw her door open wide and she was *in*. £500! £150!

Etta ended her game a tidy £1,000 up. It was a start.

A pink light shone from her Cozee messages. Her face heated: StChristopher75. She had been out of control, touching herself like that. This was trouble.

Ignore it?

She clicked him open.

StChristopher75: How r u?

DestinysChild: Not bad. Winning. You?

StChristopher75: Not bad. Winning. Do you gamble IRL?

DestinysChild: Not so far. Rilton's not really a casino sort of place!

StChristopher75: I know Rilton, not far away. I know people there. Great ice rink too.

DestinysChild: Yes, I live just between that and the massive church.

StChristopher75: What, near that brilliant all-day breakfast place?

DestinysChild: Yes, Teddy's – that's just up the road.

StChristopher75: Cool. U got work there?

DestinysChild: Nothing to write home about. Love my volunteering though.

StChristopher75: Charity shop?

DestinysChild: No, First Welcome. We advise people who need it: homeless, migrants, benefits etc.

StChristopher75: My kind of place. Wd 😃

DestinysChild: Thanks, I do love it.

StChristopher75: Still, u must need a break. R u going to the Summer Party?

DestinysChild: ???

StChristopher75: Cozee VIP Summer Party, big one cos Cozee's 10. U a VIP?

DestinysChild: No, not yet. Are you then?

StChristopher75: Too right! Keep going, u will be. Glglgl

Off went the pink light once more.

For the first time in hours, Etta smiled. She hit withdraw on £900 of her winnings. The £100 would form the seed money for the next session's investment. This was now her job. She was a money farmer, working the glittering Cozee landscape; reap, sow, reap, sow; this was post-truth era agriculture with a cash crop. Retain a cool head, and a bit of luck, and the £22,000 would be replaced before she knew it.

And now, while the luck was on her, she would do the right thing. She had to: Joyce was too important to her, always had been, ever since they used to bounce around the place with bobbles in their bunches, wearing the matching Friends 4 Eva T-shirts they had pestered their parents for; Joyce always faster, funnier, Etta shy but bright. They had grown up but never grown out of their friendship, even after boys came along; they had only needed each other more.

Yes: she would write again, a real letter, this time, to be printed onto strong white paper; she would write as she had not written in some time. The letter would kick off, disarm, guilt-trip, kick ass. It would not cuss or punch out; it would employ the argot of the powerful, shout 'injustice, you rotters!' loud enough to wake the conscience of Westminster. It would do the trick.

Forty minutes later, it was done.

•

Wednesday, 30 May 2018

To Her Majesty's Government,

I am writing to you with regard to the case of one Mrs Cynthia May Jackson. When you read my letter, I am sure that you will agree that resolution of this matter is of the utmost urgency.

Mrs Jackson has been recently threatened with deportation to Jamaica, the country in which she was born in 1942. While the reasons behind these threats are not entirely clear, it would appear that they pertain to missing or incorrect paperwork.

Bearing in mind that Mrs Jackson came to England in 1966 and that half a century is a hell of a long time in which to expect even the most diligent record-keeper to hold on to paperwork, could you please clarify precisely which documents are required to prove she is entitled to live in this country?

I have some suggestions for you. Could it be the certificate she received a few years back to congratulate her on her 40 years of service to the NHS? Or the cutting from the local newspaper that shows her, proud in her pressed midwife's uniform, surrounded by dozens of the British children she brought safely into the world? No? Could it be her marriage certificate, or children's birth certificates, the church and hospital each only two miles from where she still lives? If it's still her house: could it be the title deeds to her home? How about the four decades of PAYE slips?

(If it is her benefits paperwork you need, please go ahead and book a seat on the plane now: Mrs Jackson has accepted nothing, ever, except the child benefit and NHS pension to which she was honoured to feel entitled.)

I suspect it may be her passport you are after. On this front, we will sadly be unable to satisfy your request, as Mrs Jackson, having experienced severe turbulence during both her childhood and her flight to Heathrow, decided that she would never leave the country again and neglected to apply for one.

Whatever the paperwork you need, I sincerely doubt that there is one single document that can convey just how much Mrs Cynthia May Jackson believes she is British and how much she has given back to the country she calls home.

Yours sincerely,

Joyce Jackson

(On behalf of Mrs Cynthia May Jackson)

She emailed it to Joyce. Then she picked up the phone.

'OK Joyce, I've written another letter. You listening?'

She read it to her, the reading punctuated by the odd 'Yes!' from her friend. She finished.

'That is beautiful, Etta. Thank you so much. Should I email it or post it?'

Etta replied, 'Both.'

She shut down the email account and looked out of the window. The gables of the nearest house seemed to inch closer by the day: they were bearing down on her. For now, though, this was a minor annoyance. She was doing good deeds, setting records straight. Winning back £22,000, a sum she would consider gobsmacking, had it not already smacked her so hard on the arse.

£21,000 to go and counting.

She powered up the Cozee site.

●

The next day, Thursday, she called in sick again. Friday, spent once more 'off sick', at least brought with it respite from residual guilt: it was practically the weekend. On Saturday, Etta won, on Sunday, she lost. On Monday, she returned to work; that evening, she won again. She advanced over uneven fortunes, gathering the odd bump or bruise, but in all she was climbing the mountain: there was now £8,335 in the pot.

£13.7K to go and counting.

According to Joyce, there had been no acknowledgement from the government of Cynthia's second reply although, in the light of its exemplary logic, righteous ire and all-round badassness, Etta felt sure someone would get back to them soon. She could phone, make sure it had landed in the right inbox or on the correct desk. However, it was bound to take forever to negotiate all of Whitehall's extensions of condescension in order to locate the correct Department of Indifference, and Ola would be back soon. Every spare second had to be employed to get their money back. Etta went to the window, opened it and breathed in the back-garden air, lest she suffocate from the stench of her decaying good intentions.

As the must was clearing from her mind, her phone buzzed. Ola:

Sorry, need to stay and talk to Rob about this funding gap. Important. Eat dinner without me. x

Now she felt trapped by an hour or two of freedom. How could she do anything but go onto Cozee? Ola had no idea what she was putting herself through; it was a lonely task, and taxing on the soul, to be a secret saviour.

She ran downstairs and ransacked the cupboard and fridge. 'Yup! Need me a big one today . . .'

She returned to the spare room bearing an inordinate gin and tonic, sat and took some gulps, and clicked on her messages. Should she? She did:

DestinysChild: How's it going with you?

A minute passed. Etta spun away a few promiscuous fivers but won nothing. The pink light broke into grey thoughts:

StChristopher75: All sweet. U?

DestinysChild: Meh. Not winning enough.

StChristopher75: Try Mermaid's Gold. Paying big earlier.

DestinysChild: Thanks. Your tips are great.

StChristopher75: I try. For people I like.

DestinysChild: You like me? You haven't met me.

StChristopher75: U can tell a lot from chat.

DestinysChild: Like what.

StChristopher75: Ur smart, ur adventurous. Ur hot.

DestinysChild: Hot?

StChristopher75: Can just tell.

DestinysChild: No one has ever called me hot.

StChristopher75: Not to your face. But I can tell.

DestinysChild: Yeah right.

StChristopher75: Send me a photo.

DestinysChild: No!

StChristopher75: Please. Just your face, nothing dodge. They don't let you on Cozee. It's stchristopher75@me.com

DestinysChild: 🫣

StChristopher75: I'll show u mine if . . .

DestinysChild: So you ARE naughty 😬

StChristopher75: Ask me no questions . . . Off to check my email 😄 and play Mermaid's Gold. Remember: paying big.

Paying big. Playing big. Going for broke. Going bust. All these terms to describe the madly intoxicating interplay between hope and fortune that was now the backdrop to her every waking moment. But where had that got her? Destinys-Child needed to share; she hovered her fingers above the keyboard. He was a playmate, a laugh, but she needed a confidant more. She typed.

DestinysChild: Before you go, want to know a secret?
StChristopher75: Yes!
DestinysChild: I took [DELETE]
   I borrowed [DELETE]
   I need to win £14,000 as soon as possible.

Seconds passed. Had he left the room?

StChristopher75: Don't we all. £100,000 wud be better!
DestinysChild: I mean it. I borrowed it from my boyfriend
   and need to put it back before he finds out.
StChristopher75: Oooooh, who's a naughty girl, then?

Etta drank her gin. She had no intention of stopping.

DestinysChild: Yes, guess I am! Would rather be good
   and rich.
StChristopher75: Naughty and rich is best.
DestinysChild: ☺

A few more seconds passed.

StChristopher75: See chat – Mermaid's Gold just paid
   another £10k. Gtg glgl

Before she could say goodbye, the pink light had blinked off.

Etta raised the thick-rimmed gin balloon to her smile. She had a Cozee friend. She also had a good tip and enough funds to spin until Ola got in from a late night at the lab. There was no reason on earth why she should not drink to that.

•

The front door clunked open at 10.35 p.m. She was drunk and needed to go to bed.

'I was waiting up for you!' she called.

'Coming!' said Ola.

Moving next door, she slipped into bed. Seconds later, Ola slipped into her. Oddly for a man of no few loud opinions Ola was inclined to make love in near silence. Not even the slightest groan. He didn't command it, they had never spoken about it, but if she cried out he opened up the gap somehow, slowed and stiffened in the wrong places, so she was left echoing into a void.

When it was over, Etta lay back and they turned off the lights. Good, nonetheless, to have returned from the spare room and caught him awake, caught that deep musk of his skin on her body, caught the mood. But the shower had been faulty for months and that was the first time she could ever recall its song sharing their bed. Drip drip, bang bang, a metronome for his building desire. Was it louder or had even her ears grown distracted and disloyal?

Within the hour, she had slipped sideways out of bed, once again, to seek their fortune along the landing.

•

Come Tuesday morning, Etta felt mortified in every sense: ashamed, rendered lifeless, on a par with death.

Under the strain of trying to push her winning total up and up, and faster, she had stayed at her laptop until 4.25 a.m. At around 2 a.m., she had added a bottle of red to her nocturnal gin. She would dump the empty bottles in the FrameTech car park bin that morning, an idea that had occurred to her at 4.30 a.m., as she slipped back into bed, semi-conscious, next to her unconscious partner.

It was now 7.37 a.m. Until this minute, the more she had deceived Ola, the more elaborate the justifications and the prettier the lies, the better she had felt about her deceit. Up until now, precisely 7.37 a.m., the better she had felt, the luckier she had been. But this was not lucky, or better, this was early and sad and broken and hungover: too many illicit bottles of red wine in too few days had caught up with her. She could not raise her head from the pillow.

'Ola, I'm sick.'

'Hmm?'

'I'm not well.'

'Heh? What is wrong? I thought you were better.'

Her need took the sting out of yet another lie:

'I was, but now I think I've got a bug. Maybe a cold.'

'In June?'

'What? I'm black!'

'Heh! I hear you. But you'll be fine.'

Under an unequivocal weight of nausea, dampness where she should be dry, and vice versa – and was she imagining the sore eyes, the building catarrh? – the lack of care was too much to bear.

'Yes, I will be fine, and so might you if you're not late for work. They might still find more funding for you, right? Better keep them happy.'

Etta spun on Dragon's Layre, Rocket Fuel and Mystic Millions. An hour on, her spreadsheet total had dropped to £12,970. She still felt lucky. She could win it all back in one spin, that was the beauty of it.

She was on Treasure Temptation, mining rubies, when the phone went.

'Hi, Joyce!'

'Etta.' The voice was flat and low.

Etta nudged her laptop over to Ola's side of the bed.

'Joyce, what is it?'

She could feel her friend struggling in the silence.

'It's Mum.'

A moth-storm of panic beneath her ribcage. Were the poor lady's bags packed on government orders; was a taxi waiting?

'What's happened now?'

Silence, broken only by fractured gasps. A faint keening. A longer silence.

'Joyce?'

When Joyce spoke, there was lead in her voice.

'She's died. Heart attack.'

'Gosh, Joyce—'

'I found her last night, when I went in to check she had taken her medicines. Not breathing, her heart had just stopped and I couldn't . . . I couldn't . . . I called the ambulance and that, but it was already all over.'

'Joyce, I'm so sorry. That's terrible, awful.'

'At least she was in her bed, right?'

'Yes. Oh wow, my love. Sorry.'

'I think it was all this government stress, myself. She was waiting to hear back from them after your letter. Why did they keep her waiting? You'd even phoned to chase them, hadn't you?'

Now the lead weighed in her own throat. 'Yes.'

'Exactly. They just don't bloody care. Still, don't matter now, does it?' Her voice cracked.

'Oh, Joyce, I'm so sorry.'

'Yeah.'

'Should I come over now?'

'No, you're OK.'

'But are you?'

'No. Not really.' Silence. 'I think I've got to go . . .'

'OK. Bye, Joyce, lots of love, yeah?'

'Thanks, babes. Love you too.'

They hung up. Etta leaned back into the pillows and closed her eyes. She pictured everything as it should have been. She saw herself phoning a never-ending series of government departments in the name of Joyce Jackson. She saw herself acting fast and true, precisely as Cynthia's daughter would have done had she not suffered from a long-standing terror of bureaucracy. She imagined herself as the loyal friend she should have been, a social justice warrior standing up for love and the right thing and community, never taking an engaged tone or voicemail for an answer, just as she had originally planned. (For one unhelpful second, she also saw herself winning £12,000 on her next bonus-laden spin, but she blinked it away.) She pictured herself rising from her real-fake sickbed to make curry chicken and rice which she would take, still steaming, to her bereaved friend. She would ring the doorbell but refuse to come in as a cold – or bizarre bug – was the last thing Joyce needed right now; she would simply hand her the mother-food.

But open one's eyes and the truth will flood in, bold as daylight. Etta had not done all these good things. She had not done any of them. She would, at the right time, explain to Joyce that she had not got around to phoning the government; that her guilt weighed upon her, that she wished to stop it from wedging between them, that she would have rung that very day but . . .

But all of it was weak and wishful thinking. Except, perhaps, for the £12,000 win.

She needed air. She wrapped her coat around her dressing gown, threw a chiffon scarf around her neck to mask the v of naked skin, thrust her feet into flat shoes, picked up her keys and left. She doubled back up the road and made her way to her favourite park, the one nearest her work. No real risk: it was well before lunchtime so only fellow skivers would spot her. Safe enough. Full of green promise, almost symbolic, lying in wait just to tell her life was all swings and roundabouts.

The generosity of open space struck her from across the road. She hurried on to it, imagining herself running ahead, divesting her body of its off-the-cuff clothing and lying face down, arms outspread in the grass. Instead she walked, clothed, through the park, without aim and without sunglasses; on she walked. The day was warm, but not so hot as to render her coat strange; the air felt light, but not thin.

Face tilted to the sky, Etta walked across the park. *Bird, bench, woman in blue, clouds.* She was aware of looking with a certain ferocity to keep all thought at bay. *Bin, car in distance, grass, man on the ground.* She slowed. To her left, fifty metres ahead, a black man appeared to be sitting on a blanket on the ground. She reached into her pocket for the parking pound it always contained. Nothing. Drawn to the man's abject strangeness, she wandered off the lawn and onto the path where he sat.

He was an African man, black-skinned and lean, and he was sitting cross-legged at the edge of the main path at the far side of the park, near the swings and roundabouts; today the play equipment stood unused and none of it looked especially symbolic. In front of him he had spread out a small dustsheet. On the smudged sheet, there appeared to be two stacks of black boxes, the size of Christmas shortbread tins. Fewer than a dozen of them were laid out; Etta wondered whether he was selling out of his mystery wares, or whether that comprised his total stock. Was it jewellery, or some other form of crafty tat? Food seemed unlikely to be served from the ground. What was he doing there?

As she neared him, she could make out the slimness of his crossed legs, the dust-blown sandals, the alien lack of self-consciousness with which he called out to the world:

'Apostle!'

A man of God; perhaps they were black Bibles. As she neared him, she saw that he too had a scar, five times more dramatic than her own, running from lip to chin.

'Apostle, apostle.'

He made an exceptional prophet, sprawled on the tufted dirt of the Rilton rec.

In her coat, her hidden dressing gown rubbing across her bare skin, she felt drawn to him; he alone was odder than her in that park, on that day. As she neared him, she braced herself for the loud cry – apostle! – or even a cascading spiel of hard sell; few walkers were acknowledging his presence, choosing either to speed up their stride or to veer onto the grass and away. She drew level, casting him a downwards glance; the seller fell silent. A sharp look away from her understanding gaze, as if seeking any other possible punter. She kept on walking, too awkward to stop and examine the boxes.

He had seen her, but not called out; he had not attempted to engage her. Why? After a good fifty more paces, Etta suspected she had the answer. He saw her, but not as a customer. He saw the Africa in her skin and curls and rounded nose. To him, she was not a passing opportunity: they were both the same.

She still wished she knew what he sold.

The moment of recognition lifted her all the way through the park and back along every pavement until she was back home. Though she did feel a lingering need to warn the black man somehow; you could not just sit there muttering on about apostles to strangers in the street. His innocence might get him battered. Rilton wasn't a place that was waiting to hear the word of God, not unless God was reading out the football scores. He would not succeed here. Didn't he know? All those tacky black boxes on that grubby sheet. Why didn't he *know*?

Once inside, she went straight to the spare room.

The homepage idled, the Wi-Fi taking its time to kick in. *Hurry.* She was seconds away from the revelation of some can't-say-no novelty, a box-fresh promotion, or a virgin game promising to flash its cash: Cozee was open and ready for you, 24/7.

The display of big winners blinked from the home screen:

. . . MaeMae21 – £20,000 . . . RoyRogerz – £34,500 . . . Fabuloso – £77,000 . . . StChristopher75 – £55,000 . . .

He had won. StChristopher75, her mate, had won £55,000! She clicked on messages and found him.

DestinysChild: OMG I just saw
[DELETE]
DestinysChild: Congratulations!!! Bloody h
[DELETE]

DestinysChild: Can't believe that you won £55,000 and you didn't
[DELETE]
DestinysChild: Very well done
[DELETE]

No words would suffice to praise the brilliance of his good fortune, the genius of having chanced upon the right game at the right time. Lucky *sod*. Such prowess was unknown to ordinary folk but StChristopher75 was now the Cozee dream made flesh. He was a *winner*.

It was a sign. She too had to elevate her own sorry arse above the losers, the depressive chancers, the clichés, and become more. Imitation as flattery, actions versus words; it was *time*.

She was decided. He had money, more than enough now, and he could help her. He understood their ever-spinning world and knew that hard cash was the key. She had to get through to him, enough to secure a loan at least. She had to play the game.

She opened up old files, searching, searching. She found what she was after: a headshot of her, smiling. She was made up, but not too much; inviting, but not too much; fun times in her eyes, attitude knowing, curly afro fully out, chin up.

She attached the image to an email:

Dear StChristopher75,
You wanted a pic. Be careful what you wish for!
Stay lucky,
Etta

She had made her move. Over to him.
Etta started to spin.

Risk II

The stage looks bigger once you are standing on it, the people below far away and small. The place is filling up with men drifting in from the konobas next door where they will have eaten their fill of crni rižot which has turned many teeth squid-ink black, and savoury boškarin, and rakija-spiked fritule pastries. Still they have appetites. They look at her, wet their lips with thick tongues and drop their gaze to the beer in their hands, or to light their cigarettes. Their looks do not soften now, despite her beauty. They take on a different quality, something dark and electric.

The stage was not so big on Tuesday, when she had played it all cocky, then awed, then faint with gratitude to get through the audition that had ended in an interrupted grope and a new gig. Now she feels small.

Still, it is better than waiting tables.

As they are still shuffling in – these mostly father-age men who do not yet wish to return to their women; men who have hungers that they choose not to sate from the stocky pots waiting for them on their own kitchen table – the music starts up. It is time. She starts to bend and sway, stopping the already scant conversation, drawing hard-working eyes to the stage and – from darkness, with electricity – turning them on.

A hip out at an angle, then swung across to the opposite corner of the room; waist twisting in time to the bold sweet music; she sinks at the knees for a second's swoon, then rises high and proud. She has them. The outfit choice was good: a small flared skirt; a bright top, more camisole than corset; a shining belt wrapped tight around her middle. She grows braver and lifts one arm, then the other. Half a twirl and a fancy movement of the torso: balletic showgirl. The tension beyond the spotlight slackens a touch. Too much. She softens her own gaze, lowers her arms, sways with less force and smiles: their daughter's exotic friend dancing around their living room. There, she has them once more.

Two new men hunch in, each as tall as the door. She looks straight at them, a level gaze from her podium. They do not turn to face her; they shoot iron looks at each other and talk with urgent hands. An argument, great fists soon to strike? Blood to be shed over territory, property or politics? There is power in them, agency and heft, but none of it to be used for her ends, not tonight.

Though she works her hips harder, the men settle down and slide into a corner of the room; she catches the eye of neither.

Still, her luck could be out there, somewhere, pulsing to the beat, out there in the gloom that she has sexed up with all the might of her meticulously coy motion, waiting out there in the smoke.

Chapter Seven

MONDAY, 18 JUNE 2018

The quarterly savings account statement was not due until the following month, but at any moment Ola could check the balance and find the money gone. Etta searched her partner's face for a sudden cloudburst of anger or confusion at even the least likely moments: not only as he tapped at his phone, but as he drifted off to sleep, as he slumbered. Not a thing.

On Monday morning, Etta and Ola waltzed around the kitchen table, and each other. Hard-dough toast versus fruit bran. Coffees, black and white. Phone-checking (still no howl of outrage from Ola).

After breakfast, he grabbed a new suit from where it was hanging in the hallway.

'Hm-mm, do-di-do.' He was in a good mood.

'Nice garms,' she said. 'Is that new?'

'Yes, it is.'

'Lovely blue.'

'It's called peacock teal, the man said,' he replied.

'Bit snazzy for work, isn't it?'

'It's for the event afterwards. Remember? I'm staying over in the cheapo rooms above the conference hall tonight.'

'Oh yes. In that suit, they might even upgrade you!'

'Yes, who knows?' he said. 'We're trying to seduce businesses into extending this phase of the trial. I'm trying to look like I live in the real world, and not in a lab.'

'You'll certainly fool them.'

'Ha!'

'Seriously, it's sharp. The professors will weep with pride.'

'I'm sure you're right. Thank you, Etta.'

'It's OK, I know you never want to do these dull mingling things.'

'No,' he said. 'Not ever.'

'Ah, sorry, now you look all serious again. You're doing well at work, Ola, giving it everything. It'll pay off.'

'Hnh. Thank you. I mean that. It's been a tough time.'

'I know. Try to enjoy this one, though. We'll speak later.'

'OK. Bye.'

He left the house looking a little lost. Poor Ola, trying to dazzle his way out of trouble.

The increasing demands of his work were making him vaguer than ever. He moped and mumbled and turned away from the truth: could he really have no idea of the efforts she was making to set them straight?

On the way to work, she received a call from an unknown number:

'Hi, this is Stephan of Forthouse Insurance.'

'Hello?'

'We're calling about the car accident you had recently . . .'

Etta smiled. 'Don't think so, Stephan. I haven't had any accidents. Wrong number? Got to go, bye.'

Etta walked on, shaking her head. The phone went again a second later. A London number.

'Hello! We're calling from Cozee.'

'Oh!' said Etta, thinking of promotions and draws she may have entered.

'We just wanted to say hello.' As they had already said hello, this implied the caller was speaking from a script, a flawed one, but Etta did not mind in the least. 'And we just wanted to let you know that we've got some great news for you.'

'Oh?' asked Etta, stopping her stride.

'Yes. As one of our most valued members, we would now like to make you a Cozee VIP.'

'Great!' replied Etta. The secret club, at last. 'What does that mean?'

'Well, as a valued member, you'll get lots of extras to make your play more fun. We'll give you a monthly bonus, based on your percentage of play. There'll be competitions, free gifts, prizes, surprises . . .'

Etta was sort of listening, but she had already heard. A monthly bonus, every month, plus free prize-surprises. Whatever else she had lost – her caution, her dignity, her honesty, Ola's money – and even as her smouldering peace of mind threatened to go up in smoke, she was now a Cozee VIP.

It meant something else too.

As soon as she reached FrameTech, she rushed to her desk and opened up her private email. Something had just landed in her inbox: stchristopher75@me.com.

Hi Etta,

   Love your photo. Love it a bit too much, if I'm honest! Just so now we both know (can't believe no one's told you) you are definitely hot. You deserve to know that. Better still, you deserve to party with me as a VIP. Any joy? Would love to meet soon.

   Stay hot, Chris

She replied straight away, before she could change her mind.

> Hi Chris,
>   Great to hear from you.
> I'm now a VIP and eligible to come to the
> [DELETE]

Too starchy, crap.

Besides, he had loved her photo 'too much'? You could read that a number of ways. He could admire her. Or, he could love her sticky-tissues too much; she should know. He could be a weirdo, or freak, or ex-con. You could not tell everything from a photo but . . .

> Hi Chris,
>   Why thank you!
> Now you show me yours.
>   Etta

The emails and the phone call from Cozee continued to course through her working hours like adrenaline through veins. Checking her phone at around 10.30 a.m., her heart leapt and shimmied; an email from Chris.

> Dear Etta,
>   Please find attached a photo. But first here's what you
> need to know about me:
>   I'm old enough to know better (you do the maths).
>   I live near London (not near enough).
>   I think you look lovely. Just a friend's opinion.
>   I'm definitely bagging a dance with you at the VIP
> Summer Party.

I'm definitely not hot.

Now you may open the attachment.

Chris

Etta forced her breathing still, while her stomach clenched, while her hands fumbled, as she opened the image.

She exhaled in a puff.

White. Handsome; older good looks. Head turned slightly to the side, he was laughing a touch, eyes on the photographer. An ex-wife? Shirt collar peeking above a navy jumper. Dark hair with strands of grey in, conventional style, groomed, but not too groomed. Hint of lines at the eyes, but hard to tell. Looked kind, and fun but . . . underpowered? No, sort of mild, gentle. A gentleman.

But then: *Love your photo. Bit too much*

Ur hot

Stay hot

As Ola would say 'Food for thought . . .'

Naughty.

•

Etta pushed all such thoughts from her mind and adopted a busy expression for the rest of the morning. At 11.30, the Head of Finance, Robert, approached her desk. She tried to smile and exude competence.

'Hello, Etta, could I have a word with you in my office?'

'Yes, sure,' said Etta, smiling.

She grabbed a notepad and pen and followed him to the glass-walled corner office. Robert watched her enter, shut the door and then perched on the nearest edge of his desk, arms across his chest, leaving her standing.

As he started to speak there was a sudden rattling of weather, as if a thousand marbles were being dropped from the sky.

They both looked at the window. Robert snorted.

'Hail in June? Ha! Who would have thought it?'

'Yes, that's crazy,' said Etta.

They listened for a moment more, then Robert turned back towards her.

'Etta. It has been brought to my attention that you haven't been quite as . . . on the ball as we have learned to expect from you.'

'Really?'

'Yes. Would you say that's fair?'

'Um . . . I'm not sure.'

'The Manchester report came in late. Errors have been found, more than a few times. There have been a number of sick days that some team members have found . . . unconvincing.'

'Really?' asked Etta again, not even convincing herself.

'Indeed.' Robert tipped his bald head forward, a bull about to charge. 'Are you having problems at home that we need to be aware of?'

'No.'

'Nothing that might be having an impact on your work?'

The hail stopped. Etta hated herself as she said into the new silence:

'A family friend did die.'

Robert nodded hard and uncrossed his arms.

'I knew there had to be something. I'm sorry. Do you need to take time?'

Etta shifted her weight from foot to foot. 'Only an afternoon. There's a funeral coming up.'

'Uh-huh, uh-huh,' he was still nodding, as if thinking of HR protocols. 'You can have that time off on us. It's clearly been tough.'

'Thank you, Robert, I appreciate that.' She half-turned, waiting for him to let her go.

'Hold on, Etta.' He crossed his arms again. 'Sorry, I meant to add . . . You need to consider this as a verbal warning, Etta. OK?'

'OK,' she said.

'Right. Good. So, that's all clear. You can go back to work now.'

'OK,' she said.

As she walked out of the office, she could see through the glass walls that FrameTech life was carrying on as usual; all heads were down. All but one: in the far corner Jean was staring at her as she left Robert's corner. Etta was too far away to see the look in her eye, but her mouth seemed to twist in satisfaction as she turned back to her screen.

●

She faced an evening without Ola. By 8 p.m., Etta's £1,000 deposit had been spun down to £380. She reached for her phone.

Hope it's going well. Miss you. See you tomorrow xx

Ola replied within seconds:

Miss you too. Will try to leave work early tomorrow, just to see you sooner. Night night xx

The air in the spare room had turned. It was now poisoned with losses. Winner or not, Chris was, of course, a bad idea.

The money was tempting, essential, but ... no good could come of it. She could not yet think of a way to tell him that, so he was left hanging, his photo unanswered.

The summer light was fading; not wise to be alone too late. Dead flowers on the doorstep; what other gifts might the dusk bring? Was the spinning to blame in some way; was she inviting darkness in?

Etta shuddered away the thoughts, all the while wondering if those thoughts were taking on a fey, unhelpful quality, whether they might be tinged with madness. She could not afford to become unhinged: she had too much to do and, as all action started in thought, her thoughts needed to be fit for purpose.

Enough.

She would feel better, very soon. She would win back the £22,000 and gulp down a chance to start again.

●

It was gone 1 a.m. Still surfing waves of wins and losses, spirits doused in strong drink, head drowning in all the wrong thoughts, Etta caved.

She opened up her email:

Dear Chris,
   Thanks for your photo.
You look lovely too.
I will think about going to the VIP Summer Party.
   Etta
PS – If I dance, I dance *hard*.

She hit send and powered down. Unusually when in the middle of a spinning spree, unusually for that time of night, she felt a tiredness sweeping her body that threatened to knock her flat.

She went to bed and slumped into sleep, her thoughts bobbing on tides of rolling reels, and wizards and wins, and strange, gentle faces.

●

The next morning, already itching for intoxicants, she experienced a rare survivalist urge – she had to get out the house, that second. Air, earth, exertion . . . pulling on leggings and the *Choose Life!* hoodie from her neglected shelf of exercise gear, she prepared to take a fraudulent jog around the park.

As she entered the park, she popped in her earbuds and stumbled into a half-skip and then a semi-trot. She skirted the perimeter of the park. De La Soul playing; all cool. She saw him straight away: the out-of-place black man, once more seated on the ground, at the farthest reaches of the park.

From where she jogged, he appeared to be selling the same number of boxes as the last time. How did he live? She picked up the pace, curiosity launching her into each step. By the time she got to him, he had already raised his brilliant white gaze to her. The chin scar struck her harder today; though it had to be a historic injury it still looked sore, livid in the silvery sunlight. It reminded her of something, maybe a dream. As she neared him, deafened by a song about the magic number and wearing her sunglasses and sports kit, she saw recognition power up inside him as, evidently tossing all thought of their African commonality into the long grass, he mouthed what could only be:

'Apostle!'

He was looking at her with fire in his eyes. What was that? Pleading, hatred, desire?

She stopped the music, took out her earbuds.

'Apostle?' he asked.

'Excuse me,' she said. 'But I need to know—'

'You wan apostle?' He held up a black box and shook it; it rattled.

It came to her. 'Oh, gosh OK. A *puzzle!*'

'Yes, apostle, would you like one? Buy for your children?' Etta bent to take the box.

'What is it a puzzle of? There's no picture on the front.'

The man looked at the box without a trace of concern.

'It come like this from Slough,' he said, as if that town might be the Mecca of puzzle manufacture. 'It is as you want it.'

Etta gave a short laugh. 'Bit revolutionary!'

The man did not laugh. 'You wan?'

Etta felt in her pockets where she suspected she had left a note. 'How much?'

'Two pound.'

Now Etta, though tempted to laugh, gave the man a level look. 'That's not enough, nowhere near. Here.'

She handed him a fiver. The man started reaching for her change.

'No, no! You keep it.'

The man tucked the note into his money belt, but displeasure had flashed across his face. He looked at her as if he now saw the African in her anew. She shifted on her feet.

'I didn't mean . . .' she began. 'Like, it's not—'

His eyes had dulled. 'Nigerian?'

Etta eased; the usual chat. 'Yes, half. But I've never—'

'Who was your father? What is your tribe?'

'Yoruba.'

'Heh. Yoruba woman. I no need your money, I get food for eat.'

Did he sound *angry*?

'I know, I'm sorry. I just—'

'No sorry sorry o!' He was shifting his lean legs, as if preparing to rise. She could get halfway across the park before he could strike her.

'All right, whatever . . .'

'I am not a beggar, heh!'

'OK, jeez!'

Etta pushed her earbuds back in to disguise her hurt as petulance, and started to jog away, then run – quite fast – through the park. The air rushed past, the earth yielded in millimetres at each pounding step, the effort enlivened her lungs and blood and skin. She held on to the angry man's puzzle all the way home.

She had to shower, *now*. Ola was still out, so she stripped off in the hallway and left her clothes in a pile on the floor. She thrust the shower full on and urged herself into the cool streams. As soon as she was clean and numb, she stepped out again, half-dried and wrapped a towel around her, then went back to the hallway for the puzzle. She took the black box into the sitting room, yanked the lid open and poured the contents onto the carpet, hoping that a guide picture would tumble out along with the 100 well-machined pieces, but no. It looked as if the jigsaw might depict a countryside scene: a piece of thatch, a piece of royal blue sky, a piece showing a donkey's head. She sifted through the pieces for a moment more until it clicked. Part of a recumbent baby.

Her towel slumped to the floor in shock.

The poor bastard.

He was trying to flog Nativity jigsaw puzzles in the middle of June, here in this secular corner of the Western world. The misguided logic sat heavy on her heart. She could see him, alone and friendless in Slough, weighing up how to spend his meagre investment funds: what scene could bring more joy to the heart of the local people, his fellow God-lovers within this Christian country? Etta, naked and cooling fast, took the piece showing the two-thirds of baby and cleared a space around it. She was not sure why she cared, she only knew that she did.

Finally, she stood up and towelled the last of the dampness from her skin. For as long as she scrubbed and scoured with cotton, she thought of the puzzle of the decontextualised black man on the dustsheet, and she wondered.

●

The next day was Wednesday, the morning of Cynthia's funeral. The fiery sky was an incitement from above.

Shepherd's warning. The Lord is my Shepherd.

The shower was going, with Ola in it. Curtain up at any minute. Were it but an interval in the play of life; would that she could blast her nerves with a cold shock of gin & tonic, ice cube, lemon. Maybe an extra ice cube. Maybe an extra gin.

It was 7.30 a.m.

Normalise.

Etta pulled her mind from getting high to getting up. What might she do today?

Maybe take his wallet from the breakfast bar while he showered and filch the untouchable credit card, the one with the biggest limit. She would take no more than £2,000, surely the minimum that could now make a difference. Life was short and . . . ah. Of course, she would then shroud every limb of her body in black; Cynthia May Jackson deserved no less.

By the time Ola emerged downstairs, she had decided. She would only get to do this once, so should take out the maximum daily amount. The credit card was already in her handbag, she was wearing the black dress, breakfast was ready and her story was straight:

'I need to get into work early as I'll be off to this funeral later. You OK if I shoot off now?'

'Yes, of course. God willing, it goes OK. For the family.'

Leaning in to kiss his cheek, she left Ola eating his favourite scramble of eggs, tomatoes, onions and hot peppers. He was fine.

It took minutes to get to the cashpoint, seconds to panic as she hit buttons and learned that she could only take out a maximum of £650. She took it out. The regret was instant. She tried to get over it, fast as she could: hot-sweated it out as she walked to the FrameTech offices, swapping guilt for fear with every step. The sky, its blush now fading into the beige that coloured her working hours, appeared to thicken with weather – rain? – or take on weight from the aired problems of Rilton below, or grow gravid with warnings.

She walked on, not daring to slow her pace until she had reached her desk. Robert might have given her some time off, but she could not be late.

'All right, Etta?' It was Dana, with a laugh of delight. 'Wow, you look completely bloody awful! You OK?'

'Funeral.' She sank into her seat, drained.

£650. Too little. Too much. Worse.

She should not have done it. She should never have touched it. Bad things might now happen, such terrible things . . . She took the untouchable card from her handbag, turned it over and over until she stopped and rang the number on the back.

'Yes, hello, it's Etta Oladipo . . .'

She jumped through the security hoops and waited to explain.

'It's been stolen, my card. Our joint credit card; been nicked, I think. At least I can't find it. I need to report it stolen.'

'We'll take care of it for you. Can I call you Etta?'

Once the card was cancelled, Etta slumped afresh. Before her head had hit the back of her chair, the shakes had set in. It was one thing to deceive your boyfriend, another thing altogether to defraud a bank.

She tried to tap at her keyboard and stare intently at the screen, ever keen to exude diligence. Always, eyes were on her. But as the minutes passed, she grew lost in anxiety. Irate financial institution. Police. Prison: time and time and time again – endless, relentless seconds – trapped in hard locked rooms, hemmed in by inconceivable people. Evil food and screaming nights. The drugs and attacks and gangs and guards. *Screws.* The fear, the violence.

Muddle, it was all a muddle: but she knew she was afraid. What was she then, child or madwoman?

Etta rose and walked into the ladies' loos. Her feet failing, she shut herself into the unisex/disabled cubicle. She was afraid to lock the door and afraid not to. She left the light off, afraid all over.

Fraud! Thief.

She swallowed hard, grimaced, then gulped for air. She could not make her face comfortable. Pressure was building in her chest. She sank into a crouch. Her heart's hard thump would not stop; it was raging. This was it. All pounding and no breath. Just like Cynthia Jackson. She deserved it, end of.

'You liar, Etta. Liar. Lies.'

She chanted the words over and again in a whisper until the thoughts and feelings stopped lobbying her heart, slowed their loud demands. She mouthed the words, hoping. Somewhere within the fear, she knew this to be meditation.

'You liar. Liar. Lies.'

Guilt, peace and the tang of piss. The tiles and the half-light absorbed her whispers.

Until: a rush of air, the cheap glare of ceiling LEDs.

'God, sorry! Oh, s'you. Are you OK?'

Winston was peering down at her, his swagger softened to concern. The light from the corridor felt like redemption. She could not speak.

'Here . . .' His arm was outstretched. She could not move.

Fear, though, was beating at her skull; a thought bloomed like a bruise.

'Time.'

'Uh?'

'What time is it?'

He checked his phone. 'Ten past eleven.

'Shit!'

Etta scrambled onto her knees wondering whether anything in her life remained unfucked.

'It's too late.'

The funeral. Impossible to make it in time. Unthinkable to rock up late. She would have to lie to Joyce, say her car/taxi/bus/legs had broken down. Lies were now her stock-in-trade.

'You what?'

She took Winston's hand and hauled herself upright.

'Doesn't matter.'

Jean appeared from a nearby doorway, clutching papers. She wrinkled her nose as she watched Winston and Etta emerge from the loo holding hands.

Jean turned violent pink and her eyes went dark.

'You people!' she said, and hurried past them, head down.

Winston and Etta both heard it. They gave each other the look.

'Damn,' said Winston. 'Can I get you some water, Etta?'

'Whoa. Yeah, yes please. Thanks.'

He led her to the water cooler. She stared into the banal vista of their office, took a plastic cup in disgust – why still plastic? Did no one care about anything? – and sat back down at her desk. Her senior colleague hovered above her, awaiting further instruction.

'I'll be fine now, Winston. Thanks very much.'

Phone. She had to phone the credit card company back, no messing, or the future she had chanted to block out, crouching in scraps of no-frills bog roll and misfired wee, would crash into her present. Sipping the water, she dialled.

'Hello, could I speak to the Fraud te—?'

She hung up. The word 'Fraud' – it was too much. Fraud was what she had done. They would know that Fraud was what she had done. It was too late. She needed to take more time to think it all through. Right now, though, she could not think to any great degree, she could only see Joyce, forlorn, looking towards the door as the last guests filed in. An icy disappointment melting into hot grief as the coffin, dressed in flowers, was walked to the front of the room.

She had let her best friend down at the worst time. No way to dress that up.

Etta's betrayal was deep as the grave.

Robert walked past her desk, on the way to the meeting she was set to miss:

'Etta. You'll be off to the funeral shortly, won't you?'

'Yes.'

'Well. Sorry for your loss. See you tomorrow.'

Etta felt she had no choice but to pack up her things and go through the motions of being someone who would not ever miss a funeral. To admit otherwise might prove career-limiting; it was possible that Winston had not heard her mutter that it was 'too late'.

She felt ill as she pushed back her chair and left the office to walk home, stopping only at the bank to deposit £650 of illegal and ruinously expensive cash into her personal account.

Sick pay.

At home, she gambled.

The same heart that had somersaulted in the work loo now rocked steady; hers became the constant pulse of the serial offender; nausea subsided into nothingness as she returned to the spare room to spin, spin, spin until the £650 had become £4,300.

She did not celebrate.

●

She woke up in the dark, in the spare room, her nose touching a hard corner. Her laptop, which lay open on the pillow beside her. It took a second for her to remember why she was there: Cozee, always Cozee. She knew she should rise and go to Ola, but fear pinned her down. The curtains were open. She could not get up and put on the light. Someone might see in. Someone in the fields beyond.

She lay still, too scared to move. Her breathing grew laboured, each breath rasping like a warning. More minutes passed, long seconds. A sharp night-bird's call made her fingers twitch, breaking the deadlock of fear. She urged her muscles into action and slid herself off the bed. She got onto her hands and knees, and crawled under the window, in the dark, so no one could see her.

●

Next morning, Etta took a tub of leftover *egusi* soup out of the fridge and nuked it in the microwave for a few minutes. She removed it, tested it with her finger and gave it another thirty seconds. Satisfied, she sealed the tub and heated some *iyan*, yam pounded with vigour and care, which she sealed into another tub. She placed the tubs, a spoon and a napkin in a thick hessian shopping bag and set off towards work.

She had reached the end of their path and was about to turn right onto the pavement when she heard a noise from the houses that stopped her. Was that – shouting? Someone screaming at someone to get out?

She looked to the source of the sound and saw that Jean's front door was open. The shrieks were coming from within.

'You killed her!' the mother was screaming. 'I loved her so you killed her!'

'Mother, you know that's not true.'

'You did it. And you tell people I'm mad!'

Etta hesitated. To do nothing would be disgraceful, but she couldn't just barge in. Or should she?

A wailing started up.

'No, no, don't touch me!' cried the older voice.

Was Jean trying to embrace her?

'Leave me alone!'

The front door slammed shut, the noise echoing into the indifferent street and dying.

Etta had decided. She judged the distance from a speeding van and ran across the road to the house, trying not to jiggle her bag too badly. She tried to march up to the old women's door and was almost there when lounge curtains were violently pulled back. Both women were standing at the window looking out, pale and furious.

Etta readied herself to shout out to them, ask if they needed help, but seeing the steel in four watery eyes, she thought better of it.

She gave one last stare to Jean and was met with an anger in her gaze that seemed to burn from deep within; it was festering, it was on fire. The woman had never looked like that behind her desk. Time to cut her losses: she turned and walked away, back up their well-swept path.

Mad old bats.

She set off for work, but five or six streets away from FrameTech she turned right rather than left and headed into the park.

He was there, on the ground, still incongruous, still touting his heart-breaking haul of black boxes. A family was walking nearby; two older parents – or maybe younger grandparents – and a boy. The child broke away from his mother's grip and ran. A flock of pigeons flew up in fright. He ran right up to the African man, who would, from the boy's height, loom striking in his blackness against the pale grey cloud above. The boy regarded the man and his boxes with the guile-less, raving stare of infancy that she could sense even from where she stood. She hoped his parents would not buy one of the man's disastrous puzzles; that would make her mission harder. But no, the woman hurried after the child, headscarf slipping in her haste, throwing up her hands, crying 'Hassan! Always he be running!' She snatched her boy away from his staring and they wandered off. Etta picked up the pace, cutting a defiant diagonal across the park until she reached where the puzzle man sat, watching her approach, waiting for her.

The scar was not so prominent today, as if he had used make-up, which of course he had not. Her own was camouflaged with skill each morning; she now wished it was more on show.

As she closed in, she called out to him:

'I have a problem!'

'He-heh.' No smile; now near, the scar looked sore as ever.

'I have a problem,' she repeated.

Now he straightened his spine. 'What can I do for you?'

Etta put the bag down and delved into it.

'You don' like your puzzle, abi?'

'No,' said Etta pulling out the tub of soup. 'My *egusi*. It tastes all wrong.'

'Heh?'

'I don't know what to do with it. I think it is not enough melon seed, or too much stockfish. Help me, *abeg*. My mother is Jamaican. I have never been to Africa.'

The man met her eye with such a clarity of understanding that she felt tears start. She averted catastrophe by dipping her head again for the spoon, her jet afro hiding her expression from him. Eyes wiped, she stood tall again and leaned in to pass him both the hot soup and the spoon. Now she was here, the napkin felt foolish, a total giveaway; she left it in the bag.

He took soup and spoon with a solemn nod, unpeeled the lid and scooped out a mouthful. He tasted it and considered. Then he took another spoonful, pausing only to break out a white-toothed *ha!* before resuming the game.

'This *egusi* . . .' He looked to the heavens.

'Yes,' said Etta.

'It no taste like *egusi* from home, Yoruba woman.'

'Well, help me o.'

He took two more spoonfuls in rapid succession.

'Next time, yes, more stockfish. And the bitter leaves are too bitter.'

'Thank you.' Etta gave half a bow. 'But I have another problem.'

'Eh?' he asked, warming to his role. 'What is it now?'

'My *iyan*. Is it too hard? I think it is too hard.'

He took the second tub from her, tried the two together. He looked up at her; she knew she had to speak first:

'I can see from your face that you do not like it. Ah! Never mind, you can keep it from me. I don't want to carry that rubbish to my work.'

'I—'

'I am English woman, heh? Today, I would prefer to eat a nice ham sandwich.'

He paused his eating to flash her a smile that said he was enjoying the game even more than the food. He lit up for a second, and for that second his face held more dignity than ruin in it. It lent the illusion of handsomeness, for that second.

Etta hesitated then reached in her pocket. Would this spoil it all? She handed him the card before she could think too hard.

'I will be late for work if I stay.' There was less play and no Nigerian lilt in her voice now. 'But before I go, take this. Please phone them.'

He glanced at the card and pushed it back towards her, a hollow look of anger trying to mask his embarrassment.

'It's just this group of people who help. Listen, you can walk to them from here.' She took the card and read it for him. 'The First Welcome Project. They're good, I help out there once or twice a month and they give advice, you know? They help everyone, literally, anyone who comes through the door. They often help migr— people who weren't born here. Help them with their papers, and to find jobs—'

'Do I not have a job?' He tilted up his damaged chin and gestured at the boxes, but there was no fire in his voice.

'Mate. No one is going to buy your puzzles, I'm sorry.' He had to listen, it mattered more than she could tell him. 'Walk to 34 Grafton Road. The First Welcome Project. Please.'

He gave the card a proper read: 'Et-ta Ola-di-po.'

'That's me,' she said.

'You have a scar,' he said. 'Here.'

He reached out and with almost a touch traced the mark under her eye.

Etta's face warmed. 'So do you.'

'One man jus attack me,' he said. 'For my money. I left Nigeria from the bad men and this man jus attack me on the beach.'

'Oh,' said Etta. 'Sorry.'

'Man attack you?' he asked.

'No,' she said. 'I fell off a stool as a child.'

'Oh,' he said. 'Sorry o.'

'It's cool,' she said.

'This is not all that I am. Do you understand that? I am more than this. I had good-good life and now this . . . There is more to me than just this, the same as for you. We are more than we look, heh?'

He stared at her with an intensity that shifted something between them; she felt seen, and sad.

'I hear you. But I've got to go now, sorry.'

She forced herself to break away from his gaze and walk off; his food had to be cooling fast.

•

It was a First Welcome Thursday and she set off at a good pace: every step brought her closer to the chance to atone. The

130

credit card fraud weighed on her mind at all times, joining her other heavy misdemeanours, so many rocks on a crumbling cliff edge. But she still had to function, put one foot in front of the other.

She arrived back at Seacole Community Hall wearing an expression of optimism that she did not yet feel, for the benefit of the clients once more starting to queue at the door.

'Hello, everyone,' she smiled as she walked past them into the building.

In she went: everyone's informed and buoyant best friend, if only for a few minutes. For the next six hours, she would bury her doubts and fears in good deeds. Here, she was her best self.

The first few clients rolled up like a messed-up midsummer Christmas carol: three pregnant girls, two jobless men and an Eritrean refugee. All left with a form, or a phone call made on their behalf: tangible gifts of hope.

During a lull, Etta slipped into the tiny galley kitchen to make a coffee for her, Janie and Kim. When she returned, a broad-chested brown man with a face full of moles was hovering at her desk.

'Hi,' she said, handing the drinks to her fellow volunteers. 'Take a seat.'

'Thank you very much,' the man said.

'What can I do to help?' asked Etta.

'I must be able to stay longer in the UK.' The man had a strong Indian accent. 'I'm here to marry Nadia. I tried the Citizen's Advice in High Desford, where she lives, but they said to try here. Can you help me please?'

'OK. One thing at a time . . . Do you mind telling me your name?'

'Abhinivesh Gupta.'

'OK, Abhinivesh, let's break this down a little. When did you arrive in the UK?'

'Seven weeks ago, and I only have up to six months. It's too little.'

'Too little for what?'

'I need to marry. I'm not a ... what you might call a scrounger. I wish to stay and to find work. It is unbelievably important.'

'OK, of course. I understand. Do you have family here?'

'Nadia will be my family. Our families are set on that.'

Etta hesitated. This was delicate but she needed the bigger picture to be able to help.

'Does she agree?'

'I don't know. We haven't exactly ... spoken that much. She is a reasonable person, though, intelligent. She works in finance, but her family say she wants to settle down, you know?'

As she thought. Still, as long as the bride-to-be was willing, was it any worse than an online form or algorithm deciding who should be your life partner?

'Maybe talk to your – Nadia was it? – about this. It may help.'

'You think so?'

'Yeah, you definitely should if you're going to marry her, right?'

'OK, yes. I'll start by telling her I've been here to the First Welcome Project. I think she'd like that, you know.'

'Shows you're serious about her.'

'Exactly!'

They smiled at each other, she widely; he showed shy yellow teeth. There was a softness, an open demeanour to the wide face, under the bumps and moles.

They spent the next half an hour discussing his situation, going through possible scenarios, possible forms. Etta had gone to the largest filing cabinet, returning with a thick clutch of papers. She waved one set of papers.

'OK, Abhinivesh, could you fill in this form next?'

'So many forms!'

'Yes, and there's even a couple more we could look through which might help, if you have the strength.'

He laughed. 'A true love is worth it! And anyway, my name, Abhinivesh, do you know it means love? I will tell her that, too. Pass me more forms; more forms please! A true love is always worth it.'

His words struck Etta hard, a honeyed slap. He was right – her own meeting with Chris was a necessary sacrifice, a smart detour on her way to fully uniting with Ola. This mess with money was no more than elaborate form-filling.

'Nice, Abhinivesh; you sound like a man who means business. Now read through these, then I'll explain if you have any questions, OK?'

As her client read through the paperwork, Etta let her mind drift away and refocus on her own life. She had to risk it all to get the money, and it had to be from Chris. Who else could offer a loan of thousands? He would ask no questions, not flinch at a peek into the gory pit of her finances. He was a spinner, like her, a chancer.

Abhinivesh looked up, satisfied. 'OK, I get all this. Thank you, this would definitely help.'

'In that case, you need to sign here . . . and here.'

Yes. A true love was worth always it.

●

That evening Cozee was in more than usually capricious mood. A promising £7,300 had swelled to £9,900 then shrunk down to £3,950. Etta was starting to flag, spinning in an energy void. The feeling was this: a killing defeat; a drubbing that stuck to your bones like dried blood.

The ringing phone shook her out of her torpor. Ola.

'Hi, hon!'

'Hi. Listen, really sorry but I forgot I'm out tonight.'

'OK, no problem. Where are you going?'

'Tom's birthday drinks. He's off to Rome with his wife tomorrow so we're heading to the pub tonight. It's his fortieth.'

'Fair enough. Have fun.'

'Without you? Ne-vah!'

Etta laughed the way he wanted, then hung up. He was networking harder than ever, hoping to safeguard his role on the study. No denying it: Ola's every absence was now a double gift. They added up, these transactional sacrifices. His time away bought him hope and her time to buy their future. Strange though that he did not perceive the seismic shift in her, the tectonic movement of age-old emotional crust, that saw her waving him out of the door when she would once have pulled him closer. Did he not suspect? He mouthed his own amiable goodbyes back with his default complacency. To give him credit, he probably read her jitters as a reluctance to see him go. He could not guess the twisted truth: an eagerness that he should leave, matching a dread of being home alone.

She was, in fact, worse than alone; she was crowded by dark thoughts even on the brightest afternoons. Ola – amiable, complacent – had failed to contact their landlord about fitting a security light in the back garden. Only a thin wooden fence lay between them and anyone who might want to get to Etta in the night. What would stop a malicious chancer on the prowl?

Someone who hated her enough to deliver rottenness to her door could be observing her movements, biding their time. The back of their house was not overlooked; no concerned neighbour would call the police. The spare room gave onto their rear garden which bordered fenced-off fields; sprawling edge-of-town terrain in which unknown harms could be done. She knew she was watched, she sensed it as old women sense the coming rain in their stiff knees. The neighbours' dog was a plus, but he barked too much to be a reliable alarm. The curtains, though cheap and dated, were lined. With only the desk lamp and her laptop's glare, she ought to be undetectable.

So why did she feel all on show?

Time to take a break. She swung away from her desk and reached into the back of the wardrobe. Despite its new home of an over-sized handbag, stashed among outgrown gowns and folded woollies, the gin bottle remained cool to the touch. She filled the glass on her desk, sipped, and stared at the screen, willing it to speak.

After a few minutes, indigestion gurgled in her stomach, or it could have been a twinge of hunger. No way would she cook a dinner when Ola was not coming home. There was a long stub of saucisson sec sitting in the fridge, a shared continental weakness, and she pictured herself gnawing into it without shame or witnesses.

She went down to the kitchen and grabbed the deli sausage from the middle shelf and their best red-handled knife from the top drawer. She skipped back upstairs and sliced little meat chunks straight onto her desk, not bothering with a plate. She popped each piece into her mouth, chewing slow as if to savour each small taste of triumph. She was nourishing herself, surviving. The fatty pork should have been mitigating the gin, yet after a while the tang of triumph left a queasy aftertaste. She felt shrunken and unusual; could see herself floating on the surface of the glass and starting to sink.

She needed Cozee. She needed less challenging company than herself, alone with her night thoughts.

Chris. Time to up her game. She could email him, but that felt too formal, too slow. She wanted to communicate in closer to real time; she wanted to chat.

DestinysChild: Are u there?

It took less than a minute for the reply to arrive onscreen:

StChristopher75: Hi, what's up won big?
DestinysChild: F***** up big more like!
StChristopher75: How come?
DestinysChild: I stole twenty-two thousand pounds and lied. Then I stole and lied to fix it. Then I missed a funeral.
StChristopher75: U borrowed, remember? And who'd u kill?
DestinysChild: No one!
StChristopher75: In that case, I wouldn't worry about it.
DestinysChild: I do worry.
StChristopher75: Why? Spill.

A thrill of closeness; a surge of intoxication. Sod it.

DestinysChild: I've committed fraud. Actual fraud.
StChristopher75: You're kidding.
DestinysChild: I wish. I put hundreds on a card and rang it in as stolen. I'm drinking so I don't freak out. There you go. Hate me?
StChristopher75: Could never hate you.

136

DestinysChild: I don't recognise myself. My relationship with the truth is changing.

StChristopher75: Bit heavy. This is called chat for a reason. 😀

DestinysChild: I'm lying and I'm losing.

StChristopher75: Aren't we all?

DestinysChild: Not you!

StChristopher75: News travels fast.

DestinysChild: Yes, congratulations on your win! 😀👏👏👏😀👏🙌🙌

StChristopher75: Cheers.

Just that. He did not want to talk about it. She had over-emojied. He had doubtless endured a flock of new 'friends' messaging him since he won £55,000. She should have held off, toned it down.

DestinysChild: I'm drunk.

StChristopher75: Best way to be.

DestinysChild: Don't feel the best tbh.

StChristopher75: Try a coffee. Perk u up.

DestinysChild: Got anything stronger?

StChristopher75: Crack? 😀

DestinysChild: Go on then.

StChristopher75: My bad, used the last of it to upgrade my vodka tonic. Honestly, don't sweat it. People do worse. Maybe u need a good dance.

DestinysChild: You inviting me to all this clubbing you do?

StChristopher75: No, the party, remember?

DestinysChild: Haven't said I'm coming yet.

StChristopher75: U R coming though, right?

DestinysChild: Why?

StChristopher75: U promised me a dance. Plus u can't
    miss a night of free cocktails and retro tunes – old men
    like me dancing to Shabba Ranks.
DestinysChild: 😃 Sounds tempting.
StChristopher75: Do it. It might surprise you. We can
    hang out.

Hang out. She smiled. His attempts at cool had that effect on her. Might he affect her in other ways, up close? Full-on attraction would be a pain in the arse, to be honest, but she could do with a laugh and a dance. VIPs, free bar . . . the money that Cozee made, it had to be a decent night out. More than that, she needed all the help that Chris could give her.

Etta leaned back in her chair. Choices lay ahead, a crossroads. Ola was out. She was being watched. She had annihilated the sausage and almost done in the gin, but StChristopher75's playfulness was pulling her up from the blurred depths of her tumbler. Here was a guy for whom the sun always shone, one perhaps also man enough to help in her hour of need.

Her hand dangled the knife by her side, then let it drop into the mouth of her handbag. She did not care. Stuck at this junction, this weird and wonky intersection, she found that, at that moment, she cared for nothing at all. Impossible, therefore, to decide which way to go. How to move forward? From an unmined seam of resilience, she found resolve: she would not turn back. Etta took a deep swig of gin.

DestinysChild: They had better do crack cocktails. And
    play a tonne of Shabba.

She puffed gin fumes out through her nose, a low hum buzzed her throat.

He came back fast.

StChristopher75: Brilliant! 😁
DestinysChild: Gtg c u soon.

With that juvenile farewell tapped onto the screen, she had moved forward. Only time would tell where to.

Etta reached into her bag for the empty gin bottle and threw it into her wastepaper basket. She reached in again, with care, feeling for the greasy knife. She paused: it might be wise to keep protection close to hand. With a swift shake of her head, she pulled the handle out before it could cut her or ruin her bag. No, carrying a knife was not her at all.

Still: she was being watched.

Before she could try to sleep, she had a task; it was urgent and already too late. She opened a new email.

Dear Government,

You might like to know that Cynthia May Jackson passed away on 4th June 2018.

It's over. She's gone. Please remove her from your deportation list.

Kind regards [DELETE]

Many thanks [DELETE]

Yours?

Etta Oladipo

On behalf of Cynthia May Jackson (deceased).

She drained the last of her drink. Now she was ready to spin.

●

Several games deep, the pink light flashed on once more:

StChristopher75: Winning yet?

DestinysChild: Never enough.

StChristopher75: What did u think of my pic?

DestinysChild: I had thoughts.

StChristopher75: Do tell.

DestinysChild: Nothing like that.

StChristopher75: U don't have to worry, I won't tell him.

DestinysChild: 😂😂😂

StChristopher75: 😉 U solved the problem that u . . . borrowed?

DestinysChild: I wish. I've made it worse.

StChristopher75: How?

DestinysChild: The credit card thing. And I lost more money, lied more. That funeral I missed was my best friend's mum, so that's really not good. And I drank too much the whole time. Other than that, it's gone really well.

StChristopher75: Woman as good-looking as u should have an easier life.

DestinysChild: You think?

StChristopher75: I do. I'll take care of it.

DestinysChild: You can't. I'm someone's girlfriend.

StChristopher75: So? An attraction to beauty is in my DNA. As a friend, looking out for u is part of my job description.

DestinysChild: Not meeting up with other men is part of my job description.

There was no comment. Nothing for thirty seconds, two minutes. Five. She had panicked; a major flirting mis-step. Of course she would meet him, she needed to meet him. A loan, that was all.

Seven minutes, now. She had blown it. Come close, hesitated and failed.

Who watched? Those dead flowers had left a sticky trail across her mind.

She could not go to sleep yet; perhaps with her phone on charge next to her, and with the loo light on, she might drop off in the end . . .

No, that was a lie. She had no rest, no peace. It was all spin.

By the time she had whirred down to her last £50, the room reeked of devastation. No reply from Chris. She dug her nails into the back of her hand; tears sprang but no blood. What was this to her, a goddamn game? He had given her an easy out and she had ballsed it up. The one person who could drag her out of this diabolical mess, and she had gone and scared him off.

A pink dot blinked. Him! He was there:

StChristopher75: If I were you, I'd start looking for another job.

'Ha!'

He was still interested. She had to tread carefully, cold was bad, too keen would be worse. She put her laughter onscreen:

DestinysChild: 😂

This time, the response was immediate:

StChristopher75: So you'll come?
DestinysChild: Please tell me your full name.

StChristopher75: Chris Wise.

DestinysChild: Wise, glad one of us is. I knew StChristopher75 stood for Chris, but wondered at first if you might just like travelling, like me. I'm Etta.

StChristopher75: Hi. Here's my link to Facebook, so you can check me out there first too, OK?

DestinysChild: I will, thank you. Pleased to virtually meet you.

StChristopher75: You too, Etta whoever.

Etta waited a few seconds, her fingers wondering whether to tap out the words.

Just form-filling. Worth it for Ola, for love.

DestinysChild: OK, Chris, I'll come.

Chapter Eight

It decided to stay hot. A stout, disgusting heat steamed from the days that sweated out of the tail-end of June. It permeated Etta's limbs, browned her skin and broiled her temper. Her mother had always delighted in telling her that she was made for the heat, 'just like me, but even more like your father. African sun hot *hot!*' Right now, she was not made for the heat, she was stupid and sick and wrong with the heat, and on the 17.39 to Paddington. Was this down to the weather, or some new phase of malfunction? If she were to die of fever, or heatstroke, at least it would all go away.

'Nice party spirit,' she mumbled to herself.

She scuffed the sweat from her brow with the heel of her palm. Her phone buzzed, she checked it:

Ready for Shabba? C u in there! Maybe 5 mins late. X

That 'x'. A kiss, their first. Interesting. Was he hoping she would melt over text, send a kiss back? This Cozee player was a *player*.

The surfeit of heat surged from her chest to her forehead. Weather presenters kept chatting on about 'this ongoing

143

heatwave' as if searing English summers were still an uncomplicated delight for the planet. She fanned herself with the free paper.

Calm yourself.

The VIP Summer Party would be the perfect setting in which to eyeball Chris Wise at last. The cocktails and the music and the easy laughter of winners should make a helpful backdrop to the main action of saving her own life. Etta's plan was to enchant him at a platonic, yet compelling, level. She would not sleep with him, course not, but she would not repel him either. Some might call it a high-risk strategy but, these days, that was all she had. Others would not get it. Others—

Eyes smarting, she tapped on her phone.

Joyce, please text me back, will you?

—might call it rank prick-teasing, but she only planned to excite Chris's admiration, and intention was everything, right? They had already shared secrets and laughs; tonight, they would drink and dance. She would put in the work. She would exude the sparkle of DestinysChild, tempered by her own earnest need. She would make damn sure they got on, ignite his desire to help. She might even allow him a hint of the real Etta Oladipo.

●

Fifty minutes into her journey, Etta was stalling. She had spent the afternoon sipping with steady determination, but the train to Paddington offered neither trolley nor buffet car and was undoing all her good preloading work. She would get back on it at Paddington. Pulling in now.

Head down to avoid the eyes of commuters as they prayed to get home quickly in that cathedral of parallel platforms and intersecting lives, Etta all but ran. She crossed the concourse to her concession of choice. Expedience shone on the shelf; her eye was drawn to the gleam of a screwtop bottle of plummy red. She plucked it.

She would need a cup and the pretence of a companion.

'Could I have a couple of paper cups please?'

The man at the counter lowered his head and fixed her in a stare; the whites of his eyes creamy around black, questioning irises.

'You no wanna wait 'til you get home then, is it?'

'What?'

He raised his heavy monobrow. Had he caught a trace of stale wine on her breath, spied a purple tongue?

Style it out.

She gave a patient smile. 'We're having a picnic.'

'You like drinking, is it?'

The smile died. 'Yeah. It is.'

She took the receipt, left the judgement on the counter, and bundled herself out of the door.

Next stage: the 205 would allow for refreshment on the top deck. She found the right stop as a bus pulled up and, although still too early, she got onto it. Upstairs, an old-school instinct drew her to the back seat; a couple of kids and a pensioner sat ahead. She unscrewed and poured. Her indignation – which was in fact shame, all dressed up to go out – started to fade as the bus rumbled along Edgware Road towards the hotel; her stress receded as the alcohol bumbled through her bloodstream. After ten minutes of getting intimately acquainted with bumps in the road, her mood brightened as the sky mellowed: hard seat, scuffed handrails and yet this rose-gold, improbable evening!

●

At 7.40 p.m., Etta stepped off the 205 and was winding her way up the pavement to the Rockingham Plaza. In her bag were her heels and the bottle with its remaining inch of wine. It had deadened the worst of her nerves. Her stupid, ever-twisting nerves: what should she dread, beyond being found out? Over there, in that monumental hotel with its erect flags flying, amongst all the chancing strangers, she could shine as authentic and true.

Almost a hundred metres to go; her judgement might be fuzzing but she had been a sprinter in her youth. The beige-and-gilt monolith was looming closer; time to transform. She ducked into a side street, swigged the last of the wine, and ditched the bottle in a bin. She tugged the zip on her bag hard, swayed in surprise as a shoe hit the pavement, steadied and put both heels on. Then she stashed the scuffed trainers in her cavernous bag. She straightened, checked her make-up in her phone and moved on.

She walked through the revolving doors like a pro; first win. The lobby was echoing, busy and clean, and almost as distinguished as it hoped; only the rivers of sad swirl carpet that flowed left and right indicated that its ambitions may have been thwarted at some point in the nineties. Etta was still impressed: it might be faux-luxe, but they had rooms at £260 a night.

The party was in the Wilmington Suite. She walked on and through, not stopping to smile at the concierge, but tilting her chin up as if she was a woman who might check into such hotels often, reducing her sway and sharpening the look in her eye.

The Wilmington Suite was on the ground floor. At the doors, two women stood behind a table of name badges. Etta scanned for Chris.

'Name, please?' the older woman asked.

'Et . . .' She looked again. 'DestinysChild.'

'Um . . . yes. Here you are.'

The younger woman, more of a girl, passed her the badge and started enthusing at her:

'Hi there, I'm Lou!' She pointed at her own name badge. 'You're going to have an unbelievable time tonight! The bar is free! Go in and try one of our lucky shots, they're ace! We love all our VIPs, just find me if you need anything! Welcome, go have fun!'

As the girl spoke in her barrage of exclamations, all Etta could do was smile and nod. She had clocked that there was no StChristopher75 on the table – he had to be already in there. She walked through the double doors into the function room.

There, in her face, was a room full of proper mad celebration: silver and pink balloons frosted with '10 Years of Cozee Winners!', colossal foil garlands and miles of curl-n-twirl ribbons, posters of VIPs holding outsized cheques. In an alcove, a six-foot cake sculpted in pink and silver, gold coins cascading down its tiers. Brilliant. Diabetes-inducing doctrine: spin more, win more, eat your cake and 'ave it.

She had arrived.

Two-dozen people were milling about with drinks in their hands. More young people weaved between them dressed in Cozee polo shirts: carrying trays of branded shots, handing out free tickets for a prize draw, grinning wide enough to dazzle and disarm, using the swagger of their toned, tanned bodies and their upbeat voices to pump out the impression that everyone in the room was living it large. Etta felt exhausted just looking at them.

Etta turned and saw, alone by the free bar, a man who had to be Chris. Same eyes, same chin, although he had let his hair grow longer. She eyed him as he waited to be served; she was taking a moment to gain the advantage, drinking him in. He was exuding a strong, well-lived appeal. His faded flower shirt had a clumsy mend beneath the pocket, a touching, unexpected scar of frugality. Divorcee, she was now sure. A light kick in her guts: yes, she could get her head around chatting to him for the night. He lifted his shoulders for a moment, leaning into the bar as if stretching out a stiff lower back.

She shifted her weight on her feet and hung back for a second more. It was clear that a clumsy approach might ruin her chances: this was a sensitive man, but nobody's fool. There was something promising in the way he rubbed at his chin, put a finger to the lines at his eyes. Kindness, an open nature.

She was going in.

Etta walked up to Chris at the bar. He was texting now; her own phone could well ping in moments.

'Hi,' she said, looking for a name badge. He was badgeless.

'Hello,' he replied, ceasing his texting.

'Hi, are you Chris? Sorry, StChristopher75! It's Etta. I'm sorry, I thought I was early. I hope you haven't been—'

'Sorry? No, sorry, love.' He had a strong northern accent. 'It's not Chris. I'm Rob.'

'Rob?'

'You might know me on Cozee as MightyMouse.'

'MightyMouse!' She reached for an olive to take the taste of disappointment out of her mouth. 'Oh yes, I've seen you on there. Hi! DestinysChild.'

'Pleased to meet you.'

'Likewise.'

'First time?'

'Yes. Listen, I hope you don't mind, but I'm actually looking for a friend. StChristopher75?'

'Wouldn't know, love. First-timer too. On a mission to buy a new car so been spinning a bit crazy-like, you know. They made me a VIP.'

'Right. Congrats. Listen, I'm just going to grab a wine and, you know, circulate a bit, find my friend.'

They stood side by side in silence as the barman served them drinks, after which Etta nabbed another olive and moved away from the bar.

Which one was he, then? She had looked at his photo quite a few times, but she now realised that his face, pleasant as it was, had no startling or quirky features and she did not know whether it was a recent picture. With no idea of his height, or current weight, Etta realised that there were a number of men who could fit the Chris Wise bill. Was he the tall one coming from the direction of the Gents? No, too stacked: she had not particularly got giant from his photo. Was he the one in the linen suit, laughing with the toothy woman? Similar face, but no. Her fingers twitched to her name badge and she resolved to wander around, nursing her free drink, open-faced but cool. She would hunt him down. She felt giddy, both exhilarated and as if she could not get enough breath.

All too exciting: she and Chris would drink their way into deep friendship and she would ask him, straight out, if he would care to save her. No messing. No reverse psychology or tricks, no making him think he had thought of it. One straight-up, hands-down plea: not to advise, or support, but to *save*. This careening life of hers could only be pulled back on course by his Cozee winnings. By fifteen thousand pounds of pity or, more likely, a wish to lend her money then lead her to bed.

Where was this guy? Her cool was starting to melt; she was perspiring and needed air.

Chill.

The French doors were open and people were spilling out of the main room into the garden, clutching glasses and soon-to-be-lit cigarettes, as a sixties song lifted them higher and higher. Etta slowed at the buffet table and, picking up a cold sausage roll for company, wandered out to join the smokers.

In the courtyard garden, balloons and banners did their best to mask any natural charm. A surge of intoxication hit her. There were forty or fifty more guests on the lawn.

Ridiculous. It was time to message him:

I'm here, where are you?

As she awaited his reply, the clenching of her stomach eased. How would they greet each other: a nod, a handshake, a peck on each cheek? Shame about the pork breath.

She swallowed fast as a man with grey-streaked hair neared her, smiling. She half-smiled back, wary of clinging pastry crumbs; he walked past.

A yelp of laughter from a corner drew her eye to a huddle of what looked like VIP regulars. A great barrel of a man was holding court:

'. . . so when I said "No, my name's Leicester like the city, not Lester" she thought I was taking the piss!'

Amused roars soared into the smoke-scented air.

'What? Dad was a fan years before they won the League!'

As if to punctuate the joke, her phone pinged. Chris:

Sorry, running late. Grab a drink, I'm on my way.

Etta smiled her relief. Fun was being had all around; no one seemed to be chatting about getting hooked on the reels or excruciating losses. Here in this naff-posh hotel, under all the balloons and the froufrou, she was part of the happiness conspiracy.

She checked her phone. Nothing. More roars from the corner. Leicester-not-Lester was clearly a Cozee *character*.

Etta scanned the courtyard for a quieter spot where she could wait for Chris. She strolled towards a shaded seating area where a woman in bright peach shoes and a platinum bob sat alone on a bench next to her large green handbag, smoking. As Etta got close enough to see the woman's face, she could see that it had an unusual aspect: both vague and standoffish. Perfect.

'Mind if I sit here?' Etta asked.

'Not at all.'

The woman gave a hot burst of a smile, so fiery it startled, in great contrast to her eyes, which had the opposite problem, one of dampness, or distance, or whatever it was that Etta could not quite place.

Etta shifted in her seat, hoping she had found this party's Holy Grail: company that was not in the mood for a chat.

The woman puffed out slow, considered streams of smoke. Etta looked out at the other guests. Halfway through her cigarette, the woman spoke:

'They always put such effort into these things, don't they?'

'Do they?' asked Etta. 'It's my first time at one of these.'

'Ah,' said the woman. She spoke like the head teacher of a good school. 'I've lost count. Don't know why I keep coming . . .'

'No fun?'

'Hard to say no. Party for nothing.'

'And the drinks are free.'

The woman lifted her chin and gave a soundless laugh. 'So it would appear.'

Despite the cool words, her voice had a warm husk to it. Likeable.

'I'm Etta.'

'Josephine.'

'Hi,' they said.

Etta glanced down at the unlikely shoes and noticed that Josephine's hands were shaking; the fingertips stained yellow; the nails bitten to the quick.

'If you don't mind me asking,' said Etta. 'If you don't like these things, why do you keep coming? It doesn't look so terrible, but—'

'I come because they invite me. Been a VIP for months. Years.'

'Great! Have you won a lot?'

Josephine took a deep drag of cigarette. 'On and off. Big win of £120,000 last year.'

'Oh God, that's amazing. How?'

'This funny little game, actually. Sapphire Castle.'

'But . . . £120,000 is amazing. Isn't that amazing?'

'Ha!' Josephine gave a tight snort. She was closer to fifty than sixty and dressed for a day at the races, minus the hat and smile. 'If you say so.'

Her expression tightened and her mouth worked as Etta watched, waiting.

'The thing they never tell you,' Josephine began. 'Is that you never get there.'

Etta said nothing.

'You're new to this, aren't you? You have that excited look.'

'Happy to be here, I suppose,' said Etta.

'I knew a Barbadian woman, once.' She was looking straight ahead, not at Etta. 'Or is it Bajan now? Anyway, she was always happy too. Hair just like yours, curly-wiry.'

Irritation pricked Etta's mood. 'Stick your black friend anecdote', she wanted to say and thought of rising to go back to the bar. But the unknowable thing in Josephine's eyes kept her seated. Subject change.

'You must have loved getting a cheque for £120,000. What are you spending it on?'

Josephine took a few sips of her drink and barked out another short laugh.

'It's spent.'

'Really? On what?'

'What did I buy?' Again, she looked away into the middle distance, then reached for her handbag and turned to Etta. 'Nothing except this stupid, ugly, extortionate, fuh ... bag. Green doesn't even suit me.'

Etta agreed that it was indeed ugly, particularly when set against the statement heels in coral; orange, if you wished to be unkind. Nothing the woman was wearing suited her.

'Why don't you buy something you like? You have enough money.'

'Had, Etta. Had.'

The woman raised her eyes to Etta so she could finally see all that was wrong in them: devastation. The dark-bright gleam of someone broken.

'You lost it,' Etta said.

Josephine raised her glass:

'Every damn penny.'

'God, really? But you'd made it. You had got there!' said Etta, before checking herself. 'I'm so sorry.'

'Not your fault,' said Josephine. 'But you should know that, like I said, you never do. Get there.'

'And still, you came to this, tonight?'

'I don't like being by myself in the house. My husband left me. Two years and . . . three months ago.' Josephine shifted around towards her, a gleam in her expression at last. 'Are you here alone?'

'Waiting for a friend.'

'Ah,' said Josephine, shadows flitting across her eyes. 'Man?'

'Yes. Actually . . .' the alcohol was staring to loosen her up. 'I shouldn't say, but . . . sod it. Have you seen StChristopher75 on the site?'

Josephine straightened. 'I have.'

'What?' asked Etta.

'It's . . . nothing. We messaged a few times.' The older woman finished her drink. 'Enjoy your evening. And now, I am back off to the bar. I just want to let it all . . . wash away.'

She walked off through the door leading back to the bar. Etta had a mind to rise and follow her inside, but at that moment, her phone buzzed:

Something's come up. Can't make it now. Sorry.

The force of it tilted her chin back. He was not coming. Doubt boiled into dismay; it started seething up, up, tensing the sinews of her neck; her head tipped right back; she stared into the still-bright depths of sky. A long inhalation. She brought her chin down and looked about at the faux-luxe décor of the courtyard. This shitshow of delusion gussied up in latex and foil.

One rosy balloon broke free from a cluster, drifted to the ground, bounced once, twice, five times and burst on a still-smoking fag.

Her chance was dead.

Bar or exit? As she turned, another buzz:

Actually . . .

Chris had hit send and was now *Typing* . . .
Etta waited, one last ember of hope burning in her chest.

Our last chat changed my mind.

Typing . . .

I thought – BINGO!!!

Etta smiled and sipped her drink. He was teasing her.
Typing . . .

I should send your man – Ola Abayomi, right? – a FB friend request.

He knew his full name.
Typing . . .

Or might come straight to you and ask for what u stole from ur boyfriend.

Etta stared.

Chris was still *Typing* . . .

Might hop on the phone to Banking Fraud.

Etta read it again. Poor joke? A bad punchline?
Typing . . .
The phoned buzzed again:

Might come and collect myself 22k.

Etta groped the air, feeling for something to hold on to.

Let's call it £10,000 and I will keep quiet.

As the opening bars of 'Happy' started up, as the pointless
DJ clapped above his head in time, as Leicester-not-Lester
congaed onto the dancefloor with three women in tow, Etta
bent double, winded, as she got it at last.

Next thing she knew she was at the bar, her stomach twisting.

'Cozee Calypso, please.'

The barman made the drink, chinked ice cubes into it. 'Hot
night. Want a splash more pineapple juice in there?'

'No, but I'll take more rum, if you've got it. Please.'

The barman gave her the brimming cocktail, a knowing
smile and complimentary nuts.

She took the drink back to an unlit corner; no sign of
Josephine. Within half an hour, her glass had been drained
and she sat in the same spot with two Jackpot Juleps, to save
going back to the bar.

Only when Etta was fully submerged in alcohol did she let
her thoughts surface: Chris Wise had *had* her.

Scammed.

He had fooled her. He had plotted to ruin her. He had lied and led her here, alone, to this awful, gloating, venal knees-up just to punch her to the floor with his texts. The cruelty of it took your breath away.

She rose again. The room swayed left, her stomach swayed right. She halted. Just two more drinks, a Sparkling Spinner maybe, or red wine for greater numbness. But no: all too much and far too late. She straightened and walked, upright and in the manner of one unscathed, out of the bar, out of the lobby. Out.

Several cabs were waiting outside. She slid into the first, unable to suppress an undulating feeling of escape and defeat.

'Paddington, please.'

'Praed Street entrance?'

'Yeah, thanks.'

She tipped her head back onto cool black leather, let it fall to the side:

The world was bruised grey, but still shiny, as if someone had filmed it using a tacky filter. One street passed by, then another smaller street passed by faster; here, a peeling parade of shops, juxtaposed surprisingly with a smart square.

scammed

screwed over

The taxi slowed at the lights, then crawled behind a queue of cars onto a bridge. A third of the way along the bridge, her head lolled a degree more. She tried to focus on the view out of the window, tried not to look at her phone.

Good as dead.

•

She sat on the 23.28 to Cardiff; she changed at Reading. A black hole of a wait: twenty minutes stretched out to eternity;

nineteen of them were spent in the platform loos, vomiting, washing her hands. The bad mirror did not show a wrecked face: it was a bit rough, bit drunk; late-Saturday-night normal. The devastation would not reveal itself to strangers, but she was sure she could detect, in the blacks of her eyes, the horror.

She closed her eyes.

They would look, now, like Josephine's.

Ruined.

Minutes of darkness, until they announced the train that would take her home. She forced her eyes open, climbed into the nearest carriage, sat and stared at the filthy floor. The anaesthetic effect of free drinks was wearing off, now wearing her down. She hugged her large bag tight to her.

Let's call it £10,000 . . .

blackmail

The jolting train matched her mood: bumpy ride, dark destination.

Desperate for distraction, Etta scanned her travel companions. The rumpled Sikh opposite was chewing a wifely forethought of a midnight meal, digging it from a plastic carton. Sweet fat and fruit: mango, maybe lamb.

focus, breathe

The other woman in the carriage, sitting two seats behind the Sikh, was dressed in a suit that suggested diligence over power. Etta saw a mother, working into the night to support a Marmite-smeared brood: it was the roundness of her posture, the weighed-down shoulders. Did Etta look like a mum: catastrophe at her back? Had Josephine mentioned children?

You never get there.

Three rows ahead, a man with a shaven head nodded to the beat of music she could not hear. An edgy movement, too involved. His beat caught in her throat, her heart leapt in sick sympathy. She pushed her bag away from her chest and looked down sharply: he was not wearing headphones. There was no music. His was a dance to some pulsating imperative; a St Vitus dance of anger, a testosterone twitch.

bloody hell

She kept staring downwards, studied her feet.

'That stinks!' he yelled.

No one looked up at the skinhead shouting at the Indian's food. Not Etta, not the mum, not the Indian.

skinhead

The train stopped, no one got on or off. The Sikh kept eating, so calm she wanted to shake him, dabbing at his curry with a chapati. Or paratha. Or failed naan—

shut up

What did bread matter when they would both be murdered?

The train moved off. Next stop. Both men would be going to Rilton too, she knew it; neither had any business in the villages.

As the carriage jolted, the skinhead jumped up. He started walking up through the aisle, towards Etta and the Indian man. He got near enough to touch the man's turban, then turned and stomped back the other way. He turned and repeated his march, turned again. All the time, palpitating with aggression. Was he throbbing to sock someone brown in the eye? What would she do then?

She looked down, head swimming.

Etta's legs would not stop shivering; the cool of the late-night train and the adrenal wash of racing from the shock of blackmail and pure primal fear; the overheated blood and brain; she longed to clamber down into the concrete embrace of Rilton station.

next stop

The train slowed. Skinhead stopped his head-bobbing, looked at her naked brown face, at her bag, held by her hands. He coughed, too hard. Fear fired her muscles; her legs strained to rise. If he rose at Rilton she would be finished.

go

Her quads spasmed, her shin shuddered; her legs did not want to know.

The skinhead kept coughing, mouth uncovered, a sound like a starter motor. He looked at her as he barked.

A fresh adrenaline flood; she was up and walking to the doors.

Etta tried to appear unremarkable, to look not worth the hassle unless you had a good lawyer, to don a presumed innocence. She tried to look white.

Open, please God.

Facing the door, she heard someone rise behind her, felt them draw closer. Mad to turn around, mad not to. Mouth opening, she tried breathing down the breakbeats of her heart.

The train stopped. The doors opened.

She stepped off, still cradling her bag. Someone got off. More than one person. Would there be witnesses?

The train pulled away behind her back. At her back, a cough like a car cranking into life.

She started to run.

PART II

Risk III

This will save her or screw her for good.

She can see him in the mirror, through the dark crack. He is still sleeping, his chest a haired crest of rising-falling peace; hard to see what troubles the night brought, or took away.

Sentiment; wasted on his barbed-wire soul. She should hurry.

The wallet is thick with hundreds. No surprise: he liked to wave his wad around the club, show the girls he had money and enough muscle to break heads. Her friends feared him but envied her, his companion, more. Had they not danced better, swung their hips harder, fixed him, all the men, more irresistibly with their stares?

She looks down at the leather billfold. Will it make her or mess her up? If she takes the cash, even one note, she will have to run, run fast, and never come back.

Put it back.

Take it.

Quick.

She pushes the bathroom door open one inch more. Still he sleeps, clotted with dreams and the dissipating violence of his day.

The wallet is her passport.

England! The only place her life will make sense, now. She will blend in, make money, get by, get on, get better. She will be safe.

She has friends who have gone before, foreigners like her who set off for places like London and Luton and Rilton and Slough. They had shown courage and their reward had been to disappear.

Is she brave?

She is dressed. The wallet is in her left hand, her trainers are in her right. If she takes it, she will have to run.

Another breath-held look. The dark rumble of his snore, eyes still shut, chest in rise and fall . . .

Do it.

Out past the bed. Bending to sweep, soundless, her bag from the chair. Ten steps, barefoot, to the front door. Silent, silent; excuses on her lips at every step.

She is out, away, down the steps, foot-flesh cooling on concrete.

Done. Too late.

Runfuckrun.

Chapter Nine

She stood at the hob and cracked eggs in silence as Ola drank coffee at the kitchen table, making notes in one of his research notebooks.

The night before, she had run, gone flying, and fallen flat onto the tarmac ten feet from the taxi rank. Footsteps had approached, slowing, someone bending over her. 'Are you OK?' the Sikh had asked.

She had thanked him and got to her feet in time to see the skinhead cram himself into a hatchback and drive away without a backwards glance.

She sighed, but Ola didn't look up. Ten minutes later she was still standing at the hob while Ola shovelled eggs in with one hand and captured higher thoughts with the other. Still he did not see her; he did not care to know why her portion of the chilli-spiked scramble sat going cold in the pan as she stood and stared at the wall thinking *blackmail*. At her back he did his endless mechanical fuelling thing – fork, eggs, lips, chew.

Thoughts and stomach were churning; she had stilled her nerves with a whole pint of wine, drunk as Ola showered. She pulled her gaze from a grease stain on the cooker hood and turned to look at the man she would marry, viewing him as if from a great distance. This loving, preoccupied man, to whom appetites and absences, even her own, seemed to mean nothing at all.

Good. If he did not notice her, did not speak, she could hear herself think and set about solving the problem. She turned back to the grease stain.

blackmail

She had thought about it as she stirred egg into the onion and diced pepper: blackmail was the situation. But blackmail was not the problem. Chris Wise was the problem.

She needed to deal with Chris Wise.

How, though? Should she guilt-trip him? Entrap him with false promises of sex? Plot to end his life? Her own life had become one of those hen-party dilemma games, Shag Marry Kill. Except it was no game.

She would not delete or block him. No; she needed to know where his head was at, just to be able to function. After all, he knew where she lived, or near enough. So dumb of her, chatting on about the ice rink and Teddy's Café . . . But she had thought they were mates. He had completely blindsided her; she could not predict his next move.

Until he gave himself away, she would have to ignore him.

Meanwhile: how fucking *dare* he?

He had contacted her, rocked up in her message inbox offering tips and matesy this and VIP that. He had drawn her in, deceived her. Lied! All a trap to extort money. All a line, a merman's song, a slippery serenade to lure her life onto the rocks.

Sure, she had planned to use him, to a certain extent, but she had been right up against a wall, beyond hope, devoid of even the murkiest financing options; desperate. He had seen his chance, got his bad self in there first and charmed secrets from *her* like snakes from their basket.

Then she remembered: it had been crueller than even that.

U new yes? He must have hunted her down on Cozee from the start, waited to corner her from a coward's distance, stayed steel-cold as his texted words cut her. He would now let her bleed out.

This was not funny. She would have to act, fast. He was coming after her, wanting the one thing she did not have: money. He knew her secrets, and her failings and her dependencies and she – stupid woman – had never even shaken his nasty old hand. She would have to stop him, before he ripped off the bandage of lies and exposed the weeping sores to the man she loved. Or to the police. Who knew what this nutter would do if she did not stop him?

She could bloody kill him.

'Etta, are you not eating?'

Ola had spoken at last, pen in hand. He was looking into her eyes with such concern that she felt ashamed.

'Of course, I . . .' She shook the vicious thoughts from her head, showed bright teeth. 'Wait, just coming.'

Swallowing down her revulsion, she scraped the congealed eggs onto a plate and sank into the chair next to him.

blackmail

She stared at the pale yellow scramble, eyes swimming; her throat was tight. She could see white globs of albumen where she had not whisked hard enough. Ola seemed to be enjoying his breakfast, but then he was not paying attention. Chris Wise had paid attention. That's why she was in this mess.

blackmail

£10K

debt debt

£22K

God

The air was growing heavy around her; the dark thoughts were there, here in the kitchen, eddying around the wrong room. She inhaled in short gasps; her struggle for breath was real, the panic building. Ola looked up at her.

'Not hungry, Etta?'

'I—'

She scooped a lump of cold peppered egg into her mouth, swallowed and coughed hard, finding enough presence of mind to thump her chest, as if to clear her lungs, dipping her head to hide streaming eyes.

'Are you OK?' asked Ola.

I'm fine,' she said. It came out as a croak. 'God, sorry . . .'

Ola rose. 'I'll get you some water.'

She shut her eyes and tipped her head back as he went to the sink. She tried her hardest not to think, to find her breath, though her mind was veering high and low, and her lungs were congested.

He passed the water.

'Etta?'

'I can't breathe!'

'Oh God, really?' He started rubbing at her back, looking worried.

She was underwater. She was drowning in fear. Steer, she had to steer herself back up to the surface, somehow. Up, chin up. This had to be a bad dream.

'Etta? Breathe, my darling, breathe.'

Etta opened her mouth wide, tried to gasp. Nothing.

'Oh dear heavens. Etta! God. Oh no, no, now your nose is bleeding . . .'

Ola jumped up and away from her.

Etta twisted her head in panic, right and left.

Ola hurried back to her side with grabbed kitchen roll.

'Oh hell . . .'

Seeing her writhing like a landed fish, he dropped the tissue and slapped her, hard, on the back, his eyes wild, fearful.

The shock did it.

A breath at last, rasping and low. And another, and another. Etta gasped and cried and bled, pressing the kitchen roll to her nostrils.

'Keep taking deep breaths, my dear,' he said. 'You're OK now.'

Etta sat with hanging head, Ola's voice the only truth in the room, trying to still her thoughts.

Ola rubbed and rubbed at her back; the more Etta calmed, the more aware she grew of the towelling dressing gown scrubbing at her shoulder blades.

'Thanks,' she said, gently shrugging his arm off and dabbing at her nose. 'I think it's stopping now. I hope so.'

Hope was all she had; it was all she could do. As she dabbed at her nosebleed and sipped the water Ola gave her, she tried to force her mind back to him: to the hired home they shared and its reassuring confines. But those thoughts were dwarfed by rage and doubt; even the concept of hope was trolling her.

No, she would not rely on hope, she would sort it out with action. Beyond the absurd wish that everyone stay forever in the dark – a dank notion growing like a fungus upon her thoughts – what was the best she could hope for?

'You must be overworked. Always in our study. It is making you unwell, Teetee. You need some time out.'

'I'm OK now, thank you.'

'No, you're not. I'm worrying about you. In fact, I've been thinking . . .'

'What?'

'Well, you do so much for us both, all this housework and cooking, all the time, and you always say it's easier when it's just you. We can't afford a holiday but maybe . . . I have two conferences in the Midlands within five days. I think rather than backing and forthing I should stay in Birmingham for a week or so and give you space to—'

'No, Ola! No.' Etta brought her tone down. 'I don't want to be alone right at the moment.'

Ola sighed. 'If you're sure. Because I've been thinking that—'

'No, Ola. I'm sure. Something needs to change, but not that.'

Ola rubbed the back of his neck. 'OK. I hear you. But you should do something today to feel better. Maybe go shopping?'

She lowered her bloodied clump of tissues.

'You hate me shopping.'

'Yes, I hate it when it's for stuff and nonsense. But why not buy something good, heh? You look down in the mouth. You need a dress, something fresh. Something to lift you again. You've been talking about that new way place forever. Go there.'

Etta raised her head.

'New way? What new way?'

'That place you want to go to Way . . . Fort?'

'The Waysford Place mall?'

'That is the one.'

'I never said I wanted to go there.'

'Heh? Yes, you did.'

'Not that I remember.'

'Well. I have heard it has excellent shops. Plenty of this and that to choose from. Made for women with good men and soft lives who still need cheering up.'

'Hey!'

'Ha! I'm right, though, eh?'

'Maybe . . .' She recalled her breakfast of wine. 'I can't be arsed to drive there.'

'There's a shuttle that goes right past us. Go.'

Etta weighed it up.

'Here,' he said, passing her three £20 notes. 'Get something for yourself. I'm only joking, I know you work hard o, shutting yourself away in that room all the time. You deserve a treat.'

The stoicism in the Queen's face looked like sadness, three times over.

'Thank you, Ola,' she said and rose to shower and change.

She would do it, this normal thing, take a step away from Cozee and a step towards atonement; see what lay in store.

As she waited at the coach stop, she breathed shallow. The cheerless vehicle turned up. The journey, though: the ride to Waysford Place soothed beyond all expectation. The aircon shushed, chilling down her thoughts, numbing nerve ends. She drummed the fingers of one hand upon the fold-down tray-table to match the operatic ditty in her head.

Tock, tock-tock. Tock, tock-tock . . .

Pa-pa-pa-Papageno

Sunlight flashed across her vision, staccato bursts of brilliance upon her face. She could feel herself changing. An epiphany: Ola's work chatter was finally showing her the way. He was always going on about neuroplasticity; how our repeated actions could alter the pathways that formed the constellation of neurons in our brains. This, to Etta, was remarkable, worth remembering at least as much the effects of smoke on our lungs, or liquor on our livers. Just sitting there, submitting to the rocking and rolling of the bus, tapping and humming, her brain would not be exactly the same as when she had boarded the coach. The changes might be minute, microscopic, but she found the thought comforting. Perhaps she need only get onto the motorway, get as far as Land's End, to step off as a different woman altogether, although that might be too much to hope . . .

'Waysford Place!'

The shopping centre – tall, bright, fancied itself – also had transformation on special offer. It was part plate-glass theatre – pristine vitrines, wares polished and pressed, prices slashed from gasps to sighs – but also a clinic, promising a retail cure for the depressed and the destitute. Or it was what it seemed: a monoglot mall, speaking only the language of 'sell'. Her neural pathways were not even quivering.

Etta drifted through the acres of white tile and shop window, her gaze enlivened by neither the clothes, nor the skin stuff, nor the tech stuff, nor the food stuff. She tried stuff, anyway. She pulled on a feathered top that did not tickle her, high heels that left her flat and, with no little effort, a sale-price swim-suit that did not float her boat. After untold time browsing her purchasing options, each more banal than the last, she walked on.

After a minute, she edged close to a window displaying a kaleidoscope of fingernails. The colours were meant to con-jure up the full spectrum of femininity, to evoke the sass, quirkiness, sex, strength, sweetness and the like. Etta slowed, watching the people inside. A laugh breezed out of the door, taunting her: *smile, love.* A dark image flashed: her raking red talons across Chris Wise's cheek; him stunned, bloodied and repentant.

At the open door, she halted. Something going down: the salon's air had been shocked still. She edged inside.

A striking tableau: one dark-haired woman stood flushed and glaring, with a bleeding finger; one seated nail technician, possibly Thai, with her head dipped, a turquoise streak in her bobbed hair. Other employees were bent, blameless, over their clients' hands. All was silent, save the dryers and fans.

As Etta entered, a petite redhead rushed from the massage chair lounge:

'I'm so sorry,' she addressed the injured woman, then whipped around to her employee, arms aloft:

'What are you trying to do to me, Pensri?'

'I have never had this,' began the woman with the finger, in a lurching accent. She was young and striking. 'I am so—'

It was all too much for Pensri, who shrieked Thai disavowals, or apologies, black-and-blue bob shaking as she unplugged her phone and stuffed it into her bag. The client held up the finger before her, blood not yet clotting on its damaged tip, poise bruised, indignation swelling. The unfortunate Pensri shot up and pegged it, trailing phone and bag, glancing Etta with a featherweight shoulder as she flew out the door. Her colleagues watched her escape, gaped for a moment, then stared back down at their clients' hangnails.

'Honestly! You teach these girls everything and then this . . . She's just gone off! Always turning up late, then this! I'm so sorry, my lovely.'

Another woman, still smaller, emerged from a back room and came up to Etta where she stood.

'Your name?' she asked.

'Etta Oladipo.'

The woman ran her finger down a page in the desk diary.

'Eh? Ta? I no see you.'

No, I'm lost.

Etta stared at the smallest woman, her larynx dead. The woman stared at the boss. The boss stared at the client's finger. No one moved. After a moment, a bleached girl emerged from the back room and interrupted the Mexican standoff by handing the injured woman her jacket and a clutch of discount cards.

Etta found her voice. 'Sorry, I don't have an appointment.'

The smallest woman scoured the list once more, as if she hadn't spoken:

'Eh. Ta?'

'You know what?' said Etta. 'Don't worry.'

She turned to go, only to be pushed past once again.

'You,' said the damaged client. 'Sorry.'

Etta now saw she looked familiar. FrameTech client, maybe, low-level admin. Or a neighbour, another renter, further down the street?

Didn't matter, she was gone.

Etta turned to leave too, eager to retreat into the busyness of the glass, white and steel atrium.

She carried on, gliding through hallways that sold discount dreams to shoppers, slim-fit salvation hanging within reach, or shelved for better days; she rushed away from brittle nails and bloodied egos, putting distance between herself and the cutting calamity, hurrying away from the callousness. She turned to look behind her a couple of times, certain that someone was watching her progress, or following her steps. Her skull felt airy and strange; her brain had to be . . . forget it, enough. Enough of the mall. She was not buying it.

She still wanted to kill Chris Wise.

She could see it: the blood would pour from him, keen, hot and stark red . . . then a glorious silence.

Wicked.

Etta walked back through the retail maze, gathering pace until she burst into the sunlight. Did she look as she felt? Eyes were on her, she knew it. A bus stop faced the mall's exit; she crossed the road to shelter herself from the people, from all of their looking at her.

Twelve minutes to wait. Easy to hope, if you trusted time-tables. Easy not to panic if you trusted in luck: if you could forget about the blackmail; if you could stop thinking about fraud and debt for five minutes; if you could ignore what you had absorbed that morning from the papers about Brexit, planet-trashing and other crimes; if you fought back the dark thoughts; if you stayed strong.

Etta stood at the bus stop, seething with paranoia. She put an uplifted look on her face for the benefit of the many strangers passing by with their many, many bags of shopping. The bus would come, any minute. After a while, she toned down her expression to one of insouciance: had she been grinning? Did she appear deranged, or religious? As the bus pulled in, she noticed someone watching from across the road. The wounded woman was waiting at the taxi rank, her gaze turned towards Etta. That face, she had seen it hurt . . . blood, another nosebleeder like her . . . Yes, she was a client from the First Welcome Project.

Her face rang no bells, though; housing issue, or had it been a benefits query? As Etta tried to recall the bureaucratic stumbling-block to match the face, a bus drove between them and she vanished.

●

Etta arrived back in Sycamore Road to find Jean and her mother in their driveway, watching a man in his thirties erect a long pole. A ludicrously tall For Sale sign going up? Could be: their life in that dimly lit house hardly appeared to be happy. *You people.* Nonetheless, moving was generally an optimistic act, and Etta would have put money on the fact that the women would have stuck with that house until one or both of them dropped. That was not saying much, however; she was one to put money on many unconsidered things. She was learning this about herself.

Casting a wan smile in the direction of her neighbours, she entered her house without one bag of shopping; she suspected this would secretly please Ola, despite his frown. Pleading tired feet, she went straight to the spare room.

Within thirty minutes, Etta was down to the last of her gambling funds. The computerised reels no longer looked like a machine to her, they looked like a brain. A dreaming, thinking organ. This Diana's Diner game would conceive of her future; she had abdicated all responsibility for as long as the reels rolled.

Down to £50. Junk food churned and blurred onscreen. £40. £30 . . . cheeseburger, cheeseburger . . . *Five cheeseburgers!* Bottles of ketchup popped all over the screen, scarlet globs dripping into one great banner: £7,000.

A bonanza of cash and fake calories in one fat win explosion. She tried to feel joy, or wry amusement: nothing. There was serious work to do. With steady heart, she withdrew £6,900 and prepared to ride her luck for as long as the remaining funds lasted. Ola was downstairs, watching a film she had declared too blokeish to bear before slipping away. Now she rose and walked to the loo. Urgent dialogue drifted up the stairs, the sound of acted heroism; she and Ola would each stay locked onto their respective screens for at least another hour. By then, the whole thing, all of it, could be over. Put to bed.

Etta flushed the moment she heard: feet on the stairs. An ice-rinse of terror. She tugged up her skirt, zipped fast, had to run to check . . . She had, right?

Ola was at the desk, bent over her open laptop.

The lid was open.

Heart-stopping doughnuts and loaded burgers waiting on the reels, cartoon diner jiggling to the jingle that her head-phones, still plugged in, had silenced.

Ola did not turn to face her.

'Etta. What is this?'

His tone had no give in it; there was no hope. The £100 in the Cozee account balance was there, top right. He had seen it. She had to speak:

'Oh. That's nothing, this silly game.'

'You are spending £100 on a silly game? One hundred pounds that we are trying to save. Eh? Tell me what is going on.'

Etta felt a hot dark blooming low in her stomach; the lie growing from the soured grain of truth. All they had going for them, now, was his good faith and her reluctance to break it.

'Nothing is going on. I was only mucking about.'

'You are spending money on these children's games. Cartoons! One hundred whole pounds?'

Her eyes and mouth started to close against the coming fiction; she opened both wide to let it out:

'It's a one-off. I just this minute put in £5, Ola. Just to see. And look: I won £100! I was coming to tell you.'

'Hnh.' Ola was considering. His shoulders had dropped, his head was tilting; she had won. 'Where did you hear about this nonsense, anyway?'

'On TV, earlier. I wanted to check it out, so I did, but the whole thing is pretty stupid. They probably fix it so you win the first time. I was about to withdraw our money; it's no big deal.'

'And it's real, actual money?'

'Think so,' said Etta.

'Hnh,' said Ola. 'OK then, let's take this £100 out quick, before it changes its mind.'

'Just what I was thinking.'

She withdrew the £100, knowing that she would have no money to deposit and play with for two days, until both withdrawals from Cozee hit her bank account.

'Done. See? Nothing to worry about. The £100 is going into our account. Let's forget it.'

'Hnh,' said Ola.

'Hmm,' said Etta.

'Also,' said Ola. 'You were right. That film is too predictable. Let us go to bed and entertain ourselves better.'

'OK,' said Etta. 'Let's do that.'

The inner bloom was turning cold. She had won and withdrawn, yes. She had also diminished and fooled, faked and deceived. Presented with the opportunity to end the lies, Etta had lied more. How could she not? She was powered by a need to spare Ola pain and she could not reveal she was £6,900 better off than minutes before and yet still overwhelmed by debt. They would collapse under the burden of him knowing she contained such chaos.

What had she become in these past few weeks? Who was she now?

Etta whoever.

●

The next day, as she stepped out of the front door, she was met with a Union Jack waving at her from the tall pole opposite. Jean and Jean Senior had been busy.

It was not a high day or holiday. The Olympics lay years in the past and football was not coming home this year. The women were not dignitaries or army veterans. It was not a national moment of note, or VE Day, or any such momentous celebration of good triumphing over evil – yes, then fly flags! No, what was fluttering in Etta's face was Jean's new hobby: the revilement of unknown others.

Etta eyed the vast flag, flapping above its narrow driveway. This was not the first: on the coach to Waysford Place she had spotted at least two domestic flags which she had not seen before, plus one cross of St George above a builders' merchants. No one was going to tell them not to fly their flags, no one could, that was the point. They – the 'you people' – could do little but watch the flagpoles go up in the front yards of semis across the land, and keep schtum.

Etta attempted to stay numb in the face of all quandaries, irritations, mental assaults and homicidal thoughts for a whole day. That in itself was murder so, with Ola's encouragement, she drove an hour to her mum's for some time out. There, she spent another twenty-four hours sharing nothing of her real life and feeling like even more of a fraud until she could return home just before the £6,900 hit her account. When it arrived, life started tingling back into her financial prospects, reawakening her dazed gut.

Her phone went. Joyce.

Etta's mouth flooded with saliva, tinged with a metallic taint: guilt.

'Hello, Joyce?' she said.

'So,' said Joyce. 'You're alive then.'

'Hon. I'm so glad you called.'

'Days, I've waited. Fucking days.'

'Joyce, I've been meaning to explain to you exactly what—'

'That's the only reason I'm phoning. To tell you not to bother.'

'Joyce! I'm—'

'Of all the times you choose to let me down, Etta Oladipo, it has to be the day I can't stop crying for my dead mother. Cheers, babe.'

'I know, I feel terrible. But so much has been happening at once, you know? You won't believe it and I—'

'Yeah. You know what else happened? My mum died. I'm broken.'

'Joyce.' It came out as pleading.

'Look, don't bother coming to find me when you've got less going on, OK? Let's just leave it.'

Joyce hung up.

The shame. Etta's facial muscles tightened as two hot tears ran down. Just two. Not much to shed for a woman who was let down – by them, by her – right at the end. These days, even Etta's tears were not enough.

This had to stop. She was neither the woman she had been, nor the Child of any Destiny that she wanted. She had to climb out of the hole, somehow. Wasn't it God – or maybe Bob Marley, or the Beatles, or the Brownie Guide Law – who said the truth would set you free? She needed to own up. If Ola loved her, he would forgive her. She would make amends. Right now, it all had to stop.

I will never gamble again.

Once she had formed the words in her mind, five soundless strikes of a gong, she felt cleansed. She was no addict: she had always been free, a woman possessed of agency. She had stumbled down one wrong turn and was now choosing to step back onto the straight path, which she knew would lead to marriage. The first step would be the hardest; she needed to put some serious thought into the best way to articulate their losses to Ola.

Could she tell him at last? Stick two fingers up to Chris Wise's blackmail?

Was she strong enough to tell him before Chris Wise did?

Was she strong enough not to?

She clicked onto Cozee, went onto My Account. She clicked on every message she had received:

DELETE

She clicked on every message ever sent:

DELETE

She hovered the cursor over Delete My Account. No more withdrawals were pending.

now

Could she kill all access to her dreams, finish off this loaded friend called Cozee who was meant to save her?

Could she finish off Chris Wise?

DELETE DELETE DELETE

Risk IV

At last, the time has come.

She had been too smart to simply hand over her money and hope for the best. She had traipsed down the steep stairs to the closed blues bar tucked away in Petrinjska ul. having texted her mother first to tell her the what, the where and the who, as far as she knew. (Her mother took her word as gospel, and her occasional donations as a gift, and never tried to stop her escapades.) She had called the mobile number at the door and waited. When the squat chunk with the beard had let her in, she had smiled enough to soften his gaze, but not too much. She had not chatted too freely, just followed him to the back room and nodded at the spiel of a larger man who told her 'two days to Dover, leaving in ten hours'. She had committed, paying the vast deposit. She had dropped the names of 'friends': two powerful men who had watched her dance in the club – she had danced well, despite the cramping stomach – and had bought her drinks after. Men rumoured to hate Josip. She had made the traffickers laugh, brief surprised grunts, about the food and the weather that awaited her. She had reapplied her lipstick in her phone camera to snap a secret selfie that captured the head man, what-ever good that might do her. As she left, she had looked back, sharp and sweet as the Malvazija wine with which she would toast her departure, at last, from Marta's shitty sofa, her hideout in this shitty place.

That had been nine hours before. Now it is nearly time and she is doing everything right. She is early, ready with her backpack, wearing her mashed-up Adidas. The same men are there, standing before a white lorry; they tell her to pay the rest of the cash – all her savings, some borrowed, most of it stolen from Josip as he snored – twenty thousand in the local currency, all in. She is warned that the wrong eyes might clock them. Told to stand aside, get back, wait at the café.

During the next twenty minutes, seven more come to pay up and hang back in the café; they sit at pavement tables next to her, texting and smoking, not wasting their money on coffee, hoping not to get shooed off by the flapping owner.

The sun grows stronger as they sit and wait, warming like hope. Then, movement across the street: men frowning into mobiles, gesticulating, husking blunt words at each other; not looking at their charges, watching them from the café; not opening the vehicle's back doors. Getting into the cab of the lorry. Starting the engine. Moving off.

'No!'

She needs to break them, as they are breaking her.

She snatches up the loose chunk of cobblestone and lobs it hard and fast at the lorry. The crash of wing-mirror glass as it explodes into shards; the stone hits it dead on. Hey! and oi! and cursing; the other dupes, leaping up and waving. The men swear out of the window, revving up big as if to say: 'We could end you, bitch,' and drive off. Acid shock smarts in her gorge. Now she has nothing.

She watches the lorry grumble away up the street, taking its own sweet time because what are that bunch of goddamn losers going to do about it, anyway? The lorry is leaving, its drivers newly rich, carting its cargo of washing machines, tumble dryers and cookers but without the humans. Humans who had begged, shafted, borrowed, blagged, thieved and sold all but their souls to crouch in the spaces between the cheap white goods, covered in plastic sheets, hushed and yearning, on their way to new English lives. The lorry men are liars and cheats.

The light refracts, a prism of tears; her future glinting from the tarmac in twenty thousand broken pieces.

She is dead.

Chapter Ten

THURSDAY, 26 JULY 2018

Every day Etta waited for a message from Chris Wise and every day nothing came. She could not pay him, could not forget about it, could not dare to hope he had changed his mind. When it came to the last Thursday of the month, she was relieved that she was scheduled to work at the First Welcome Project.

She turned up early, ready to drown herself in other people's sorrows. Janie met her at the door.

'Just so you know, we were broken into last week.'

'What, really?'

'I know, bizarre right?'

'Horrible. Is everyone OK? What did they take?'

'We're all fine thanks, and that's just it: they took nothing you'd expect. Our computers were untouched, nothing smashed. They just took our paperwork: a load of client files, staff files, forms and that.'

'Damn, OK. At least no one was hurt or anything.'

'Exactly. No one was here. It has been creeping me out though. Glad you're back!'

Etta spent the shift talking to clients, handing out leaflets and filling forms as usual, but all the time she wondered when she could next check her mobile for a message from her blackmailer. She got through, while waiting for the axe to fall.

It came to the last Friday of the month. Payday. Ola's quarterly savings statement was due any day; she would have to destroy it. Also due were the loan repayments. Payday profligacy versus payday pledges: her salary was, in the best of times, gambling funds. But she should reduce her debt. She should not gamble. All action seemed to incur privations and consequences. The struggle followed her on the walk to work, through the whim of a detour to the park to find the puzzle man, who was not there, and into the office; it was crippling, a killer. She got through the morning, but the afternoon was a walk in the fog. At around 3 p.m., a short-circuit, something shut down in her. She did not want to speak, or look out at her colleagues, or tap on a keyboard. She sat, eyes open, seeing nothing.

'Cat got your tongue?' Dana, a cream-and-blue blur barging into focus.

Etta started from her trance as if caught in an illegal act.

'Sorry, sorry.'

She was not sorry. She was sad, confused and somewhere else, somewhere not good, but better than reality. It was happening to her more and more.

She got through to the end of the day and rushed home to not gamble and to not pay debts and to not function in privacy.

Although a month of silence had passed since the VIP party, when the world had turned upside down, the thought of Chris Wise was still pure fire, flaming her multifarious fears so that they jumped and popped like corn in a pan. The central deception, while not undone, was undiscovered. It was agony.

She was fighting, at every moment, not to lose more money, not to *lose it*. Her mind had rewired itself into a tangle of fear superhighways and mad B-roads, dead ends and twisting paths that could only lead to another calamitous error of judgement.

Etta whoever

No Cozee, no gambling. Hours of strenuous effort; unending minutes of forgoing and refraining, stretching on through her fretful sleep and into Saturday morning when Etta woke up late, alone and hungry.

She dialled:

'Hi, Ola.'

'Hi, sleepy-head.' He sounded like he had been running. 'You did not move an inch when I got up.'

'Where are you?'

'At the gym, of course. I will be back in two, three hours, or about that.'

'OK. Enjoy.'

Within the first minute of waking, she was craving a solid hit of brunch: a hot bacon bap with egg moin-moin and fried plantain, plus bottomless orange juice, as if she had done the workout. By the second minute, her throat itched, with disregard for the stomach's health, for gin; the gin, also bottomless, would soothe her palms, which were also itching.

Her palms were aflame, the skin of each hand tingling. It was not her new hand cream, no antihistamine would help. This itch could be cured and she knew how to cure it.

Her abstinence had now lasted almost a month: surely, she was no addict. Not indulging was not *stasis*, after all; she still had to decide, twenty thousand times a day, not to gamble, or worse. She had been fighting. Trying and fighting, with no let-up. That had to say something encouraging about her character. She was no animal, she had mastered her baser instincts, she – surely – had nothing more to prove.

But now, this itch . . .

She had to get out of the house. She would do something she had not done for weeks. She dialled:

'Hi, Jada? Yeah, hi, it's Etta. Could you fit me in this morning, please? Perfect, thanks. See you in a tick.'

She ditched breakfast. Ten minutes later, she was around the corner, on the ninth floor of the flats on Wellington Road.

'Babes!' cried a woman with a wide smile and a short burgundy wig. 'Get yourself in here, it's been ages. Need a steam, is it?'

'Yes. I look a mess, right?' said Etta, lifting her head, searching her friend's eyes. At last, she was being seen.

'No, come, come. Make yourself comfortable. Want a coffee?'

Jada made her a drink and set about her work.

'I've been wondering where you've been. All OK?'

'Been better.'

'Oh, sorry, love. Why, what've you been up to?'

Etta swallowed hard:

'All sorts. Nothing special. It's been OK, I suppose.'

Jada hovered her hands above Etta's head.

'OK. We're going to sort you out, babes. Leave it to me.'

Jada stroked and pulled at a curl to test the strength of her hair.

'Your hair been breakin'?' she asked.

'A bit,' said Etta.

'You should look after it, you know. You've got good hair. And your skin's *beau*tiful. You're lucky.'

'I've been a bit . . . under the weather.'

'OK,' said Jada. 'No need to worry now. Put your head back.'

Etta leant her head into the freestanding sink in the front room.

'D'ju remember that guy, Matteo? Hardly my type, right?'

'Mm,' murmured Etta.

'No, so that was a pain in the arse and then what was worse, his dickhead mate decided to try it on . . .'

'Mm.'

Reading her friend's silence, Jada wound up her chat.

'OK, we're gonna wash you now. Just lie back a bit more. That's it.'

Etta closed her eyes, felt the porcelain of the neck rest cool her. Her stomach muscles tightened as she heard the *whoosh* of the pump dispensing a squirt of shampoo into the hairdresser's hand. A shiver ran through her as Jada turned the water on, let the temperature settle. Water was scooped and gently tipped onto the back of Etta's head.

'Is that OK?' Jada asked.

'Yes. Lovely,' said Etta.

Her eyes stayed closed as *whoosh, whoosh* . . . Jada gathered more shampoo and applied it to Etta's hair. There, at last: the hands set themselves upon her head. Warm water coursed over her scalp; soft fingertips firm, pressing the neglected flesh stretching around her skull, circling, kneading in gentle sweeps, not judging but caring, not doubting but knowing. Tears pricked the corner of Etta's eyes.

She drifted. In the dark there was only comfort; the warm water, that restorative touch.

Her tipped-back head grew heavy in seconds; it lolled to each side as the fingers rinsed, massaged shampoo in again, and rinsed.

'OK, let's towel this dry.'

A rough-soft tussle of hair in cotton, ears rubbed, neck patted dry.

'Right, my love. Here comes the hair mayo. Mayohhh.'

Now the hands, scooped and slathered, scooped and slathered the creamy conditioning treatment all over Etta's hair. Then the hands worked it through with a stout comb; divided the hair into four sections; wet the hair and pulled it into twists. Finally, she was crowned with a shower cap.

'Chill a bit now, yeah? Twenty-five, thirty minutes. I'm going to check on Ionie.'

Etta settled back, eyes still shut, and breathed. And breathed. All was dark and peace: too high up for traffic noise, no one hollering, no TV. Peace.

At some point, soft footsteps, a voice coming through the dark:

'OK then, let's rinse this out.'

Warm water, cleansing from brow to nape. Again, again. Hands towelling her hair dry. A spray of leave-in conditioner: the scent of warm skin, split coconuts, a cove . . .

Click. Hairdryer on.

Etta opened her eyes and shifted in her seat. She was being blow-dried with care, her hair blasted into its full glory.

Click. The noise died; a hand on her shoulder.

'You're done. You'll be all right now.'

A mirror was propped in front, another held up behind.

Etta stared. She looked so orderly; so cared for.

Tears were streaming before she could stop them.

'Hey! Ah, no need for that. You're OK.'

Etta's eyes closed tight against their weeping and she tipped her head back again, right back, into the warmth of Jada, stooped behind her; her head tipped back and the tears ran and she croaked out her pain while her pampered crown pressed into soft thick thigh, or breast or stomach, she knew not what; she could only feel the love.

●

Back at home, Etta examined herself more closely for change in the mirror. She had to look away. She prepared a single poached egg on toast, coffee and orange juice instead of gorging. She drained her mug and set it down. Minutes passed; one long inconceivable moment. A tingle, a light burning grew on her skin. Compulsion began to crawl once more across her palms; the urge was back, stronger than ever.

Etta was itching to gamble.

Her body was breaking out: her thoughts starting to flutter, her breath coming faster. She patted her palms to her hair, trying to feel the love again . . . but no, there was just the *itch*. She rose, went to the cupboard and forgave her shortcomings with a whisper of gin, her thoughts growing hot and sweet in her head as she drank it down. She poured another half-glass for luck and went up to complete her breakfast of champions by playing slots, hard and fast.

This time, she would also play smart. She planned to diversify, to spread her new eggs across the optimum number of baskets. Not on Cozee, never again. She joined Winners Kingdom, despite the lack of apostrophe (the omission of champions); she joined Spin City, because of the joining bonus – *£30 now, plus £30 when you recommend a friend!* (the incentive of champions); she stopped at just the two sites, because she was now back in control; what restraint! Even her pulse played along, never rising above a trot as she joined first one site, then the other. An excellent sign.

Etta's handle in this new realm was 'Nemesis'. Hands steadying, she downloaded the Spin City phone app, to maximise her opportunities. She deferred the outstanding payday loans and took out two more. Everything cool. She was doubling her chances, getting a grip. She would be as smart as she hoped she was, this time. She had good sense, good hair. She would get through it.

●

Etta was strolling around Spin City, dipping into games with the most appealing shopfronts. A text arrived: Joyce!

> I told you, we're over. Don't send me any more of your goddamn junk mail.

Etta stood up from her chair. Sat down. Stood up again and picked up the phone.

'Joyce, it's Etta.'

'Yeah?'

'I think you've made a mistake. I didn't send you anything.'

'Bollocks, I've got the email here. Hold on . . . Yes. From these stupid arses: "Your friend Etta Oladipo has sent you £30 to start spinning on Spin City. Don't miss this outstanding chance to have fun as you spin and win!"'

'Oh, yes. I'd forgotten about that. I just wanted you to get a break, you know, have a bit of luck. I've been thinking about you.'

'I need more than thoughts and prayers right now, thanks, Etta.'

'I was trying to be a friend.'

'Bit late for that.'

'I am so sorry, Joyce, you have to believe me. I should never have let you down like that.'

'You should never have done a lot of things, including sending me that stupid link.'

'It was just a gesture, an apology. I thought—'

'*I* thought, fair enough, I'm having a low day, let's give it a go. Wasn't gonna sniff at a free £30, was I? Thought I might win enough to top up my FOF—'

'Sorry, your what?'

'The Fuck-off Fund, you know this, for when you need to get the hell out. So, I had a few spins, won a bit first game. Thought, brilliant; few more spins. Then I figured it wouldn't hurt to have a bit of a longer go. Next thing you know, I've spent all this week's rent and half of the next.'

'Oh shit. Joyce, I—'

'You blow out my mum's funeral and then, just as I'm finding my bloody feet, while my head's still a mess, you send me a link to these bloody crooks. What kind of bloody friend are you?'

'Joyce, I am so sorry. Those games are never a dead cert, of course, but I thought—'

'You thought "that stupid mare hasn't got enough grief in her life, let's shovel some more onto her, quick".'

'Joyce!'

'It's OK, Etta, no need to act surprised. My own stupid fault. We're fine. We're cool. Let's just stay well away from each other from now on though, yeah? Because nothing calls to trouble like trouble.'

She hung up.

Etta sat down and stared into the screen of the laptop. A goggle-eyed cartoon dentist was testing his syringe, shooting a serum of pound signs into the air, to the amusement of the cartoon nurse.

Drillionaire could take a running jump, for now. Her palms had stopped itching – no anaesthetic more effective than a friend pouring scorn on an open wound. From her heart to her fingertips, she felt numb.

The front door went, Ola shouting:

'I'm back. Did you miss me?'

Etta clocked the truth before shouting back, 'Of course!'

●

Up early on Sunday, at 6 a.m., because this was a bright new dawn. Chris Wise had clearly thought better of his blackmail plans. She had funds and time. Today, Etta would begin to put things right, starting with Joyce. She would win £300 or £400 for her friend, whatever it took to cover her lost rent money. This was a priority and it would leapfrog all deficits. She would spin, win and transfer it to Joyce. Straight away. This time it was serious.

Leaving Ola sleeping in bed, she went to the spare room and fired up Spin City. She played Pandora. But Pandora played her back; within half an hour she had lost it all. The gambling stake, plus every penny she had earned that month: her whole July salary, gone in minutes. Devoured.

Etta stared at the screen without any tears, or twitching, or flutterings of panic; something darker but more patient sat heavy in her chest. Something like hate.

An alert popped up onscreen:

You are now a Spin City VIP!

She leaned forward in her chair, her eyes closed, and let the bad times roll, a raving, rambling movie in her mind. She drifted through the day, making meals, making empty conversation. That night, she drifted into a restless sleep; rolling inside her counterfeit dreaming, memories flowering and fading like colours in a kaleidoscope, until the metallic slap of Monday morning jerked her awake.

She ran. Downstairs, five envelopes had landed on the mat. She scooped them up and shuffled. There it was: the grenade. She dropped the other post back onto the mat and took herself off to the downstairs loo.

She locked the door and opened the bank statement. Only two months mattered:

June 2018 – £22,018.34

July 2018 – £0

Etta's eyes filled at the sight of the figures – the brutal reduction of their future to zero; the financial chasm between her and Ola; the betrayal tallied in black and white. With her vision swimming, she tore, tore, tore until there were at least thirty pieces of betrayal in her hands and – there! – they were floating in the toilet bowl. She flushed. A few shreds bobbed at the surface; she kneeled and flushed again, forcing them down into another turbulent stream before they could settle. One last scrap clammed itself against the porcelain, so that she had to grab the loo brush and shove at it, but it got caught in the bristles and then only her fingers could work it out, and her gullet contracted as she choked back nausea, the better to free the filthy white mush, only to flick each last bit of it into the bowl and cry freely as she flushed and flushed again.

Once the cistern had shut up its grim song, Etta tried to think about moving away from the toilet bowl.

But now there came knocking. Ola.

'Are you all right, Teetee?'

'Fine, Ola, I'm OK,' she replied. 'It just wouldn't flush.'

'Oh. Sorry o. I'm going to work now, if you're sure you're OK. Got to go.'

'OK, thanks, I'm fine. See you later!'

Etta tipped her head back against the loo door and tried to visualise the moment, seconds from now, when she would rise up from the mat and walk out into the hall, regaining the day. But she stayed sprawled on the ground, bent over and spent, floored.

●

Work was a slow-motion replay; she fast-forwarded in her mind. Monday evening brought no text, again, from the man who haunted her thoughts. Maybe he felt too bad to go through with it. Or had bottled it. Whatever: he was not chasing her for £10,000 she did not have and that was enough light in the darkness to see her through another day.

One further point of light: life off Cozee was starting to feel better. Safer. She could whirl around Spin City and explore Winners Kingdom incognito: a true player, with no loyalties and no connections. The right way. Pure madness to have engaged with another gambler – another *spinner* – outside of the confines of that shifty, ever-shifting world.

Real-life friendships had been neglected – or blown apart – and she would put that right with a win. Money Meteor, next. She blazed a trail from £10 to £380 in a few spins.

Etta was winning.

Minutes later, money at the £440 mark, the roll, roll, roll of the reels set her mind drifting. This £400 would make everything right with Joyce. Withdraw now and the friendship was fixed. But the Meteor Shower bonus was still out there, waiting . . . Maybe Joyce would forgive her if she just called her up to explain once more?

addict

The word rang in her head, but she rolled on.

●

It was late when the neighbours' bulldog went mental. Then the doorbell rang.

Ola had stopped at the pub opposite the uni and was on his way back. Etta went downstairs alone.

'Hello?' she called, tucking her phone into her dressing-gown pocket.

The light above the front door had been left on, as usual. She could see through the glass that no one was on the front step.

Bracing herself, she went to open the door.

She breathed deep, waited, then yanked the door wide.

No one. Her eyes darting into the dark corners. Was someone hiding behind a car?

Then she saw them: glasses, on the doorstep, one lens smashed. Ola's reading glasses. Propped up on their arms, placed central and straight on the porch mat. Etta snatched them up and threw herself back into the house, slamming the door shut.

Chris Wise. What had he done to him?

She fumbled for her phone and dialled.

He picked up:

'Hello?'

'Ola! Thank God. Are you OK?'

'Whoa, slow down, it is noisy in here. Hold on, I'm moving through to the garden . . .'

Etta waited as she heard Ola close a door, voices fading out.

'So. Speak to me. You OK?'

'Not really,' said Etta. 'Have you been attacked? Hurt?'

'Of course not? Why would you think that?'

'I just . . . Someone's been in the house.'

'What?'

'Seriously.'

'Are you hurt?'

'They haven't touched me. I found your reading glasses on the front step. Broken.'

'What?'

'Yes!' Etta gasped at her own honesty. She had no choice.

'Are you sure they're mine?'

'Yes, the ones normally on your bedside table. Broken. A lens is broken.'

'Ah,' said Ola.

The two of them were silent for a moment.

'They must have been in the front pouch of my rucksack. Fallen out, eh? Smashed.'

'You reckon?' she asked.

'Yes.'

Time to pull back. No good could come of the truth.

'Yes,' she agreed. 'You must be right.'

More silence.

'Sorry for bothering you,' she said.

'It's OK. As long as you're all right.' A door opened, a burble of voices. 'Go to bed now, heh?'

'OK,' said Etta. 'Night night.'

She went to the kitchen, turning on every light as she went, checking the large cupboards, looking. No sign of him. More lights on upstairs, all the lights; the house blazed with her fear. He did not appear to be in here and yet he had been here.

Dead flowers, her lover's glasses broken: these doorstep messages were enough to tell her that he wished her harm. That he was watching.

Etta locked the bedroom door and sat on the edge of the bed, still dressed in her robe and ready for flight. She sat, waiting for the sound of the key in the lock to tell her Ola had returned. She sat, wondering whether she might first hear the sound of breaking glass, a stranger's footsteps on the stairs.

Her eyes were tiring in the glare by 11.24 when her phone announced a WhatsApp. She tapped the screen. Her mouth formed the O of a scream.

She had been right. Chris Wise.

You owe me

Chapter Eleven

THURSDAY, 2 AUGUST 2018

It was three days later when the doorbell rang.

Ola had returned soon after Wise's late-night message and she had feigned normality ever since: working, waiting, watching out.

Now, the bell. She had only been back from work for five minutes, again skimming looks over every passing face as she hurried home. She had felt Wise's badness in every step she took, just as she had sensed his gaze upon her as she strived in the spare room. Had he followed? The front door was not that sturdy and the back of the house, the garden, the watched windows . . .

The bell went again.

A lurch of horror as she realised that if she did not get it, Ola would. She ran downstairs.

A man's shadow behind the dimpled glass. His imagined height, his imagined build.

'Who is it?' she called brightly, reaching for an umbrella in the stand.

'Did your windows the other day,' the man called through the door. 'We left you a note.'

'Oh!' The umbrella crashed to the floor. 'Sorry! Give me a minute, please.'

'No problem, love.'

She replaced the umbrella and opened the door.

'Whoa, hello!' said the man.

'Hi.'

It was not Chris Wise, but a young man with ready wit and bucket, eyeing Etta as if he would like to clean her, limb by limb, with a tiny rag. She turned her back on him, buying time. She trembled as she made a show of looking in the coat cupboard for her handbag; her thoughts were oscillating and her hands and legs were quaking. The shock, of course, but also another night of no sleep and a 2 a.m. rendezvous with gin. The spirit had not done its usual trick, so she had stared blank-eyed into the dawn. She was tired of gambling, of lying, of stressing, and of not sleeping. She was tired of being tired of all of them: at least the trembling was a fresh tribulation.

She hauled herself out of the cupboard, holding up her handbag.

'Just a minute.'

She continued her fake searching, this time rifling for her purse in her bag, which would contain nothing; she could offer this hard-working man not a thing for his trouble. The window cleaner watched; he whistled something vaguely familiar as she searched and shook.

The rifling went on for too long; she knew it had to look like a bad joke, or a mime of desperation.

The whistling died. An awkward noise: a laugh, quickly strangled.

'You OK, love?' The window cleaner was craning to see into her bag from the doorway.

'Yes, I'm sorry. I can't find it.'

'Take your time.'

She leaned her bag on the hall table and rummaged more forcefully. His smile slipped from patience to concern.

Etta shoved the bag hard off the table onto the floor. Out spilled receipts, mints, a lipstick, a guilty corner of purse.

'It's just . . .' she said, standing straight and looking right at him, 'there's no money!'

The shaking got harder as she cried. The man took a step back from the door, palms raised. The thud-thud of Ola coming down the stairs.

'What is this, eh? Are you unwell?' He took in the bucket in the man's hand, the ladder on the path, and reached for his wallet, tucked under some papers on the side.

'I'm so sorry, Ola.'

'Sorry o? Wah?' he laughed without joy and handed £30 to the window cleaner. 'Come now, Etta, all done.'

He closed the front door, but not before Etta caught a look of understanding pass between the two men, as if to say 'funny creatures'.

Etta spoke first:

'I'm sorry, Ola, I don't feel right.'

'I can see, poor-poor thing. Come here.' He opened his arms wide and she leaned in. 'Are you ill?'

'I don't know. Yes.'

'You couldn't pay him?'

'No money!'

He tipped her head back and gave her a look.

'I have been pressuring you too much, Teetee. What is a man if he cannot ease the purse strings from time to time, eh?'

'But Ola, we haven't got enough—'

'We're fine. Are you telling me that your man cannot take care of you?'

'No. It's me, I'm sick.'

'Go upstairs, I'll bring you tea.'

Etta went up and got into bed without taking off her work clothes. Her head was pounding with an unholy trinity of thoughts:

Chris Wise

£10,000

blackmail

She drifted off, breathing shallow, dreaming of ruin. By the time she woke up the light had a different quality to it; Ola was standing by the bed, shrugging on his shirt.

'Morning!' he said.

'Morning?'

'You needed to sleep.'

'Oh. It's Friday?'

'Yes. Listen, I have an idea. But I have to go to work now, OK? Tell them you're sick, go back to bed.'

'OK. Oh, no.'

'What?'

'They won't believe me. I'm already on thin ice. Could you phone them please?'

'If you want me to.'

'Tell them you're Doctor Abayomi, that should work.'

'OK, I will do.'

Etta spent the day lying where she had awoken. The tremors had persisted, on a lower frequency throughout her long sleep, but had subsided altogether by lunchtime. To celebrate, she opened a bottle of red. At some point, it went dark. She awoke to the sound of the front door shutting.

'Ola?'

It came out muffled, crushed by the weight of worry and the duvet. Clearer words sat, useless, in her chest. Even, upward steps that did not sound like him, steps coming to the door. It opened to dark skin, a brilliant smile.

'Oh! Thank God.'

Tears that shamed her – too easy, too few – started once more. Ola sat on the bed.

'This is my fault,' he said.

'No, Ola. I'm just not right.'

'I've stressed you out too much, but don't worry. I've got the answer, let me show you.'

On the side of the bed, he powered up his laptop. The hard metal sat between them, blocking off any true closeness and comfort.

'This. Here, look.' He turned the screen towards her.

A turquoise credit card sat large on the screen. Words featured above and below the image, but all Etta noted was 'Up to £5,000 limit' and 'Apply HERE'.

'You're letting me have a credit card?'

'Letting you, heh? When have I ever stopped you doing what you want?'

He smiled, and she smiled back rather than pull instances from the well-catalogued library of their relationship. All in the timing.

'Thank you, Ola.'

'Take your time, Teetee. Relax and do the application. I'll go and make us a drink.'

He rose to leave but paused at the door.

'Etta, another thing. Have you been drinking wine?'

Etta said, 'A little, with lunch. It helped me sleep, my darling.'

She did not say: 'It *was* lunch; my lunch knocked me unconscious.'

Ola nodded and left; she tapped at his laptop. This was it, the big break, the credit ladder up which she could clamber from the hole. She heard the kettle boiling downstairs within moments of hitting 'submit'. By the time Ola came back in, bearing two steaming mugs, she was crying once more.

'Very poor,' she said.

'What?'

'Very poor. My credit rating is "very poor" and I've been refused. They won't give me a credit card.'

Ola passed her a mug and sat back down on the bed.

'How can this be?' He turned the laptop towards him, shaking his head. 'What nonsense! It must be a mistake. We've been so careful. Why?'

Rather than respond, Etta cried louder, in part weeping at the blow to their joint-mortgage future, in part salting her distress to make it more palatable to him. If she stopped, he might probe further.

'There is no sense in this decision. Eh? Why?'

'I don't know, Ola.' The ache behind her ribs spread. 'I'm sorry.'

'Ah! Don't cry about this silly-silly card.' He pushed the laptop aside and pulled her towards him. 'The interest rate was not that good, anyway.'

She gave a little caw of amusement, deep into his shoulder so that he would not hear it ring false. But, all the time, her eyes kept soaking his shirt, salting his collarbone, salting the truth.

●

They spent an evening saying little of value, avoided all friction, then got an early night.

Etta rose to brush her teeth at 10 p.m., then again, around midnight, to get wine from downstairs which she brought back to sip next to the sleeping Ola. She woke up staring into the dark, an empty glass pressing into her side. It was 3.12 a.m. There was another WhatsApp waiting:

Isn't it great that u can message anyone on Facebook, even if their not ur friend? Beats all other social media hands down for REAL communication, right?

Typing . . .

Although, u may have noticed that my grammar is not great. Maybe u could read this message over for me? It's a goodun.

Typing . . .

Dear Dr Abayomi u don't know me yet but u will . . .

Typing . . .

I really should write 'you' shouldn't I, for a doctor? And do I need a comma? Sloppy. What should I say next, any thoughts?

Etta wanted to slap him down as if she were a woman who feared nothing.

No. Cheque's in the post you fucker.

She hit send and started to weep. What had she done? She was not strong or brave; Wise was not just a blackmailer, he was clearly crazy and knew where to find her. He could come and kill her in the night, kill them both.

She waited for five minutes, tears drying. Nothing. Maybe she had called his bluff after all, seen him off. Or had he fallen asleep? It was the heart of the night, but to full-blooded spinners that meant little, and insomnia frequently ate up all hope of rest. But no bleep or buzz came in these darkest hours. Not a murmur from her phone, even after the granite sky had warmed to pale gold; nothing as Ola ate his Saturday morning breakfast, insisting that she should not trouble herself by making him egg moin-moin, that he would just eat bread and milk; nothing after Ola left to go for a run . . . Until there was.

A beep. She knew it was Chris Wise before she saw the words:

You don't rate the good doctor, then.
£10,000 or I'm coming for you.

•

Wet-faced, wiped out, Etta leaned up on her elbows and breathed something flimsy and distracting to her partner about hormones and nausea and troublesome aches. His usual reflex would kick in at the mention of the biological and yet strangely unscientific problem of her femininity.

'I'll go and make you some tea.'

She muttered thanks as he left.

Unwitnessed, the tears kept coming. She writhed and wrung her hands and heaved her shoulders. Bent double under the duvet, wracked, she hit at the mattress, stuffed inches of pillow into her mouth to strangle the sound, or choke herself.

209

He could tell Ola everything in a Facebook message. He might even go to the police. He would blow it all up, every last hidden thing – the spinning, the theft from Ola, the credit card fraud, the party – showering everyone she cared about in the gore of her life.

They always said you should never pay them off, that that was the worst thing you could do. But it was starting to look like the least worst option. Ten thousand pounds was not so much. While so much money had the sheen of myth or folklore, a unicorn's horn in the middle distance, what was it really, within the realm of fantasy finances? She could win enough in one day – one spin! – to pay him off and to save her relationship, her sanity and her arse.

She would have to pay him off.

A gentle pushing open of the door.

'Here's your tea, my love.'

'Thank you, Ola.'

She wiped the last of her tears with a tissue. She could do this. One good spin.

Time to bag a unicorn.

●

The only problem was, she needed more funds; she needed another payday loan. This time it was no joke: Wise was *here*, around, waiting. Was he hiding in the garden now? She edged up to the spare room window, pushed her cheek flat against the curtain and looked out sideways. Grey sky and sun, slow-moving air and cloud. The flowerbeds appeared to be fertile with secrets, the lawn seeded with intent. The bushes that hugged the fence, keeping the back fields out, what did they hide?

focus

Etta slipped back into her office chair, away from the window, and searched for a lender, floundering, flailing and falling at hurdles. Her stomach ached, but she dismissed a trip downstairs for a quick fry-up. Ola would be lost in the papers, and she would like him to stay lost a while longer. Loan, a loan; who would accept her now? Her stomach complained as the screen replied:

**We're sorry but we are unable to offer
you a loan at this time . . .**

Some unorthodox borrowing and a few late repayments and the rumour must have run like bacon grease across a burning hotplate: Etta Oladipo was hungry for money, but she must not be fed.

All the bigger lenders had already coughed up. After that, she had fallen prey to the broker portals which masqueraded as lenders. Their trick – and it was a goodie – was to disguise their filthy warehouse as a stush boutique. You paid and paid, and when you emerged you felt dirty, and you felt had. But the money was yours.

Etta googled, scrolled and checked reviews; she could barely credit the credit on offer. She might falter in her own morals from time to time, but this was another level of exploitation. One camouflaged cesspit offered to charge her £25 for a 'Recommended Loan' with another company altogether which would lend her £100 (repay just £350) when she needed at least £700. Cartels of chancers, skyrocketing interest. It was a carnival of crap.

She knew these to be the daily trials of the skint and unconnected. She knew she ought to swerve the lot. But Wise was after her and without £10,000 she was dead.

The phone went.

'Hi!'

'Hi.'

'Hi! It's Roxy from AVS Bank. How are you today?'

'Fine. AVS Bank?'

'We're calling as there's been a security breach on your account. We need you to—'

'I'm not with AVS Bank. This is a con. Goodbye.'

Etta hung up. She pushed the laptop aside and, for the first time that morning, got out of bed. She edged along the mattress, moving limbs that felt disinclined. If she did not succeed, Wise would finish her off. She had to have a loan. The T&Cs and the APR did not matter, in the end: she needed to borrow a stake, any stake, to win back her life.

Etta went back to the window and pushed it open; breathed in the air from her scheming yard, then got back into bed. She needed access to more than £100. She had to enter the furnace that powered all of gambling Hades: No Credit Checks! loans.

The excitable punctuation was compulsory. The terms were appalling.

Her new financial home.

No Credit Checks! loans tended to find you. They were always just passing by as a friendly text or email, no pressure. They found everybody, in the end. These, the hard nuts of all loans, albeit suited, booted and under their Sunday manners, lobbed you a few pennies at monstrous interest . . . but what the effing hell were you going to do about it?

Of course, she borrowed. The maximum: £750 from Flying Pig Loans. She did not try to calculate the interest because there was no choice. Wise had taken all her choices from her.

Funds secured, on to unicorn hunting. Etta tried Diana's Diner, Meteor Shower and Merlin's Miracles, for old times' sake. Within forty-five minutes she had won £7,300, forty minutes after that she was down to £2,800. She blamed it on her lack of focus; she kept checking the window, checking her phone, checking her state of mind. Neither she nor her luck could settle.

In the spare room, where she had offered to sleep as Ola had an early Monday morning start, she gambled through the night with red wine and undiluted gin for company.

Come the dawn, she had £1,270 in the kitty and chronic indigestion.

She resolved both issues with a capful of milk of magnesia and a 6 a.m. spinning spree that promised much – a bonus on the first spin! – but stripped her of every penny.

No unicorn. Just £0.00, a still-cramping stomach and a chalky taste in her mouth.

As she walked to work, numb with losses, she retained enough feeling to twitch at the sudden movements of pedestrians; blaring radios buzzed her nerves, car horns jarred. Yet at every step she was cogitating an abominable new plan: could she do it? She couldn't. Could she? She might be able to, but she shouldn't. Should she?

By the final few streets she was in a near trance, a good one. Her meditation had brought a clarity: she knew what she had to do next.

Anxiety pumped through every limb as she made her way across the car park. She had to commit this terrible act.

At her desk, she deteriorated fast. Winston looked weird, Dana was watching her, Jean was full of dark thoughts, the temps could not be trusted. She spied danger in each corridor. She could not function, she could barely simulate normal, she could never face the mission she had set herself.

Verbal warning or not, she needed to get out.

'Just popping to the doctor, OK?' she said to Winston.

'No problem,' he replied, intent on a document. His face definitely looked a bit puffy, or twisted. 'See you in a bit.'

Robert was off. Jean was going into a meeting. She might just get away with it.

She rose and walked out of the office. She kept walking, right and left and a long way down, all the way to the least popular supermarket. The drinks aisle. She took bad red wine and she took overpriced gin, putting them on the household card. After a moment's thought, she picked up a packet of sausages that looked under-refrigerated and unsure in their plastic wrapping, four potatoes and some frozen peas. *Et voilà*: dinner.

She walked on to the park, deciding that her defrosting veg would cool the meat products. No sign of the puzzle seller, yet again, and she was glad of it; she needed solitude, just there, 200 metres away from his patch. She needed to slump against a tree trunk, legs outstretched, and drink.

First, she checked her phone. Nothing. Chris Wise's moves were becoming easier to read: he wanted her to wonder and to stress and, above all, to get the money together. She might have been tricked into this fresh torture by his cunning, but she knew enough of their world to smell out another spinner's desperation.

drink up

She took her time: a Malbec starter, followed by a main and pudding of gin. Sure, why not call this lunchtime at the doctor's? The alcohol made a sweet and strong anaesthetic. You had to take the sting out of the savagery of the world. Friends turned nasty; stood you up or disappeared; they stabbed you in the back; others lied, or died; the unmourned haunted you. All too heinous to handle sober.

Growing lighter now though, brighter, a cheese course of Malbec dregs gave her the strength to rise and start back towards work. She dumped the wine bottle in the recycling and stopped to lean against a wall while she hunted for a mint in her handbag.

'I know you.'

Etta straightened, her vision smarting.

'You!'

'I knew you would be here.'

The puzzle seller was watching her, too close, too earnest. Shame surged like nausea. Had he seen the bottle go into the bin?

'I want to thank you.'

'Thank me?'

'The First Welcome Project. But I do not see you there.'

'I only work there on the odd day. Not very often.'

'Ah. The people there have helped me. God is good o.'

'Great,' said Etta. The surging was in fact nausea, not shame. She had to go, now, or vomit at his feet.

'I am not economic migrant. I am asylum seeker!'

'Good for you,' she said. 'Nice one.'

'The bad men at home. Ah!' He ran a finger down the scar on his chin.

'Sure,' she said. 'I get it.'

'I can never leave England. Not even to go to my cousin's wedding in Paris. She has found a good man. I will never get back into this country. You understand?'

'I understand,' she said.

'This help from your people is therefore a blessing. It is making my life.'

'I understand,' she repeated, knowing she would never fully understand what he had suffered while trying to get here.

'You think I am beggar? I had a job in Nigeria, my father had a good life, I had a good life. These men . . . they try to destroy me.'

'I'm so sorry,' said Etta.

'No, no sorry o. You have helped me. I have job interviews. They are sending me for *meh-dee-cal.* Medical! You have been good to me. I cannot believe you came to talk to me that day. I must be so lucky!'

He smiled wide, better fortune now his.

'It was nothing. Well done.' Etta moved her palm along the wall, to feel the saving coolness of the next brick.

'I've had the first medical. At the hospital, Dr Mishra from Kerala. You know him?'

'No.'

'Incredible man. Ah-ah! Clever man. Whole family killed in fire when he was a boy. Clothes factory. He tell me this o. Good, good man. Only ever want come to England, become doctor. Fix hearts.'

Etta dropped her bag at his feet, scooped it up again.

'Listen, sorry, I have to go. Nice to see you.'

Before he could thank her, or bless her, or praise God again, she was off, sweating up the path.

The act of walking was beneficial, if precarious; it zipped fresh air over the mint on her tongue so that, after a few yards, she felt less sick. Even so, her stomach lurched at a grey man in the distance; no, not Chris Wise. A runner broke into a sprint and she started as if shot. But there was no trouble. As she walked on, her vision snagged on buildings and bin sheds and large bushes; she did not pause by alleyways and checked each road before turning onto it; she was as calm as she could hope to feel.

By the time she had reached the office she had adopted the expression of benign competence that would see her through the afternoon.

'All OK?' asked Winston.

'All good, thanks,' she replied, shuffling papers.

There were no other comments as she took her place at her desk, no visible disapproval. One hour and twenty minutes was a credible doctor's trip, all good. She would spreadsheet and document and diarise until everybody left.

Three hours later, she sat alone in her corner, bar the mixed blessing of the cleaners. She went to the loo, taking her shopping with her, the now-toxic pork and the deliquescent peas, still chilling the remains of her gin. She sipped slow and breathed deep, keeping the queasiness at bay with juniper fumes. She had endured worse cocktail hours aged seventeen on the Paynton Road.

A rattling of the handle. Etta jumped, staggered into a crouch, steadied herself.

'Is that the cleaners?'

'Yes!'

'OK, I'm coming out!'

She sprayed the can by the loo, choking the air with lemon to obliterate the gin, and walked past a short, bored woman in a tracksuit, back to her desk.

The cleaner walked into the loo and began to mop.

now

She rose and walked across the office, trying to look as purposeful as possible. She stopped at the desk nearest the fire exit, Dana's desk. Etta sat down in her seat and searched through the pile of ring folders on her desk. Office protocols, forms, nothing. She tried the drawers, the top one was locked.

A brief rifle through the unlocked ones revealed nothing Etta did not have in her own desk. She needed the key.

Etta tried to picture Dana, to recreate the movements of a woman she often tried to ignore. She lifted piles of paper, checked the back corners of the open drawers. Maybe she took the key home with her? No, all Etta could do was work with what she knew of Dana: she was not bright, and indifferent to her job . . .

Pen pot.

She dug her hand into the royal blue container full of biros and pulled out a tiny drawer key. It fitted the lock and in seconds she had pulled everything out. The notebook was the thing: it contained a list of passwords, including those for her PC, email and the work intranet. The folder beneath it held the treasure: the Funshine Club accounts. This voluntary scheme funded outings for the employees who paid into it each month: meals out, spa days and other organised fun to brighten their lives.

Could she do this?

Why not? Her cards were marked at FrameTech. Jean had it in for her and she had more power, always would. Nothing to lose.

She powered up Dana's PC. Her own breathing sounded unusually loud and nasal; everything weird today. She scrolled and clicked on the correct file, the one with the numbers that matched those in the ring-binder.

In another window she opened the right online banking page.

Her vision tightened up, shocked sober as she stared from paper to screen:

Sort code: 19-55-24

Account number: 62019607

The password was right there in the notebook; more pitiful than even she had predicted:

DanaL0vesFunshine!

The trick was not to think about it; if she hesitated, she would be finished. She ran her eye down the list of debits that past year: small amounts for this and that. She took the money out in unnoticeable £100s and £50s and £30s, and then blew the bank with one £3,000. Now she could gamble bigger, get lucky faster and pay Chris. Dana wouldn't notice for weeks; Etta would replace it long before that. It was her colleagues who paid into the Funshine Club, but she was no thief; no one would lose a penny.

gin, calm

She finished the bottle in long bitter draughts and set it down. Now the numbers on the screen swam freely. She was not stealing. She was borrowing to save her life. In fact, she should go larger, take £10,000 from this vast corporate-matched pot. Why not? In fact, £20,000 would do it in one go: ten to get rid of Chris and ten as funds to process, to save herself.

Etta stared at the numbers until they appeared to stare back. Madness. She should have bought more gin.

fuck it

She did.

Then she returned to her own desk, thinking at each step of the security cameras.

She sat there, stiff with horror, numb with drink, for many minutes.

Then she tilted forward, slow, slower, until her forehead was touching down on the desk. She closed her eyes and tried to gauge whether she had, in fact, lost her mind.

She had to get out. She straightened, swept her essentials into her bag, dropped the gin into a colleague's bin and went to the lifts. The lift doors opened and closed. She checked her phone during the eternal descent. A text from Ola two hours before, alerting her that he would not be home for dinner and was staying over at Christopher and Josie's so they could iron out a niggle with the research for as long as it took. Luck might be on her side after all . . . the doors opened onto reception.

There sat the same security guard who had eyed Joyce up for a beating. Roy? Robin?

She slowed. 'Night, Roger.'

He looked at her as if she were Joyce:

'Working late?'

'Big project.' He would have seen her, keeled over, on the security cameras. 'Almost fell asleep!'

'Right.'

'Been working like a . . . a . . .'

stop

Her tongue was growing thick in her mouth but she smiled as he jangled keys, swiped a card. Moments later, she was out. Out in Rilton: a liar, a thief and a fraud. If she walked slowly enough, she might catch her death on the way home.

Etta survived the walk. As she neared her house, she looked right, across the road. The lights were on and there was Jean, hunched at the windowsill. She was looking out at the road. Some motion as she drew near, the ghost of a nod, but Etta felt no desire to wave. The flag hung limp in the night air, on its pole; a black abdication.

A mad flurry of movement in the hedge. A spectre lurched out of the bushes, white and wild-eyed. Etta cried out.

'Have you seen her?'

It was Jean's mother, barefoot in her nightie.

'Have you?' the old lady grabbed at Etta's arm. 'She killed her, you know. My Ruby. Put her in the bin!'

Jean was hurrying out of their house, up the path:

'There you are, Mother. Come inside!'

'No!' The mother looked like she might run.

'Can I help, Jean? Let's—'

'We're fine!' Jean snapped, tugging at her mother's hand and trying to lead her in as if her parent were the child. Seeing the look on Etta's face, the words spilled out of her:

'Ruby was her cat. *She* put it in the bloody recycling one night and I pulled it out just in time. Now the bloody thing's scarpered anyway and I can't blame it – and just come on, come inside, Mother!'

They shuffled past Etta up their path, the old woman now completely calm. Jean however, was red-faced and turned back once more to shout:

'What are you looking at? This is so . . . You shouldn't even be here! Come *on*, Mother!'

Etta recoiled and turned away. A binned cat, what the hell? Had that been what she had seen in the middle of that night? Whatever: it was all too much, she also needed to get inside. Reaching the doorstep of her house, she slumped inside, upstairs and turned into bed, holding down a resurgence of nausea.

She wanted Ola. She wanted to confess everything, to apologise for her incontestable weirdness, to tell him she had turned a corner, to tuck herself inside his shirt and hide from all that she had done. Unreasonable, impossible, sentimental. She had clearly not slept off the gin.

sort it

Etta opened her laptop and transferred the £10,000 to Chris Wise: it took ten seconds. She texted him:

It's done. £10,000. Now leave me alone.

She waited. Five minutes went by, fifteen. She stared at her phone until the rearing nausea threatened to wash her away. She shuffled down the bed, lay her head on the pillow and her phone by her cheek. Was this it? No thanks, no acknowledgement, no receipt. Was this to be her peace?

Still trying to fathom it out, she fell asleep.

•

She woke up to a violent banging on the door. Shrugging on a robe, she stumbled downstairs. On the doorstep stood the puzzle man.

'Hello?' she said, pulling the cord of her dressing gown tighter.

'I have it!' he said, the triumph hard to miss.

'Sorry, what?' asked Etta. She forced herself not to look around; there was no Ola, no one else.

'Your purse!' he cried, holding out the red leather wallet. 'You dropped it in the park.'

'Did I?' Etta rubbed her brow. 'Gosh, thank you. Sorry.'

'No trouble.'

Her driving licence card, her address on full show, was facing outwards.

'Thanks for coming to find me,' said Etta. 'What's your name?'

'Bankole Motilewa.'

'OK, thanks, Bankole. I appreciate it.'

'I am happy to help you, Etta,' he said. 'I will always help you, just as you have helped me.'

'Blimey,' Etta smiled. 'That's sweet. Bit early for me, sorry.'

'Do you have to go to work?'

'Yes. And I can't speak before a coffee. I can barely move.'

'Ha! He-he-he,' the puzzle man enjoyed the joke, although she had not been joking.

'OK. Well. Thanks for returning this, see you then.'

'It was no problem. I should do more than this for you. Maybe I make you my own *egusi* soup. I am a man who can cook and do many things besides. I will bring you my *egusi* one day, show you the real deal o.'

'Is that right?' She laughed despite herself. 'In that case, I'll see you and your soup later.'

'Goodbye, Etta Oladipo.'

He turned and went up the path.

She survived the remainder of the working week. The Tuesday walk into the FrameTech reception shimmered and warped like a hallucination, but after the first nod from the guard she felt more grounded, her lies ready ballast in her chest. She kept her head down, stayed sober enough to think, steadfastly refused to tremble, did nothing obviously un-toward. She repeated the formula on Wednesday.

•

Sobriety had its benefits: on Thursday she woke up, clear-headed if not fully rested, before 6 a.m. She dressed, whispered goodbye to Ola and got into the car. She drove to the 24-hour petrol station, put in a tenner of petrol and drew out £100 from the forecourt cashpoint. She paused, as she went to pay, by the plastic tubs full of cellophaned chrysanthemums. Not for her. She got back in her car and drove out of Rilton, up near-silent A-roads to the flower market in Pitbury. There, she wandered through the hand-slung avenues of lilies, roses, sweetpeas, gerbera, and others the names of which she did not know, strolling among the buckets of flowers, breathing in the scent of them in the morning dusk. Did she have a favourite flower? She did not know. She asked their names, gathered a great armful. She drove, then, back towards Rilton. After three miles, she turned off. It was lighter now and she did not let herself entertain the darkest thoughts as she walked up the well-tended gravel path of the crematorium grounds. She knew where to find Cynthia: Joyce had discussed her resting place with Etta before.

Etta knelt with her flowers and laid them down in order: iris – alstroemeria – meadowsweet – sweet peas – orchid – stocks – orchid – rose … With a slow hand, she laid them all out until they fanned in a thick bouquet beside the grave, bearing the weight of the words she now always carried with her. She stayed next to her in silence, until it was fully light. Then, she drove to work.

But, above the ineradicable scent of bitter, burning regret, life lifted with the veil of night, a touch brighter, and sweeter.

●

On Friday, at 6.12 p.m., Chris Wise at last confirmed receipt. He messaged her as she was watering the plants in the back garden, the sparse primroses and tough rosemary, the first time she had spent outside in weeks.

Got the money

She wanted to feel the weight of her hate lifting, feel the closure people spoke of, but she only felt a fleeting relief from the fear, and a sadness. She was still in debt and in trouble; she still had to fight for her life.

She was standing wiping her face with her palms when the next message came.

That Merlin's a right dodgy bastard, isn't he?

It took a moment. And then it rose, this permanent low tide of nausea, into a cresting panic. She texted one word:

What?

She stared at her phone, not moving until it buzzed again:

That beardy old git took my £10,000. Some Miracle!

Etta closed her eyes. The levity was the worst, that vicious gloating humour. Too much.

She groped her way inside, and sat at the kitchen table, sipping water. Her phone was on the table. It buzzed at her again.

Another £10,000 should do it. Thanks!

PART III

Chapter Twelve

SATURDAY, 11 AUGUST 2018

Etta was winning. What she was playing was not clear, but she was winning enormous sums and explosions of joy and light detonated behind her eyes. The pleasure was intense, but greater than even that was the sense of freedom; she was flying high. Little by little, consciousness seeped back and she grew aware that she was dreaming. By the light she could see in the bedroom as she opened her eyes a crack, she knew that it was morning. She roused herself enough to say:

'Happy birthday, Ola.'

She raised her head from her pillow and pressed dry lips to her partner's cheek. She sipped from her bedside water, letting the elation of the night drain away from her. The emotion that replaced it was not despair, however, as she recalled there was no need to jump up and rush downstairs before him. Now that the bank statement had been flushed away, she did not have to wait, coiled and stricken, for the steel smack of the letterbox.

Not today. The tensions that flooded her from the head down every time she thought of Wise could also chill, for today. Today, the two of them would celebrate big style; it was all in hand. Today was a game-changer. Today, she would tell him.

She slid out of bed to open the champagne for the Buck's Fizz brunch. As Ola showered, she saw to the spicy eggs, moin-moin and custard, fruit platter and toast. She forced Wise from her mind every time his face came into focus. But as she cooked, the rogue thought skittered and exploded across her consciousness like water drops over hot fat: every crumb of their feast and every last present – from the noise-cancelling wireless earbuds to his favourite palm wine, all of it – came courtesy of the Funshine Club.

She put on his favourite music to drown out the searing notion and kept on his preferred lace-elastane robe. He wandered into the kitchen with a clutch of envelopes and she greeted him with a smile; for now, she was safe.

She poured his sparkling cocktail, sat on his knee, laughed low, *ha-sha-sha*, her mouth's flesh against his ear.

'I think we should go back to bed for a while, Ola, after we've enjoyed all this fine breakfast . . .'

He weighed her behind in his one-handed grasp:

'Good, then I can enjoy all this fine you.'

Throaty laughs; he grabbed at her, playful, as she rose to scramble the eggs and make toast, while Ola settled back and tore open his post.

'Phone bill, knew it. I'll ignore the bills until tomorrow, eh?'

'Yes. Birthday prerogative.'

'Hnh,' the rip of another envelope. 'No, this one is not a birthday card either.'

More laughter.

'Ignore them, now. Your birthday brunch is ready.'

'Brunch, hey? What is it with all this brunch business, anyway? What's wrong with breakfast?'

'Eat!'

'I'll eat, woman, I'll eat. It smells so good! Where's your drink?'

An opportunity to reassure. 'Bit too early for me, birthday boy.'

'Hnh. Good.'

Both of them ate as if they had made love all morning: every scrap of the eggs and two rounds of toast, the moin-moin, the custard and fruit. Etta topped him up with champagne until the final splash had disappeared into the flute. As they shared his neat slices of what had been a dripping, indecent peach, Etta felt sleepy rather than aroused; perhaps they could take time out, lie down and rest their eyes for a while before tucking into each other.

She forced herself to rise and tidy up, transferring plates to the dishwasher as Ola unsheathed the final letter.

'Oh, sorry o. This one is for you.'

'OK, I'll read it in a—'

'Hold on a minute. What the hell is this?'

She spun around. A shattering as she knocked her plate to the floor, ceramic shards ricocheting to the farthest corners of the kitchen.

'Pass it here, please, I think it—'

'Freedom Loans,' read Ola. 'You owe £11,900. What the bloody hell is this, Etta?'

'I . . .' She had nothing.

He shook a page at her. 'Etta?'

'I'm sorry. It was this . . . stupid mistake. I took out a loan but—'

'Hold on. They say it was £7,000 and now it is £11,900. Are they serious?'

'I think so.'

He leapt up, arms raised. 'What have you done?'

He had never hit her. He would not. She shot a look at the door. He was rigid and vibrating with anger; she wanted to vanish. They were somewhere entirely new.

'You took it out . . . only a few weeks ago. And now, nearly £12,000! Eh? You lied and you hid it from me. Why, Etta? What else are you hiding? What are you doing with this money? Are you giving it away to some man?'

Etta's right eyelid pulsed; it was a twisted truth. But all the loans – £8,300 here, £6,000 there and the host of £1,000 top-ups – had been taken out with good heart, in good faith, to fund their escape from the hole. Tell him, now, confess all? Was there any way he would understand?

'Answer me, Etta.'

'I will. I am.' She groped for a lie that lived somewhere within the truth. 'I borrowed money from Dana, ages ago. I was hoping to surprise us with a holiday.'

'A holiday?'

'Yes.'

'We don't need a holiday.'

'We do, Ola, badly.'

'So why did you not ask me?'

'I know, stupid, but I wanted to surprise you. I also blew too much on presents – I've been planning your birthday for weeks – and then Dana needed the money back faster, so I took out this stupid, stupid, loan. I didn't tell you because I know how much you hate chaotic money business—'

'Yes! This is *chaos*. This is terrible. *Terrible*!'

'I'm sorry, Ola. I love you. I'm sorry.'

'Don't give me all your loving-loving now. Bloody hell!'

He stomped out, banging the door, and thundered upstairs. Etta stood, staring at where he had been, in the kitchen. She could not go to him with cold comfort and lies, she would stay put with the dishwasher and the broken pieces of plate and his leftover inch of champagne. She would have it, too, that tepid inch.

She swept the floor and stacked the intact crockery in the dishwasher. What else might he say, once he had considered?

Footsteps, movement. Ola was coming downstairs holding an overnight bag.

'What, Ola? Olala, no, don't be ridiculous!'

'Ridiculous, am I? Me?' His stare was dark. 'All this time, we have been so careful. We saved, even when I was studying—'

'Yes! I saved for you. Made sacrifices. For you!'

'I know, eh? In case I am in danger of forgetting that I owe you, so much, you never let me forget it. Not for one second.'

'I hardly ever mention it!'

'What? With your marry-me, marry-me guilt. With your eyes when we row.'

'That's a bloody lie!'

'No. You are the liar, Etta Gabrielle Oladipo.'

He walked towards the door, out the door and out of sight before Etta could tell him she was all kinds of terrified.

She was in debt, beyond anything he could imagine, forget the statements; she was being blackmailed and had stolen and had broken the law.

Above all, as she had been going to tell him, she was five weeks late and had taken a test that morning. She was pregnant.

Risk V

She sits, unmoving, as the doctor looks over the onscreen notes.
Ten seconds on, she shifts, twitches a finger against the desk.
Look at me, she wants to shout. See me.

'It is early stage, so we could go in with a simple hysterectomy.
It's not in your lymph nodes, as we know, which is great news,
so—'

'You'd take my womb?'

The doctor turns to meet her stare at last.

'The cervix and uterus, yes. There's a small chance we'll need
to remove the ovaries and fallopian tubes, we can't yet say.'

'No children, then.'

'No, not naturally. But there are other ways.'

'I know.'

'Nothing's certain. We'll need to investigate further.'

She does not feel fear, or the sadness spreading through her,
numbing that fear much as would the anaesthetic; she feels an
incision of hatred: for the disease, for the months spent ignor-
ing her aching abdomen, for this drab grey-beige room, for the
sharp understanding of this doctor, for her dealt cards turning
out to be something else entirely.

The doctor is saying something about 'next steps'; the words
are going in, but her own thoughts win. Who would marry her,

incomplete like that? She would become a chicken who cannot lay; a barren bird fit only for the pot . . . stop. Bird? She is not livestock. She is woman enough for any man: that means everything. Go through with this horror?

'What if I say no?'

The doctor scrolls through the notes on the screen for a second, then at last fixes her in the eye.

'You will greatly reduce your chance of surviving this cancer.'

'I know.'

She is not mad. No choice, in reality. Here, in the capital, far away from Josip but no nearer England (those thieving dogs, she should have smashed their heads). Here she could fix herself up, choose her path.

There will never be a man she could trust enough with this truth, in the years to come. It would turn her from a beauty into that sad eggless hen and she would be left alone. No man has left her yet.

No, if she goes ahead and does this, it will stay a secret inside her: as raw and cavernous and unshared as her eviscerated core.

A wet trail bisects her cheekbone; although she is make-up free she rubs it hard away once, twice, like a black mark.

The doctor rises from the desk, gives her a smile that crushes the wind from her chest; a breath escapes as the older woman indicates the examination bed.

'Lie down please, miss.'

Chapter Thirteen

How many ways was it possible for a woman to feel heavy?

Etta felt weighed down and swollen with portent. She felt ponderous, overburdened and gross with guilt. She felt pulled down by the gravity of her situation, leaden-hearted and, apart from all that, she felt pregnant.

She also felt profoundly alone. She had been on the cusp of talking to her mother about the baby but could not face telling her that Ola had left. It would blow over and then she could share the news in the right way, without giving her mum a breakdown. She had hidden her true self from her mother for months and was working up to restoring that closeness. In fact, since Cozee, all her key relationships seemed to have fallen off a cliff: not just Mum, but Ola and Joyce . . . she would make it up to them, regain all her best people. In the meantime, as a poor but informed substitute, she had the internet. Google the previous week had told her to avoid runny cheeses; that, sadly, there was no need to eat for two; to take B-vitamins, to restrict alcohol intake, of course, and to indulge in the right forms of exercise. What googling could not tell her was the stuff she really needed to know: how she, her, Etta, would feel when this tiny life-changing life – meant to be the first of four-plus – finally arrived and how they would cope, let alone thrive. She could not countenance coping alone. The signs were not hopeful, she knew this. However, if she lingered on it, or rehearsed sad words to share with her mum, the shadows descended, the dark thoughts danced.

To counteract these effects, she gambled. It was a novel experience, sober. Now, she noodled around with modest £100 deposits, banging out £5 spins which, she recognised, did more to scratch her itch than achieve monetary gain. The gambling lightened the load; it also worsened the guilt, but she would write that off as collateral damage.

Thoughts of Chris Wise still coursed through her, heating her blood, singeing her nerves. She was not planning to pay him off with a further £10,000; he was showing all the signs of being insatiable, a one-man money-pit. But the more money she won, the more options she had.

And so, she spun on.

•

The key turned in the lock as Etta was standing in the hall, looking in the mirror to see if pregnancy showed in her expression.

As soon as Ola came in, she could only see herself through his eyes.

'I need to get my things,' he said.

'Hello,' she said. 'Coffee first? We can talk.'

'No.'

He went upstairs and she was tempted to follow him but knew that would end in shouting. She waited at the foot of the stairs. The sounds from above, the opening and shutting of doors and drawers, sounded like a man selecting shirts and jackets for a new life. She wanted to cry out but kept her lips pressed tight.

Ola had left the front door ajar, apparently intent on a quick exit. Etta glanced out and saw Jean's mother being helped into the back of a car by a young woman in carer's scrubs. Jean followed behind them with a suitcase and a bulging carrier bag; she looked directly at Etta as if she could see her through the crack in the door. A hard, bitter look. Etta caught a breath of rotten flowers, a glint of smashed glass, and pushed it to.

She felt a tsunami of panic rising in her lungs; if it broke it would wash them away.

'Ola!' she called up the stairs. 'Let's talk!'

'Etta!' he shouted back. 'Do not come up here . . .'

Etta withdrew her foot from the bottom step and stood, looking up the stairs, willing him to slow down, calm down, come down.

He did, after a while, holding two cases.

She stood between him and the front door.

'It's just money, Ola, I can pay it off. Please.'

'It's not the money,' he said still edging forward. 'It's the lie. I have to go.'

'Ola, please! I only did this for us.'

'It's all lies. All of it is lies.'

'I don't understand,' she said. 'It was only a bad loan. Why leave me?'

He looked down at the two suitcases in his hands as if someone else had packed them.

'I don't know what is true and what is lies any more. I just know it is none of my business. Not now!'

He tilted the cases onto their wheels and nodded at her to step aside. She took a step to the left and started to weep as he walked out of the door, down the path.

'Ola!'

He did not look at her; he unlocked his car. He swung the cases into the boot, swung himself into the driving seat and reversed, muttering as Etta stood frozen. She lip-read 'mad liar' as he drove off. It could have been 'bad liar'.

•

Etta spun on the slots early that evening. The worst had happened, at last. Ola had gone. There was an air of stillness, but not of calm – the hall table was pushed against the door and the back door double-locked and rammed shut with a chair.

She did not want to talk to family or friends. What to say? She did not even feel the need to drink. For what?

The reels rolled, doing nothing of note; the blip, flash and chime of taking her money.

A phone message buzzed. Wise.

She tapped with no discernible increase of heart rate; she was now as good as dead. She read:

See you soon.

Etta typed swearwords, and deleted them, typed them again, re-deleted. He could not now blackmail her, Ola was gone. And she knew how to defend herself.

She went down to check the front door was double-locked, and checked the back one again, then closed a missed inch of loo window and put her phone on charge.

Downstairs made more sense to her than the spare room, for once. More exits, downstairs. She needed to stay alert, awake and distracted, so she sat in front of the TV, flicking channels. She stopped as an item came on the local news; an upcoming art exhibition had been inspired by the Windrush Scandal. One installation featured African-Caribbean residents, captured in black and white, giving one-liners to the camera with both sound and subtitles.

One man, eyes like washed pebbles in a pool that broke into ripples as he laughed:

'Some of the people like us, some of the time.'

A large woman, unsmiling:

'We do not know what to expect as we arrive; will we get a royal welcome?'

Then Cynthia Jackson, looking so untroubled tears rose in Etta's eyes:

'We take our chance at a better life; we are all gamblers.'

Had she misheard? She rewound and played it again. And again. And once more as the tears tracked over her collar-bones.

There it was, at last: absolution. One last act of generosity from this old woman she had failed, whose daughter she had failed. Etta counted the wrongs that had accumulated since joining Cozee, gathering still faster since she had failed to see Cynthia off from the world. Her friend's mother had years of understanding; she had gambled on men and babies and countries; she had wrung out truths, drop by drop, from the twisted skeins of life, much as she would have once handled her daughter's braids after a swim.

'I'm sorry, Cynthia.'

We are all gamblers.

●

An hour later, she knew what to do.

She had to take the ultimate risk, or this would never end.

She was alone, now, and unprotected. Until he was out of her life, she would not be able to rest, or sleep. And sleep was vital for those who were expecting . . .

She would stop him now, tonight.

It was time to be super-smart and play dumb as. Time to finish this.

She sent the text:

One last payment. Cash. Harder to lose.

The reply was immediate:

OK.
Where do you want the money? I can drive there.
You know High Desford?

Etta's first job after leaving school had been there. It was not too far away in the car. Easy getaway.

OK. The big Leigh Road Car Park, the end near the boarded-up Barkers bingo hall.

After a minute, he came back at her:

Poetic

She fired straight back:

Convenient. One chance only. Repeat, last time. Be there at 9pm.

Wise replied:

I will. Don't want to talk. Don't come near. Just leave the money.

OK.

Where EXACTLY will cash be?

Etta, fizzing with adrenaline, barked a short laugh.

You like doorsteps, right? On the doorstep of the dead bingo hall.

He came straight back:

Whatever. Just no police.

Etta wanted to swear as she typed:

No police. You know I can't do that.

She waited and waited more. No reply. Game on.

Her plan was simple: she would go to meet him with the parcel of cash and wait in her car, watching as he collected it. Then, as it was 9 p.m., he would probably go home. But wherever he went – home, pub, club – she would follow him. Then she would do whatever it took to make sure he never troubled her again.

For now, she grabbed the printer paper.

She also grabbed her bag and the sharp, red-handled knife. To take it with her had to be tempting fate. But she could not go into the unknown without her . . . no, not weapon, ridiculous, she was no gangbanger. But it was protection, her lucky talisman.

She placed the knife in the bag.

By 8.30 p.m., she was in High Desford, dressed in black and sitting in her car, the tightly wrapped package beside her on the passenger seat. She was parked between a hatchback and a 4x4; many more cars were parked further away for easy entry into the nearby supermarket, still open. At this scuffed-up end of the huge car park she was neither obvious, nor dangerously isolated. The boarded-up doors and windows of the old bingo hall faced her: a dozen blank, beige, blinded eyes. They had seen nothing as she had placed the package on the wide door-step before the graffitied double doors. No one had yet gone near it, but Etta was looking out for the slightest movement.

Light was fading, it was overcast, but she could still see every last thing. Minutes passed. At 8.35 p.m. she stopped playing with her phone in case she missed him. At 8.40 p.m., chest already tightening, she put the radio on to a dance music station, very low, to build her energy, steady her nerves, and keep her mind alert.

Movement at 8.47: an older man, at the right of her vision. He was walking a young German Shepherd. Etta sat straighter, not breathing . . . No, he turned left up an alley leading away from the car park. She took a breath.

At 8.58, her eyes were still trained on the package. Movement: to her left, someone was coming! Overcoat on and blue hoodie up, this had to be him. He was hurrying, head down, straight to the bingo hall doors. Etta weighed the risk: not that tall or stacked, she could probably take him. The rage that was brewing inside her at every step he took would give her the strength. She could make him see reason, if she kept her cool. She was smarter; he was slight. Yes, she could take him.

He was bending now, back still to her. There, he had picked up the package and was hurrying away, towards the alley. Etta started the engine and turned away from him, left. She had to hurry, but she knew exactly where the alley came out. She turned left out of the car park, left again, and accelerated up the road. She could see him fifty metres ahead: he was not hanging about. Etta set about following him. She would get Chris Wise in his own home.

She drove closer to him, not too close, determined to keep him in her sights. He was going head down past a parade of shops, past the laundrette and the bookies, moving fast in that heavy winter coat, getting closer to the dodgier end of town. Wise turned right at last into a residential road, Felcham, one of the worst. Etta followed at 5 mph, heart hammering. Cars were parked along the road, but she was the only one moving; he could notice her at any minute. But he did not turn, he stopped outside a small terraced house and, barely pausing, key ready, he went inside.

Etta's breathing was coming fast and shallow. If she stopped to think about it, even for a minute, she would be lost. There was a space to park three houses along. She parallel-parked into it, getting it right first time. She was taut and focused, on a knife-edge. She had to get to him before he opened the parcel which was stuffed with nothing but cut-up printer paper; she had wound it round and round with parcel tape and packed it into bags within bags. When he looked inside, he might come out of his corner swinging. She had more than herself to think of; it could not become a scrap.

In seconds she was out of the car and at his front door, with her bag open wide, just in case, ringing the bell before she could think. Lights on all over, a kid's plastic trike by the gate. Wise might not live alone. He might—

'Hello?'

A slight and wizened Indian man had opened the front door.

'Oh!' said Etta, pumped up but thrown. Landlord? 'Hello, Chris Wise lives here, right? I need to talk to him.'

'You've got wrong house, sorry.'

'It's definitely his house.'

'No, this is Choudhury house. Sorry.' The man started to close the door.

'No! Wait. I saw him come in here, just a minute ago.'

The old man narrowed rheumy eyes, bright behind his glasses.

'What does he look like?'

'What? Oh, I dunno . . . He's wearing a big old black coat and a blue hoodie. Trainers.'

The old man scrunched his mouth in displeasure. 'Hold on.'

He pushed the door to, but not closed, and started to shout up the stairs calling to someone in what could have been Urdu, or Hindi or something, Etta had no clue. A voice called back, at least two others joined in. Etta could see the old man gesticulating excitedly behind the glass. Now someone was coming fast down the stairs.

The door opened again: a young woman was standing there, a defiant look in her eye.

'And?' she said.

She was still wearing the long black coat and the hoodie, pushed back off her head.

Athletic build but not healthy, Asian brown. The nose she was sticking up in the air at Etta was pierced. She could not be more than twenty years old.

'Who are you?' asked Etta.

'Who are *you*?' said the girl, chewing her lip.

'Why did he send you? Chris Wise. Has he—'

'I don't know anyone called Chris Wise, sorry.'

'What? Why did you take my money then?'

The girl looked straight into her eyes.

'You're not . . .'

The girl did not blink, her mouth twisting a touch. As if proud.

'Ah!' Etta puffed out a breath and leaned sideways in the doorway. 'You? You're the one who—'

'Hush up!' said the girl, glancing over her shoulder. 'I can explain.'

'You'd better,' said Etta. 'Get out here!'

'No.' The girl looked over her shoulder. 'You need to go.'

'I want to hear what you've got to say for yourself.'

The old man – her grandad? – came back and started waving his arms around again and berating them in a rapid stream of incomprehensible words. Etta thought she caught him addressing the girl as 'Nadia'.

'Look, you're getting me in shit with my people . . .'

The man, still spouting angry foreign words, leaned between them and started trying to pull the door to. Now the girl started up her own angry stream of words. The old man was giving in. He was definitely calling her 'Nadia' and was so furious that he did not notice the door catching Etta's arm as he yanked at it again.

'Fucksake,' said Nadia. 'Either piss off or just come in.'

Etta had to call it: neither the grandad nor the girl was intimidating. This was the only chance to a shine light on this havoc. Before she could lose her nerve, Etta had put one foot over the threshold and then the other.

Nadia immediately leaned in, reached past her shoulder and did something complicated to the door. What, was she locked in? The old man gave another burst of babble then disappeared off. Etta glanced back at the closed door behind her.

She was inside. In this strange liar's home. This had not been the plan.

'Come on then,' said Nadia, who seemed to be standing taller now. She took off her coat, threw it into a corner, slid the hoodie's cuffs up to her elbows.

'I'm not staying,' said Etta, the panic rising. 'You just need to tell me what the fuck.'

'Yeah, yeah,' said Nadia. 'Let's sit.'

Etta tried to take the girl in: a sleeve of tats that made her look more fragile, not less, shadows contouring her face. Chewing gum and an attitude worked her bony jaw.

She spoke as if she were speeding. 'Knew it, just knew it. Recognised you straight off. Etta, yeah?'

'Hm. What's your real name, "Chris"?'

'Karen,' the girl spat back.

Etta gave a laugh that did not touch the sides, a dead hard sound.

'Sure, Nadia, OK.'

The girl stopped dead at the foot of a staircase and shot her a steely look.

'I thought you were smarter than that.'

Etta realised her mistake too late.

'Listen, I don't care who you are. Not like I'm going to tell anyone. If I was going to involve the police, they would be here by now.'

The girl raised her chin and looked Etta in the eye.

'You're chattin' about police and that with everyone able to hear? Come, we'll talk in my room.'

She did not want to move forward, but she could not move back. The front door was locked. Etta felt a sensation like cold lead dropping into her stomach.

The stairs were wider than expected, the house seemed to go right back.

248

Nadia, jaw still working her gum, jerked her head upwards.

'Come, yeah?' She bounced halfway up the stairs and turned, waiting.

She looked and spoke like a jittery teen. What could she do, really?

'OK,' Etta exhaled a touch. 'Just a few minutes.'

As she walked upstairs, she noticed scuff marks on the wall, small craters of gouged plaster. Not a cared-for home, not upmarket, but bigger than it appeared to be from the front. A long landing carpeted in dark red stretched ahead and faded into darkness. It looked like a run-down B&B.

'OK . . .' said Nadia, seemingly to herself.

She walked ahead, slowing. As they edged into the dim hallway, it smelled dirty: old grime and stale herbs, a definite tinge of marijuana, plus a weird chemical tang that caught at the back of the throat. No grandparent would want to live here. What was this place?

'Wait,' said Nadia, pulling something from her pocket. She leaned into the door and it opened.

Etta glanced up to the dark end of the corridor. Behind the closed door opposite, she could hear a woman enunciating loudly on the phone: *No, I said Higgson . . . (something muffled) . . . Yes, INSURANCE. We're calling about the car accident you had recently . . .*

'Come on,' said Nadia.

Etta half-turned but the girl's arm was outstretched. She moved into the room – bed, chair, desk, lamp – after her scrawny host. Only as she stepped inside did she glimpse that it was not an ordinary bedroom door. It had a card reader, like a hotel.

Nadia pushed the door to and indicated that Etta should sit.

Etta took a seat on the hard plastic chair by the desk as Nadia flopped back and sat cross-legged on the bed, trainers still on.

'So,' Etta tried to put flint in her voice. 'Let's just get this done. You totally catfished me and—'

'Hush,' said Nadia. She leaned hard to her left, stretched one arm down, then rocked back up holding Etta's package.

She waved it at her visitor. 'You think I'm an idiot?'

She flexed her wrist to turn the package, which had a slash across the parcel tape on the back. She had already opened it.

Nadia's dark eyes gleamed. She reached into the package, pulled out a handful of white paper and threw it at Etta, who blinked, went rigid.

'What is this shit?' said Nadia. 'Trying to pass off this . . . rubbish. That's what you think I am?'

'No, I—'

The girl dropped another handful of paper onto the bed with slow contempt. Her face was taut and waxy, giving less away than her hands. She looked cold, or unwell. Or like she was hiding something.

Nadia bowed her head right down to where her legs crossed, letting her long dark hair fall in a thick curtain that hid her whole face.

'Huuuuh,' she gave a low growl of annoyance, then flicked her hair back. 'You've got me in serious shit, now.'

'I didn't have much choice. I don't have that kind of money.'

Nadia picked up her mobile, dialled and waited.

Etta was starting to feel clammy, breathy, a bit sick. Her eyes scanned the room. Sparse, crusty carpet, no wardrobe: more dilapidated office than bedroom. Boxes stacked in the corner, the top one full of maroon booklets. Were they passports? As Etta stared harder, Nadia hung up.

'Not picking up. You're gonna have to chill your boots here for a bit.'

'Who are you phoning?'

'Never mind.'

Etta needed to get out. She rose and rushed toward the door, started tugging at the handle before Nadia could unfold her legs. Definitely locked.

'Whoa, listen.' The girl had not risen from the bed. 'Chill, yeah? It won't take long. Sit down.'

Nadia jabbed at her phone again. Hung up.

That was when Etta saw what was hiding behind the glassy brown gaze. Not hate, not fear: total indifference to Etta and to whatever might happen next, as long as she made her call.

This was bad. Maybe she could connect with her, some-how.

'So. What did you do with the first £10,000?'

Nadia raised her eyebrow, said nothing, and started texting on her phone.

'Come on, please. That was a lot of money.' She tried to force amusement into her tone. 'Merlin's Miracles, seriously?'

'Needed funds, babe.'

'But why?'

Nadia looked up from her phone, eyes fiery. 'You think I'm working for fun? Reckon I should just marry myself off to some fat moley bloke? Fuck that.'

Her mind working overtime, it clicked fast.

'You know that man, Abhinivesh, from . . .' she stopped herself.

'No, I don't, that's the point. And I don't want to know.'

'Sorry. Sounds rough.'

Etta was doing all she could not to look at the door. She had to talk herself out of this place.

251

Nadia smirked.

'S'fine. Man's not a problem. Do I look like the type to get hitched for the fam? Please.' She started chewing faster again, buzzed with another surge of energy. 'Still, useful, him being a twat. Loved to shoot his mouth off, chatting on about First Welcome this Rilton that, the lengths he was going to for his fake love and all that bollocks. Helpful lot, aren't you though? Handy for prospects.'

'You know about First Welcome?'

'Just told you: mutual friends, innit? Good information. Crap security, though.'

A beat. Etta breathed out in confusion, 'The break-in?'

'Break-in? Hardly, drama queen, s'no biggie. Paperwork, yeah? They keep their records nice and tidy.'

'Is that why you came after me again, after that Cozee party?'

'Don't be dumb, you hardly registered. I don't give a shit about your virtue-signalling, do-gooding bollocks, I just needed to check you out. What, you think I'm weak, or clueless? Good little Indian girl gone bad, right?'

Etta's eyes flicked to the door, desperation growing.

'No! No. I'm sorry. It's just . . .' Etta slowed, held her hands up. 'It was *all* my money.'

Nadia gave her a look, exhaled long through her nose, and started texting again. After a moment she said, 'Well. My girlfriend's got expensive taste, yeah?'

At last, a chance. Etta leant forward. 'Yes? What's she like?'

'Why do you care?' said Nadia, with a naked sneer. 'Fancy some?'

She was jiggling her phone in her hands. Etta sat back again, biting her lip.

The phone started buzzing. Nadia picked up.

'Hi. I know, it couldn't wait. Bad news, yeah . . . Piss-taker. Mm, that one.'

Etta had one last shot.

'Honestly, if you just let me out of here, I'll forget everything. Wipe my mind: the money, the dead flowers you left on my doorstep, and the broken glasses and all—'

'What you on about? That weird shit's nothing to do with us.'

'Us?'

'Leave it, seriously.'

The door opened. Nadia jumped up, phone in hand.

A man stood there and looked at Nadia, then Etta. He was in his early thirties, with a dirty blond crop, wearing an elite streetwear brand on his chest. The tattoo of some woman-faced reptile or oriental succubus snaked up his left bicep and under his sleeve.

He looked at Nadia again.

'This is where your stupid fucking hobbies get you, yeah?' He spoke in a punchy London accent.

Nadia stopped chewing her gum, her jitters stilled by dread. No indifference now.

'Sorry,' she said.

'Going awol to pick up. What've I told you? And all this fake-name bollocks. You wanna be a man, is it? Don't I give you enough proper work, is that it? What, you still have time left to arse about, trawling the internet looking for mugs to rip off?'

He was fixing her with a stare so hard that Etta could feel the fear coming off Nadia in waves.

'I've said: my bad.'

He said nothing for a long moment.

Nadia shifted on the bed, tugged a lock of hair.

'I'll go sort the other things, yeah? I've got this, honest.'

More silence. Etta felt like her heart was battering her lungs from the inside.

'OK, go.'

Nadia slipped past him and out of the door without a backwards glance. The door was pulled to a click behind.

Etta was alone with him.

Her mind went blank. 'I need to go.'

'Etta, right?' he asked. 'Are you mad? What you doing here?'

'Sorry,' said Etta. 'I just want to go.'

'Bit late for that.'

'Please. I need to go.' Etta did not run but her mind raced, clutching at anything at all. 'I've got a kid at home alone.'

He barked a short laugh. 'No you fucking don't. I know exactly what you have and have not got. Don't try it on.'

Etta shrank back into the hard chair.

'Please.'

'Reckoned you could get one over on us? Do we look like fucking jokers?'

Etta shook her head.

He crossed thick arms over his chest, cracked a thin unamused smile.

'I won't say anything,' said Etta. 'About this.'

He stepped nearer, until his shins pressed into her knees; she tilted the chair back until it hit the desk. Trapped.

Etta pushed back hard as she could into the seat.

'Nice skin. I like my coffee milky.'

He leaned harder into her.

'What you gonna do?' he said low.

She writhed, kicked out a leg; he shifted back, unharmed; she lifted herself up from the chair, leaning back away from him. 'Let me out of here.'

He lunged onto her and clamped a hand onto her nape. She was forced right back, hips forward, head nearing the desk.

'Filthy bitch.'

He grabbed her head, trapping hair. A hard yank, twisting her neck.

Shit.

An explosion of motion. She jerked hard away from the desk, her hands flew out to stop his clawing. He barged her hard, bending her sideways. She thrust back, body contorting, but he was *pulling*; they lurched towards the centre of the room, in a close dance of violence. She could not think, could not see. Carpet. Bed. Window. A smash of something as she was pushed onto her back on the desk. His mean-fleshed mouth on hers. Lights in her face.

'Nadia!'

The scream was weak, stupid; no *voice*. The force of him was overwhelming: his bristling skin, his saliva, sweat, hands.

She struggled, twisting sideways and then she was on her stomach being shoved up the desk, head dangling; his hands were pushing, searching, pulling; he was pulling up her skirt. Below her face was a bin, scrunched paper and tangerine peel. Next to it was her open bag. Her hands were trapped beneath her stomach; she worked one free and thrust it into the bag. She clutched. In one great surge she twisted again, halfway onto her back, rearing up and sticking her fist to his chest, pushing pushing . . .

Only when he fell down to the ground did she feel the true weight of the knife in her hand.

●

She was on the windowsill, with her hand bleeding, and the dark alleyway below her and no trees to break her fall.

She jumped.

Her right foot hurt as she landed, but still she ran to the car and somehow got it started and drove off, back towards home. Roads and houses and gardens and people raced past, unseen, not mattering.

Ishedead?

She had probably killed a man. That bad man, knifed, by her.

Ishedead?

Nadia would not be hurrying back to that. She might have done a runner. Him bleeding out on that dirty carpet . . .

He would have killed her. Who even was he? Who was anyone: Chris was Nadia? Nadia was a girl. Nadia, not the leaver of dead flowers, or broken specs. Nadia who was a cheat, a proper criminal. Who had left Etta for dead, locked into that room with that psycho rapist.

She refused to feel anything, in her head, in her foot. She just drove.

The worst thing of all was that when she arrived home, Ola would not be there to pull her out of this nightmare.

Chapter Fourteen

MONDAY, 13 AUGUST 2018

Bang!

Etta rocketed upright, a scream caught in her throat. Her heartbeat was machine-gunning her ribs.

She swung shaking legs out of bed and listened at the locked bedroom door. What was that? Was it them, breaking in?

She stood behind the closed door, trying to hear any movement downstairs over the rat-ta-tat-tat of her heart.

She stared into the gloss-white door. Time meant nothing. All she knew was *now* and this staring, snow-blind terror.

The machine-gun heartbeat slowed, but only as aches set in, the bruises on her thighs and scalp and lower back complaining that she had been conscious for a good many minutes; only when the most perfect silence had been observed for what had almost certainly been a quarter of an hour, did she unlock the door, opened it a crack.

When she was sure that she saw nothing, heard nothing, she padded onto the landing.

On a hunch she crept to the top of the steep stairs. There: a scattering of envelopes on the doormat.

That bloody, cheap, banging, tin-can letter box.

Before she could change her mind, she walked downstairs, just to feel OK for a few seconds. She scooped up the post, turned and went straight back up the stairs. She locked herself back in her bedroom, sifted through the envelopes.

Letter for her, mobile bill, garish pizza menu and one last white missive:

Dr Ola Abayomi

●

Etta emailed in sick from her bed, knowing but not caring that Robert and his spy Jean – who only looked more haggard and tense since sending her mum off in a taxi – would doubt her excuses. She scrolled for news of a stabbing in High Desford and, seeing nothing, closed her eyes again.

The horror of the night before clung to her like cooling sweat. She writhed in the T-shirt of Ola's that she had pulled from the wash basket to sleep in; she struggled to raise her head from the smell of him on the pillow. To comfort herself for whatever damage she had done to her throbbing ankle she wrapped herself in the duvet she hadn't washed since he left; it was gross not to wash it, or the T-shirt, or her body, but it seemed unthinkable to get naked with action-replays of the night before still spooling non-stop through her mind; it seemed unthinkable not to be wrapped in Ola; unthinkable to blast away what was left of her life with water and detergent.

The curtains stayed drawn. She kept her eyes closed long after waking. She was trying to black-out stress; it could only be bad for the baby. In that willed darkness, batting away a barrage of thoughts about Nadia, or whoever she really was, and that brutal man, attacking her, falling to the ground in that horror of a room, and her terrifying jump and the lies and the cheating that had led to this mess, she breathed Ola in, drew down draughts of scent from where his skin had been, not in gulps, but gently, as if he simply *was*.

He was, but he was not there.

Despite the pain and bruises and fear, she was alive. She was also confused, not least about the dead bouquet and smashed specs. Had Nadia really not done that? She was a professional liar, after all. When had it all started? If not her, who? And why? Etta rubbed her forehead.

After a few more minutes, she sat up on her elbows and looked at the letter. Tempted though she was to open it, this could be a chance for something more. She thought about the wording for a full minute before simply texting:

Ola, an important letter has come. Will you come and collect it?

The response came back in seconds:

Just send it.

Where to?

A longer pause this time. Then:

87 Peartree Avenue, Rilton, Bucks, RL2 3HG

●

Etta stood on the front doorstep for over a minute before she could bring herself to knock.

A woman answered. Etta knew her at once. Same dark hair, although now damp as if she had just stepped out of the shower, that sharp look and matching cheekbones.

'You!'

The nosebleed woman. The cut-finger client from the Waysford Place nail bar.

'Can I help you?' the woman replied, tilting her chin up.

Etta went blank and asked: 'Is Ola here?'

'No,' said the woman. 'Wrong house.'

Etta glanced again at the house number. It was the right one. She shook her head, to get the confusion out; she knew this was the place.

Unable to turn away, she peered instead past the woman's shoulder and saw Ola's jacket on a hook, alongside two other men's coats she did not recognise.

A fire started up in her.

'Here. He's here and I know you, right?'

'No, please,' said the woman, moving to close the door.

Etta stepped up, arm out to keep the door open.

'Where've you popped up from? You're not his landlady.'

'That's not any of your business.' The woman glanced at the top of the stairs.

'You've made it my business. You asked me for help at the First Welcome Project.'

'I don't remember.'

'Your nose bled all over my desk. Where is he?'

'I don't remember.'

'Where is he?'

Etta kept her voice soft, her movements slow.

'I don't know. You make mistake, I'm Bosn— I came over from Croatia. It's not me you want,' the woman shot another look upstairs. 'Now go away.'

Etta stepped up onto the front step, from where she could see, past the woman's shoulder to one, two, three pictures of this person and Ola together. Framed pictures, hung on the wall: a beach selfie, a black-tie pose, a smiling embrace.

'What the . . .?' Etta could not take it in.

'Who is it, Medina?' This was Ola, calling from upstairs.

The woman tried to push the door closed. On pure instinct Etta pushed back.

'Go away!' Medina hissed in her face with such vitriol, Etta took a step backwards on her bad ankle, and lost her balance. The door was shut in her face.

She stared at the closed door for a moment, mouth still open. Croatia. She had finally met Zagreb, and she was a beauty. Ola was already living there, had to be. In one hallway photo, the woman – Medina he had called her – had shorter curly black hair, now it was past her shoulders; Ola had been captured wearing clothes she had never seen. So that house, maybe only twenty minutes away from where they lived in Sycamore Road, had been Leeds, and had been working late, and the endless networking events to stave off the unemployment; it had been the pub with the boys, and the stag dos, no doubt, and the friend's birthday party. This house was where he played house with another woman altogether. She had thought him to be preoccupied and he was just that – already occupied by this other woman's needs and affections. Ola had lied and lied and lied.

Rage surged up her spine and she was banging on the door again before she could think.

'Ola! Ola, I need to talk to you, really important. Ola!'

Medina tugged the door open and leaned out at her: 'Go away. You took our bloody money!'

'Medina . . .' Ola said behind her and was silenced with a look.

'Your money?' said Etta. 'I don't think so.'

'You're a thief.'

'So are you! We were getting married!'

'Never. We marry.'

Etta took a step back.

'You're getting married?'

She then saw the diamond on her finger. Not small. Behind it, the platinum band.

'We already marry,' said Medina. 'Weeks ago.'

Etta swallowed the words as the woman, this other fraudulent woman, this *wife*, dripped them. Some, when you were down and flat out, would drip honey into your mouth. Others would drip poison.

'All this time,' Etta said.

'Hm!' said Medina with a sharp toss of her head.

'I helped you, Medina, at the First Welcome Project. Can't believe I bloody helped you stay!'

'You want medal?' said Medina. 'Thief.'

'Ola?' asked Etta.

He looked past her shoulder, eyes bright; shook his head. Was *he* angry?

A firework went off inside her.

'Nothing to say, Ola? Silence now? Always silent when you should open your mouth. Yes! That's why you were so damn quiet in bed – didn't want to cry out the wrong name! Am I right?'

'Come, Ola,' said Medina, turning to bring him closer. 'Let's talk to the police.'

'Police, Ola?' asked Etta. 'Really, are you kidding me?'

He looked at the ground, his jaw working.

'Yes, Ola!' said Medina. 'We must call the police like I say, now!'

'No,' said Ola. 'I've said, we can't just—'

'Yes, we must!' Medina was shrieking now. 'We must tell the police she stole our money!'

'Well,' said Etta. 'OK, let's all go! I can tell them how you sent me dead flowers. Stalking!'

Medina glanced at Ola. 'Who told you?'

Etta smiled. *Drip drip*: her own noxious nectar. 'No one. You just did. Who else could want to scare me off that much?'

Ola looked at Medina, the flare on her cheeks.

'Didn't she tell you, Ola?' Etta went on. 'She left me that stinking bouquet to freak me out. Then your glasses, broken, on our – my – doorstep. QED she's a piece of work, Ola, your perfect match, QED you're both total—'

'I knew you would be stealing from him!' Medina's face was flaming, scrunched in rage. 'Women like you—'

'What do you mean "women like me"? What about you? How could you be with him, knowing he was with me? We were already together!'

'You were nothing! We were just trying to get our money together so he could leave you for good. I waited, took a risk. So many risks. But now you've stolen from us!'

'Us?' said Etta. 'My God, you dare say "us" to me. Go on, say it one more time—'

'Stop now,' said Ola. He stepped forward and pulled at Medina's arm, something like pleading in his eyes, meant for his new wife, or perhaps Etta.

'Stop?' said Medina. 'What do you mean stop? She should stop, she's taken everything.'

Etta could feel Ola, unable to look at her.

He spoke, the dam burst: 'Yes! She is a thief and a liar and she's screwed us right over!' He lowered his voice. 'But let's leave it for now, yes?'

'What?' cried Medina, outrage contorting those memorable features. 'Ola. We have to go to the police, Ola, we have to—'

'Medina no. I said leave it.' Ola turned back towards the house, waiting for his wife, his souvenir from Croatia, to follow.

Etta had a window of seconds. She should tell him. Destroy him. Tell him how, as his now-wife had held a tissue to her bloodied nose, she had told the helpful stranger at the First Welcome Project how she had been operated on, her womb removed, how she needed this new start with her British boy-friend more than anything.

They rarely asked even your first name, the First Welcome Project clients. Just sat down, drank the free tea and told you their life stories. Shared the secrets; showed the worst scars.

She should tell him: that Medina had said she would do anything to stay; that she had done just that, trying to pull him out of his living situation, scare off the unseen rival with devious tricks then race back to their hidden nest to coo and woo and flutter at him like an innocent; that this woman was desperate and had nothing to lose; that she would have been unlikely to register the vibrations of true love in the midst of the earthquake that had been her life; that Medina would rather destroy *his* life than forfeit his support, or England. And as for his four-plus kids . . .

No. Etta did not have to give him the answers. Let him live them out for himself. She did not have to give him anything any more.

As Medina moved to go into the house with Ola, Etta called to his back: 'I'm pregnant, Ola.'

Ola turned and stared at her, lips parted. Medina looked at her too, her eyes dark.

'You're not, you can't be. Etta?'

'I am, Ola. A baby, like we wanted.'

Ola took a step towards her. 'I can't believe it. We weren't—'

'Our child, Ola.' Etta fixed him with a clear stare.

Again, he stepped closer to her.

'Don't,' said Medina, 'she's obviously lying.'

He gave the smallest dip of his head, almost a nod.

'Let's go in, Ola,' said Medina. 'Now!'

Medina reached out, rubbing at his forearm; the urgent pressure made him turn.

'Ola?' said Etta.

His face remained turned away from her as he walked towards the door and said:

'It is nothing to do with me.'

●

Etta sat up. She was in bed. Alone.

Still no news of a stabbing. No knock on the door. She would have to keep lying low.

Her head felt . . . No! She no longer cared. Her ideas did not matter any more. Her mind had failed her; any higher thoughts had sodded off when Ola had left, packed in with his know-it-all chatter; carted away with his clothes, his tooth-brush and his endless research notes.

He was married to his Zagreb woman. His betrayal could not be more obscene.

Their life together was not just over. It had been murdered.

Her head was numb and dead.

But her heart . . .

Time to get busy. She needed to spin, to win, or she would go mad wondering if Nadia's crew would be coming after her. They had to know her exact house by now; did they watch? It was all falling apart: she needed a clear shot at something, anything but this present. But to make choices, she needed money; always money.

Etta powered up.

She waded through the crap in her inbox. Since her first payday loan, it had become infested by a swarm of missives with short, sharp stings. Untold phishing and spam, not to mention the nuisance calls. Desperation was big business.

She should know.

Etta hunted out a stinking brace of loans, shot down from the cloudless skies of No Credit Checks! They would have to do.

Now to find the right opportunity to win.

She was in luck. Spin City was starting a leaderboard promotion, with a top prize of £10,000. The beauty of leaderboard promos was that it was all about how much you wagered, or spun through, not deposited. About how much you *wagered* not won. It was fundamentally important for you to know that you could win as you won and win as you lost. This was the purest possible translation of the spinners' creed.

For Etta, it had been lucky that she had secured the funds to gamble. She now had to swing back the blade of her critical faculties and chop down the mad labyrinth in which she was lost. One last shot at making it good. All of it.

Which is why, to maximise her leaderboard chances, Etta spent the next hour taking out as many No Credit Checks! loans as would have her, planning to feed the sum total of £1,495 into the grinning maw of Gregor: The Jackpot Giant.

Gregor was new to this virtual metropolis of speculation. Etta slipped him a few tenners and he turned up, roaring and gargantuan, brandishing a club and a sackful of sovereigns, on reels 1, 3 and 5. Bonus round.

The giant proved as generous as his height, his girth. Sovereigns rained from the skies with every thwack of his club. He turned the very ground to gold; £1,017 more was added to the funds. Reason to hope.

Lunchtime: Etta did not eat, she played on. At 5 p.m., guilty, she forced herself to go to the fridge and swallow three slices of supermarket ham. She had more than just herself to think of.

Gregor, though, turned nasty. Him too: fickle. Spiteful, in the end. He took from her too fast, gave too little.

A £10 spin. Then £20 spins. She raised the stakes, again and again, feeling nothing as she hit the button, feeling nothing as she spun.

£100 . . . £100 . . . £100 . . . £100 . . .

She rolled £100 spins, the stake of madmen and millionaires, feeling nothing, not one thing . . . Until she crashed.

Game Over

Now, the numbness wore off and *feelings* rose back to her surface like bruises: the waste and the pain and the gigantic loss.

She looked to the wardrobe, where there was an empty gin bottle, to the bottle in the wastepaper bin, which might contain one last sip of red. Not now, she was on her own.

A hand fluttered to her stomach. *They* were on their own.

She fanned a palm out on the desk, stroked her fingers across the wood, thought of Ola's skin. A Post-it had been forgotten, left on the side of the printer. She unstuck it, read his writing:

Science It! 1,500 words
Rewrite paras 1–5: molecular lock and key
Opiates v dopamine – in layperson's terms

She scrunched the note, binned it. Her thoughts did not need feeding; no call for layperson's terms. She already knew.

Gambling was not a financial plan.

This was not a hobby.

This was not an itch.

This sure as hell was not salvation.

Addiction.

This was addiction.

She was an addict, pure and simple. Squirming, abject, hooked and caught. Player, member, VIP, high-roller, spinner, punter? She was bleeding *prey* and the leaderboard losses spelled out, in a neat microcosm, the true nature of the trap. Amass spins as she might, another VIP would be spinning faster, climbing higher up the board. Spin to win more spins and you would still lose. Win on the rolls, chase, and you would lose: win £100 against the pre-programmed odds, against the entirely legal 95 per cent RTP, that risible Return to Player, and it would never patch up the £1,000 that had gushed from your funds the week before. Bet £2,000 and you could never staunch the £8,000 wound of last month. Spin your way – in insane £100-a-spin bets – to win £10,000, £15,000 even, it would be no gauze pad to heal the livid chasm of £22,000, plus change.

She was an addict.

•

Midnight. She checked the leaderboard. Chumbly71 had won the £10,000 with 4,257 points. She, Nemesis, had earned a mere 2,783 points. She had spun through £13,915 and was tenth, last. Tens of thousands may not even have made the leaderboard, but there were no prizes for coming last.

And this really was it: the last.

The phone went.

'Hello?'

'Hello! This is Neel.'

'Neil?'

'Yes, Neel. From Windows Technical Department.'

'Oh, Godsake no. Why, Neil? Why do you have to lie to people? Why draw people in?'

'I'm sorry, ma'am, I'm calling to tell you that you have a problem with—'

'I have a problem, Neil, yes. I have many, many problems, but my computer's fine, so I won't be sending you my bank details.'

'But—'

'Neil, Neil. I have ninety-nine problems, but a glitch ain't one.' She laughed, a short sick bark.

'I'm sorry?'

Neel sounded almost innocent.

'Oh, Neil. I'm joking! It's all quite funny, really.'

The torpor of gravity; her hand felt so heavy that she lowered the receiver for a moment.

'Yes, ma'am . . . Hello?'

She raised him back to her cheek.

'Did they teach you to say all this crap, Neil?'

'Ma'am?'

'They could at least have told you. Done a bit of background research in Brixton or Bangalore or wherever you are. I mean, "Windows Technical Department". Really?'

'Sorry, ma'am. I don't—'

'They are liars and they've made you a liar.'

'Ma'am? I'm calling you from . . . um . . .'

Etta's free hand reached up to her face. She caressed her small V-shaped scar, the smooth rough-edged dermis, barely perceptible to the touch; that ancient damage.

'How much do they pay you, Neil?'

'I'm sorry?'

'Your pay. How much is it?'

At last, the long pause. 'Ninety rupees an hour.' His voice was now stripped of the smarm.

'What's that? So, hold on . . .' She started googling.

'I'm sorry. I have to go.'

'No! Wait! You're kidding me. You get 90p an hour for this?'

'Sorry I have to—'

'No, stay. Talk to me.'

The dense silence of a suppressed sigh. 'I also get bonuses.'

'Ah,' said Etta. 'Bonuses?'

'Yes.'

'Have you any idea how many rupees I've spent gambling?'

'No. Sorry.'

'No, nor have I. Probably many millions. Yes, here it is: more than four million.'

A gasp. 'Four million?'

'Sick, innit?' she said taking a sharp breath; an acidic stab in her stomach.

'Crazy world,' said Neil.

'Yes! Yes, isn't it? Thank you. Ninety rupees an hour,' she went on. 'Cheaper, much easier.'

'Pardon me, please?'

'Easier to cheat others when you yourself are being cheated, right, Neil?' She closed her eyes, wishing she could see him.

There was no reply.

'What have I done?' she asked.

Silence.

'Win the lottery, suicide, or get myself killed . . . What, Neil? What have I done? What—'

Click.

The call had been cut off. Etta hoped some manner of crooked supervisor had levelled her and Neil's shared edifice to the ground. But to help insulate against a world where the alternative was probable, a midnight feast of wineless water and the last of the ham could do no harm.

Ola was never coming back.

●

Etta woke and reached for her phone. It was 3.07 a.m. She paused, growing alert within that moment of held breath, wondering what had woken her. She rarely started, scared, in the night. No noise from downstairs. Had a window been smashed, or a knocking broken through her wall of sleep?

Sleep-stiff limbs, a numb fuzzing in her belly. She should have eaten more than ham. She wandered to their bathroom. The shock of the strip-light jolted her at the door; she turned to the mirror and saw grey-brown skin, with darkness beneath the eyes. She sat back on the loo and pulled down her knickers. Blood.

Much blood. Everything had gone away.

Etta tugged off her pants and threw them into the bin. She felt nothing she could name bar a need to get clean. She stripped off Ola's T-shirt and crammed herself into the bath, turning on the overhead shower and not minding the weakness of its flow as, too slowly, water mingled with blood and no tears.

After many minutes she stepped out, no longer smelling of Ola. She dried herself, pulled the bag with her underwear in it from the bin, added the T-shirt to it and walked downstairs. She was naked, and didn't care. She unlocked the door and walked to the bin, lifted the lid and tossed away her future.

Risk VI

ZAGREB – MARCH 2016

His skin is a reminder of every prejudice she once left behind. Dark and surprising, pitted in places with tiny, heart-breaking flaws, not unlike her father's worn but polished work shoes. She had friends, real friends who would, even as he sat there, call him 'негър', but she cannot help thinking, despite these too-bright lights which do not help her own cause, that he glows, he shines. He is all beauty and power. Just like Denzel Washington.

He will not want to come up to her room, but he will come. He is solace and, more than that, transformation: the night has been flipped over by his presence; she is no longer alone after being stood up by her dead-end date, called back to heel at the eleventh hour by his wife. Now, she is giddy-lipped and laughing; a touch of her drink sloshes onto the bar; she cries out in a bright rising arpeggio as she sloshes herself a touch off her stool. He puts out a hand, as if to catch her.

'Be careful.'

Yes. She is sure he will not leave her to get to the fourth floor all alone. This thought lights her up from the inside. No, not the thought, they must leave all thoughts to chill; thought is the ice at the bottom of their glasses. This dark man: he is the light.

●

He watches her thinking of moth-flame clichés, and rank impos-
sibilities. He cannot. But he feels responsible, having chatted to
her at the bar for so long. He has involved her, asking her about
her city, her country, as friendly travellers do; he had engaged
with her, at first, to mitigate the dullness of his colleague who
was known, with the laziness of collective irony, as Dan the Man
and spin-offs thereof. Only then had he fully taken in the triple
threat of the woman's hair, the lips, the jutted hip. After an age,
Danny Boy, hay-feverish, myopic and missing the point, had
bored himself into an early bedtime and left him with nothing
to do but buy the woman – Medina – several glasses of wine
that turned out to be full of blackberries and spice, not the thin
vinegar for which he had braced himself.

After an hour or more of that hair, that curious hip and pout,
their movements playing off each other and working in concert
to draw his eye, the small talk has taken on weight and mean-
ing. Earlier, the heart of the evening had blazed with humour
as they joked over rakija and dried figs, all set out on a small
wooden tray as if they were old family; now their night glows
like the last of the embers in the grate. With the ailing Dan-
meister long gone, there is a shocking lack of hindrances. No
witness. No alibi. No excuse.

Yes, he will help her to her room.

•

She is unsteady on her feet; he is stronger than he feels. She is
laughing too loud for the time of night. He laughs and shushes,
then stops; too conspiratorial. She leans on him now as he leads
her, one dense arm resting at her back but not touching the waist
above those hips, up the corridor to the lift, then from the lift to
the room her date had booked, 428.

'Are we here?' she asks. She sounds like a child now.

274

'This is it,' he says. He takes her key card from her and holds it to the door.

She does not say goodnight but leaves the door open wide. She rushes in, twirls 180 degrees and flops onto the bed, letting the bounce from the mattress flip her dress high up her thighs. She lies there on her back, eyes closing.

'Sit with me, please.'

'I've got to go, Medina.'

'Please.'

'OK. Five minutes.'

He pushes the door to and sits on the edge of the bed while she notes with regret that she is growing ever more clear-headed. The alcohol fuzzing her brain feels as if it is draining into the pillow beneath her head, and all her best ideas seeping away with it. He looks ready to stand.

'Tell me about England, please.'

He does not refuse; he does not move.

'It's beautiful. It rains. There is way too much traffic. The people are proud and kind and like to laugh. We love our NHS.'

'I . . .' She swallows the words. 'Yes.'

'And, of course, I am best friends with the Queen.'

'The Queen,' she smiles, her eyes now fully shut, the better to absorb his bedtime stories. 'Is that so?'

'OK, maybe not. But I did see the Duchess of Cambridge, once.'

'Who?'

'You know. Princess Kate Middleton? From about a hundred metres away. I'd gone out to get a coffee.'

'I am going to England.'

'When?'

'I am not sure, but I am going. I look for job.'

'Really? Good for you.'

'They don't want Bosnians here.'

'I'm sorry. But—'

'I will go.'

'I believe you. Thousands would not.'

'Ah.' She did not understand. 'Please, I need help.'

'What?'

'I cannot undress alone.'

He barks a short laugh and then gives a groan that echoes around the painted grey walls. But he does not move off the bed.

She flips over onto her stomach and makes a big intoxicated show of struggling to unzip the back of her dress while lying down. She can hear the hesitation in his silence; she wriggles more, lifting her hips, banging them down again in mock defeat. When she feels the weight of his hands on her lower back, she knows a decision has been made.

He turns, kneels on the bed and pulls; the dress falls open across almond milk shoulders.

One palm lifts away, the other presses on, sliding up onto the expanse of back just below her bra. As it rises, the touch grows firmer; he is holding her beauty, which flows as strong as the Sava river, away, at bay. She knows this. She knows it's no use. She can feel the wondering in the heat of his hand.

'Lie down please, Ola,' she says.

Chapter Fifteen

Etta rolled out of bed as soon as it was time. She was thirsty, longing for the right liquids; a bottle she could only buy in another seventeen minutes' time. She rolled down the stairs, into the car; rolled up the road and padded, too numb to feel ashamed, into the express supermarket to buy its excellent own-brand vodka. A moment of relief when she felt the incontrovertible weight of it in her bag. Whatever she had lost in the night, at least she could now drink without fear.

Reaching her own home, again, she could not face going in. She was frightened of revisiting the scene of after-dark misery. Home, but it had no heart in it.

She placed her handbag in the passenger-seat footwell, reached into it for the bottle, cracked the cap and tried to lift the whole handbag, swaddling the bottle to her mouth. The jangling mess was too much; a lipstick slipped out, a tissue fell to the floor without her getting it to the angle where she could taste vodka. She pulled off the handbag camouflage and held the bottle aloft, relieved; she took two, three, five gulps of a clear no-frills spirit that few Russians would recognise. The heat bloomed in her stomach, but she felt no compulsion to get out of the car, no pull towards the house.

She drank again, looking around at the surrounding area out of the windows, in the rear-view mirror. A slow-passing car or two; Jean chatting on the landline in the half-light of their lounge; a man walking his Labrador. Otherwise, no one. She put the radio on, not too loud, and took a congratulatory swig of vodka as she realised that it was playing Joan Armatrading's 'Love and Affection'.

She surprised herself with a few impassioned croaks from her vodka-warmed throat, then decided to shut up. A dry laugh as she took down more of the spirits and Joan faded out. Many more songs: divas came and went, soulsters gave their thoughts on love, lust and regret. Then started up the wistful piano and chunk-chunk-chunk intro of Eminem's 'Lose Yourself'.

Life could start again, if she could just force herself to go inside. She went to open the door. Then she saw them.

A black 4x4 was parking up across the road. Nadia was in the passenger seat, staring at her. The driver had big shoulders; in the back were two men, one white and one black, both in black shirts.

Etta threw the bottle down hard; it clanked loud against metal under the passenger seat and gushed into the footwell.

She started the car and rammed the gear into reverse as the pungent alcohol stink burgeoned out, filling the car. She swerved out of the drive and hit the accelerator so hard her bad ankle shot pain up her leg. Jean was at her window, looking straight at her. The bulldog owners were crossing the road with their now-placid pet, coming back from a walk. They got in the way of the 4x4 which was trying to steer around them all. She owed that dog.

She sped up the road, drunk, dangerous, desperate.

'Oh God. Oh, God . . .'

The 4x4 had edged past the neighbour and was coming up the road behind her. Without thinking, she was turning right, speeding away towards Ola's new house. The motorway lay five minutes beyond that, and her mum would always—

The petrol light came on the dashboard.

'No. No no no!'

Ola was her only hope.

He was across town but she would have enough petrol to get there. They could not catch her, or she was dead.

She was too scared to feel fully drunk; adrenaline trumping the alcohol. She was flying along on pure fear.

Etta sped past pedestrians and parked cars, seeing the 4x4 coming closer in the background. Every few seconds her eyes flicked to the petrol gauge. 'God. Oh dear God.'

There were traffic lights coming up. No cars ahead. Fast, faster. She sped through on amber and huffed out a breath as she saw the 4x4 slow on red while she raced halfway up the next road. Ola's new house had a garage. She could hide the car, hide herself. He would help, wouldn't he? He bloody owed her. Car, heart and mind racing, she had to pull it together. She had to call ahead. She hit the hands-free and shouted, over-enunciating:

'O-la mob-ile.'

It connected:

'Hello Etta.'

'Ola, I need your help. Please, please, open your garage, get your car out and you have to let me drive straight in, I need to hide, I need to—'

'What are you talking about?'

'Don't ask. I'll explain. I'm minutes away. Just hurry!'

'Have you lost your mind?'

'I told you, I'll explain later. Got to go!'

She hung up and was forced to slow the car as a family stepped onto a zebra crossing. The 4x4 was there, far behind her; not speeding, but there. Sure of itself. Determined.

Etta felt sick.

The family crossed and she stamped her right foot down on the accelerator.

Twenty streets away? Fifteen? Speeding used more petrol. The car had to be running on fumes already.

'Please, please, please . . .' chanted Etta as she sped.

She was close, two streets away when she saw it: the police car turning out to follow her.

She wanted to stop them and beg for help. But she had stabbed, maybe murdered, and stolen and lied. She turned right into Ola's road, and drove not too fast. The police car also turned right. She cruised, sitting upright, puffing her breath until she was just approaching the house. Then several things happened at once:

The police car started blue-lighting, siren screaming.

Etta slammed her numbed bad foot down too hard.

The vodka in her blood finally swamped the adrenaline.

The phone rang, making her jump while she was looking at the police car in the rear-view mirror.

A loud smash. She had driven up onto the pavement and crashed hard into a wall, three houses down from Ola.

She wailed, the siren wailed, terrifying blue flashes: the police car pulled up. Two white male officers got out and approached Etta.

One knocked on the glass.

'Are you OK?' he asked.

'Yes, I think so,' said Etta.

'I need you to get out of the car.'

Etta clambered out, her limbs heavy, her head light, her stomach swimming. She was moving with the grace of a rhino; she wanted to blame her bad foot; she was coming across as drunk. She was drunk.

'Name?'

'Etta Oladipo.'

The officers looked at each other and one wandered away to radio through to the station.

'Etta Oladipo,' said the remaining officer. 'Is this your car?'

'No,' she said, clutching at technicalities. 'It's my partner's.'

'But you were driving it.'

Etta nodded, as it felt less incriminating.

'We saw everything. A responsible member of the public alerted us to your movements and . . . activities.'

'Bloody hell, Jean!' Etta cursed before sense could stop her.

The policeman reared his head back. 'Have you been drinking?'

'No.' The rush of fear was strong and clear, secreting from her pores like ethanol. 'Are you going to breathalyse me? There's no need, is there?'

As she breathed, the officer lifted his chin, an ominous tell; she turned her head away.

'No need. But we'd better, eh? Maybe down at the station. We need to talk to you about some money that's gone missing from your work. FrameTech, isn't it?'

Etta looked around. The 4x4 had seen the police car blocking the road and was doing a three-point turn. They drove off, back the way they had come.

Etta shook her head. 'I'm sorry, I can't help. I need to go—'

'We need you to come with us, for a chat.'

'Please, no!'

'OK then. Etta Oladipo, you are under arrest on suspicion of theft. You are further arrested on suspicion of being unfit to drive through drink or drugs. You do not have to say anything but it may harm your defence . . .'

On they went, saying words she could not bear, could barely comprehend. A hand protected her skull as she ducked into the back of the panda car. The time had come. Not ready; her head swirled, a suffocation of bad thoughts and strong breath. The policemen got back into the car and they drove off. There was nothing she could do: she was a criminal.

Risk VII

She was trembling, the phone shaking in her hand. She had let her fortune come and go. She had missed her chance and she knew it.

Ola was speaking slower than normal, treating her like a child.

'Please, my love, stop crying,' he was saying. 'Listen to me: we will get you to England. I won't let you down.'

'But, Ola, you keep saying this and you say that you love me but I am still here, so far away from you . . .'

'Medina, Medina, hush now, I have been thinking about this, all day and night, my mind turning over and over and—'

'I am losing hope, Ola.'

'No! Never say that. Please. I am making enquiries: my cousin, Akin, he knows people in his town, High Desford. He knows serious people, people who can help, if we pay them.'

'But you keep saying that we have to be patient. How long must I wait?'

'It will be soon, I promise. I am getting the money together for these people, my love. I think this will work.'

'How will I get to England?'

'They have not told Akin all the details yet. There are lorries, there are ways. He swears it can be done, he knows other people who have used this . . . team. They can do it: paperwork, transport, the whole lot.'

'I've been lied to before, Ola. By men promising me a journey to England in their lorry, men I paid. I have been lied to by many men, people I thought I could trust. Why should I trust you? Men lie.'

'I have never lied to you, Medina. My cousin is not lying. They will get you to England – the person who can help is no lying man, heh? She told Akin to call her Nadia. She will do it, if we pay her right.'

A silence of a long moment.

'I am afraid, Ola.'

A beat more silence.

'Do you remember, Medina, the first time I flew back out to Zagreb just to meet you again. Do you?'

'Yes.'

'I told you I would do anything to keep you.'

'Yes.'

'Well, this is my anything.'

'OK, Ola,' she said at last. 'Please, just get me to you.'

Chapter Sixteen

The policeman by the door clears his throat, a fist up against his dark beard. The blond man rises and moves away so his colleague can approach the desk. This other man, PC Howard, who she had assumed to be a junior officer, sits down in the vacated seat, taking his time about taking up space, telling her – with his amused stare, and the entitled set of his arms and chest, stretching back, now leaning close – he is in charge.

'How?' he asks.

'How what?' she says.

'How the hell have you got here?'

She looks up. The losses, and the risks, and the lies; the terrible fun, and the wrong men, and the surprising choices, and the victories; the boundaries breached and the many rivers of cash crossed; the unknowable connections, pathways and turns, a constellation spreading backwards to infinity; all that has brought her to this point.

'Just lucky, I guess.'

She cast him a wan smile. The urine glare of the overhead lighting would be doing regrettable things to her face, not that it mattered.

'Etta, you have been arrested and charged under Section 4 of the Road Traffic Act. You have been informed of your rights and declined to see a solicitor, to inform a third party of your presence here or to consult the Police Codes and Practice.'

'That's right. I believe so, yes.'

'OK then. Etta, is this your first offence?'

'It's the first time I've been arrested, yes.'

She tried a smile.

PC Howard allowed own his teeth some controlled exposure.

'One more time for the record: have you been drinking today, Etta?'

Now Etta did smile, which surprised her. 'You know I have.'

'According to your breath samples, you had well over 100 milligrams of alcohol in your blood. You're looking at a serious penalty here, Etta.'

She wished he would not say her name. As if he liked her. As if he owned her. As if he hated her and everything she had done and everything she was, which is why she was here. Hate was currently beyond her, what with the walls closing down and the piss-yellow light accentuating her flaws, but she could not get past his power to destroy her life.

'I know I'll get points. Will I—'

'You could be looking at prison.'

'Oh.' Her shoulders dropped and she eyed scuffs on the table. Teeth marks, maybe; police brutality?

'Why did you drink this morning, Etta?'

Howard judged her to be a booze-battered loser, but she would make him see. She softened her features into a more likeable expression once again.

'I was upset.'

'Why?'

'Because my partner has moved out and he's living with this other woman. This woman he met years ago. Probably been with her, too, ever since. And I'd just miscarried his baby. I thought I deserved some vodka.'

'But why did you drive?'

For a second, she saw Nadia, glaring from that monstrous black car.

'It was stupid. I thought I would go to confront him again, tell him about the miscarriage, and I sat in the car for a while, then just ... drove. I should never have started the car, I'm sorry.'

'You could've killed someone. You really have been lucky.'

'Doesn't feel like it just now.'

She looked at him, straight and clear-eyed, trying again to connect.

'Your first offence,' he said.

'Yes.'

She gave another smile that was working hard to shine; too hard, it was a grimace of desperation.

Howard puffed out his cheeks and sat back in his chair.

'We need to talk about other possible offences.' He leaned forward again. 'What happened to the money in FrameTech's Funshine Club accounts, Etta? You took it, didn't you? That what's really been getting to you, right?'

She, the detainee, started to feel the walls push back an inch. He also wanted to be liked.

'I want to tell you everything,' she said. The words dislodged the mound in her throat that threatened to choke her. 'But you have to promise ... I'm afraid.'

Howard leaned back. He looked scoured and firm-fleshed, but softness hid there, too. The man seemed generous.

'Etta, you really should call your solicitor.'

287

'I'm not sure we, I, have one.'

'You're in a serious situation. Use the duty solicitor; I really would.'

A clenched fist now started opening and closing low down in her abdomen.

'I can explain—'

'You need legal advice.'

Etta had to get out. It was madness to draw things out like this, police stations were no place for people like her. But agreeing to a solicitor . . . it was the point at which the girl started running in the fright movie.

Howard shifted in his seat, flexed his fingers, stilled his features.

Etta stared at the table.

Seconds ticked on.

When the realisation kicked in, Etta nodded, as if one of them had spoken again. She nodded and nodded, not sure she could stop; she looked at the man who was waiting for her, so wide and tall and patient.

'PC Howard,' she said. 'I need to tell you something.'

•

Etta straightened her shoulders, took a sip of water.

'Gambling.'

The word rang in the air.

'How often?'

'A lot. Every day. All the time. Usually drunk.'

'Why didn't you let your husband know that you were struggling?'

'Partner, ex.' She took a breath. 'I wasn't, at first. It wasn't the drink. Not in itself. I was just trying to . . . you know.'

'What, Etta? What exactly were you trying to do?'

Etta groped to unlock the door in her mind that had trapped her for weeks, months. Could she set herself free, here in this policed room? Her chin drooped to her chest. This left her no more breath so very quietly she said:

'I wanted to win.'

She could see PC Howard flipping over a fresh page in his own mind.

'Win what?'

'Win everything. Everything. Or at least a few good things. Or one massive thing.'

'What do you mean?'

'Marriage. I wanted money to get married. What a joke!'

'So, you gambled to save for your wedding.'

'I think,' she said, warming up, 'I was trying to buy a proposal from a man who was not worth it. That's all.'

'That would be . . . Doctor Abayomi?'

'Yes, Ola.'

Howard was still leaning in.

'So, how did you try to win, precisely? On the horses, scratchcards, what?'

'Online.'

The officer shifted in his seat.

'If you could only understand,' she said. 'It started out well. It was amazing, really. I won, at first. But then I lost and I won, then I lost more and I could not escape from it and it was *everywhere* . . .'

'What?'

'Slots, online slots. I just played the bingo at first, for a short while, then I went onto the slots. Then I couldn't stop.' She looked back down at the table. 'I can't.'

PC Howard seemed to be processing her words and tilted his head further forward; a groove between his eyebrows.

In that moment, she could feel and hear everything in the room: the scrape of fingernail against hair and skin as PC Howard scratched at the back of his hand; the scrape of the chair leg as the other policeman shifted an inch; the exact quality of the light, which struck her as not just tainted grey-yellow but, like her smiles, too weak and uncanny; the squeeze of her gums as her molars pressed hard into each other and released; the slow drift of a rogue strand of the other policeman's hair, as if teased by her breath; everything.

The police waited. She suspected they were aware of her new hyper-awareness – maybe every detainee experienced this advanced state.

The second policeman coughed.

The heft and generosity were now overlaid with something else. Purpose.

'So, Etta. You have a gambling problem.'

'You could say that.'

A moment's silence. His eyebrows worked themselves higher.

'How exactly have you funded all this gambling? Where did you get the money?'

'Loans. Payday loans, mostly . . . I'm sorry. Would it be at all possible, please, to call my partner now?'

'You changed your mind,' said Howard.

'Yes. I'd like to speak to him.'

Howard rose. 'I'll go and talk to the Custody Sergeant, then I'm off duty.'

'You're going?' A plaintive note hung in her question, close to a whine.

Howard said, 'Let's get that phone call sorted out for you.'

'Thank you.'

'Wait here.'

Etta was left sitting at the table. She looked up to the CCTV camera. She was not going anywhere.

After some minutes Howard and another officer returned carrying a phone.

'You can call your partner.'

'Thank you.'

It rang just once.

'Ola, I need—'

'What the fucking hell have you done? Your work called me. Jean? You stole from work too? They said they were going to contact the police, Etta! Etta?'

She hung up. Her mind was stunned stupid, drained of thoughts.

'All OK?' Howard asked. He was giving her a look that pinned her to her chair.

'Not really.'

'Well, what happened?'

She shook her head.

Howard held out his hand for the phone.

'I'll take this back, then. I've got to go now. PC Jameson will finish up here. Goodbye, Etta.'

'Wait!'

PC Howard turned.

She could tell him everything, now. Better than being finished off by Nadia's gang of thugs. She could tell about the vast sums of money wasted, about plundering of bank accounts, tell them about the credit card fraud and, yes, every last thing about taking the money from the Funshine Club before Jean got there first. Spit out all the poison in one fast confession. Cough up every dirty sin and hope for clemency. She could do it. Or . . . She could keep her counsel, hope for some piece of luck to change the seemingly inevitable path. Twist or stick?

We are all, at heart, gamblers.

'Nothing,' she said.

●

Outside, it was a dry afternoon. The sunlight was still a glittering, eye-hurting, white; too much, the planet was running a fever, the climate was hotting up. The rays kissed her face as she walked away from the police station. Long-dead emissions from the sun's photosphere, dangerous and yet welcome on her cheeks. This stark bright shining. She had thought a lot about the nature of light and dark, what each meant, in recent weeks.

No rain today or coming storm.

Out on bail. Her stomach was still twisting from the fear that she would never leave the station. But freedom brought more fear. Could she go back to the home where the gang had found her? Was she hurrying to her death?

She turned away from the police station, back towards the eerie calm of that moment. The afternoon had set in, the sun no longer at its highest point; illumination was everything. She wanted to move her feet, but the thoughts billowed and swirled; she could not move.

All that waiting and hoping to marry him. The whole £30,000 target – all of it, one huge lie, an easy excuse. The coward had been buying time to gather more money then leave.

He would have gone sooner had he not been worrying about losing his post; he had clearly planned to lean on her little salary until he had secured his job. Medina's demeanour did not speak of hard times. Etta's wages had pretty much paid for that ring. That symbol of together-forever that she had been a fool to want from that man. The worst though was even worse than that: she had lied and stolen and cheated and gambled and drunk a whole lake and swerved living and sweated and lost everything for *absolutely nothing.*

•

Home. There was nowhere else.

She shifted from foot to damaged foot on the pavement, bruised, uncertain, waiting for a sign. Ola was furious with her, that was completely out. Maybe it was not too late to reach out to Joyce; maybe Joyce had forgiven her or could be persuaded to. Maybe—

Her phone buzzed with a text.

The name 'Chris Wise' flashed up; Nadia.

One word:

Laters

Her final option closed down. The gang would be at her house, waiting. Death was waiting.

She edged to the roadside and stood, waiting to cross, not sure she would be able to move her feet when the way was clear. This was what it meant: to be petrified. But she did cross the road, one foot following the other; she reached the next road and waited again. A middle-aged couple with a small dark boy passed before her on the opposite pavement. The boy, aged around four or five, broke free, making a run for it. A flock of pavement-pecking birds flew high up out of his path. Etta feared he himself would fly into the road, but he stopped to stare at a fluffy dog.

'Hassan!' his grandmother cried out. 'That boy. Always he be running.'

Etta felt a jolt. Why not? Why not run into this road, like a free woman, like a child . . . Her eyes locked with Hassan's for a moment. His brown stare was so pure, so undoubting.

run

Etta walked on, then picked up the pace and started to almost jog, pain pounding in her right foot. When she reached a road, she ran into the traffic, looking straight ahead. A white van was racing towards her. Etta kept running. The van braked hard, invective streaming out of the half-open driver's side window. Etta reached the far pavement unscathed. She turned left, raced past a parade of shops. She pushed on faster, into a hobbling sprint, pain to bludgeon the fear at each step, doing damage now to save herself. Nadia's lot were coming after her, she knew it.

When they caught her, they would kill her.

She had nowhere to go, nowhere to run but home. They knew where she lived and they were on their way.

She ran. But with every step she knew she was out of time. Out of luck.

•

At the end of Sycamore Road, she stopped dead.

This was it.

She looked as far up the street as she could. Parked cars up both sides. No black 4x4 that she could see. It meant nothing: they could be in any car; anyone could jump out from anywhere.

All she could do was get inside the house, get safe. She delved into her bag, scrabbled until she held her front door key between thumb and forefinger. She needed a plan, but her mind felt as battered as her right foot.

run

She pounded raggedly up the street, her feet on fire, her mind too alert not to feel; this was blistering agony now.

Legs, lungs and heart were throbbing, sore as her head by the time she reached her front door. No sign of forced entry.

Her hand shook as she jabbed the key at the lock.

She hurried inside and ran upstairs to the landing. Already short of breath, it winded her, being back. Gasping, she looked into the bedroom where she and Ola had lain and lied together for so long. She struggled for air in the bathroom where she had lost whatever promise they had in blood. She limped into the spare room where she had made a world out of chance; tried to build a life on ever-spinning foundations; where she had risked everything.

How could the ceiling hold it up, all this?

One last roll of the die.

She had to hurry.

She powered up her laptop. Straight to it: not a gambling site, but to the copy she had long ago made of the file Mots-depasse. In seconds she had the details for the account she had spotted on his list, MO Money. She had wondered, at the time, whether it might be secret savings for a honeymoon. A super-luxe, someday honeymoon. That had been the only reason she had not touched it, this shining £11,542, this undeclared amount that could have seen them over his lie of a £30,000 finishing line. MO, Medina-Ola Money; it made sense now. It could well be meant for a honeymoon, just not her own.

She tapped in the password on the old doc:

ETTAO1!

Cruel, making her the shrieking guardian of their secret lovers' fund. A violation of her—

The password did not work. Caps lock was off. She tried again, in case she had mis-typed.

Again, no entry.

Etta closed her eyes. He had changed the password since she had copied the document, securing himself against further theft, against her. What the hell was the password? If she got locked out now, it was all over.

Think.

She had thought she knew Ola. But he was someone else altogether. What words would he use, this other Ola? She had no time, no more chances.

A click at the back of her mind. Eyes wide open, with growing horror, she typed:

MEDINAA1!

Click. She was in.

A simple substitution. No time for the grief, the rage, the indignation. No time. She hovered the cursor over the button that would move the cash into her account.

She should not.

Two wrongs did not make a right.

But they could still be very happy together.

TRANSFER

Her FOF. Joyce had been right and she would get on her knees and beg for the chance to thank her, if she survived all this. God only knew if she would see her ever again, or anyone she loved.

It only took another second to then transfer £1,600 from her account; half a moment more to text her former friend:

Rent x 4. Sorry 4Eva Exx

An engine revved hard in the street below. A violent surge of fear.

Them, already? She was as good as trapped.

She opened the top drawer of the desk and rifled for the envelope where she kept her passport. Snatching it out, she ran downstairs to the sitting room. From where she stood, she could see the dim lights on across the street, feel that grim old soul willing her to fail, to lose for good. Perhaps calling the police on her again.

It was no use. What had she been thinking? She had just dug deeper, made it all worse.

She leaned her back against the wall and sank down onto her heels. The shadows danced in the far corner. As she stared at them, she dreamed, seeing the reels rolling; they turned and merged until they became one globe; the whole world spinning, fast and tilted and light.

She would stay, close her eyes at last and let death come for her.

A vibration roused her. Light glowed from her phone; an unknown number was ringing. A landline, official. Her thumb hovered, trembling.

That second another ring: the doorbell. She let out a whimper. Run out the back door, or would they be waiting? The side window was high; what if she turned her ankle again and could not run? But if she did not answer? She could not cower in the dark forever, the police would learn all she had done at any moment.

She had to see.

Phone still ringing, she walked, slow and shaking, to the hallway and looked through the ridged glass of the front door: black clothes, black skin.

Etta killed the call. She reached for the handle, and paused, all her thoughts fluttering up, a flock of startled birds. One thought alighting, at last.

His long scar appeared to brighten; touched by the porch-light through the warped pane: the moment's puzzle reformed into the complete picture.

'It's you.'

His eyes locked with hers, full of light; as bright as his silver badge: B. Motilewa. He was holding a sealed tub; a strong savoury smell came from it.

'I should have brought you my *egusi* sooner, I'm sorry, but I have had to work. You will like it!'

A coming down from horror; something good swelling beneath the fear.

Etta said, 'I thought—'

'Are you OK?' Concern creased Bankole's face. 'Why are you looking like this?'

Etta blinked hard; no tears should splash this new dark uniform. He made a smart security guard.

'I need to get out of here, Bankole,' she said, looking past his shoulder. 'Fast.'

'Why,' he asked. 'Is someone after you?'

'Not just now,' she said. 'But they will be.'

'Don't worry, I am here. Your First Welcome people, they told me about this . . . place. I have cash job for this week. And I have this for you.'

He put the tub back in his bag, reached into his breast pocket, pulled out a small package wrapped in red paper and held it out to her.

'Bankole, I can't—'

'Please, Etta,' he said.

With still shaking hands, she ripped the paper. It was a small dark wood carving; a man or god bearing a double-headed axe.

'It's beautiful,' said Etta. 'Thank you so much. But I have to go.'

'Shango. He will strike down your enemies with thunder. He is also the best lover-god in all Nigeria.'

Etta gave a small laugh, despite herself.

'It is for good luck,' Bankole went on. 'I had to see you.'

'Just in time,' she said. 'I am going to prison, or—'

'Wha? Non-*sense*. I will protect you, Etta Oladipo,' he said.

'You can't,' she said, taking a small step back. 'The police or the bad men will get me.'

'Etta. You have man?'

'No,' she said.

'I am a good-good man.'

'I believe you,' said Etta, leaning forward again. 'But right now I am good for no one and I have shedloads more to worry about than dating.'

'You need to get away,' he said.

'Yes,' she said.

'We can go to Paris, stay with my cousin,' he said. 'She arrived last month and married her businessman. We are a good family; she is always good to me. You must come with me. Then, we shall see. I have been thinking about staying or going, staying or going . . . My head has been turning and turning. Like the Earth itself. I will go away, for you.'

'But you told me that if you leave this country you will never get back in.'

'I know this.'

She felt hurt as she looked at that long crescent scar, running from lip to chin; she also felt pure gratitude. Thankfulness that such a man should exist. Damaged, still he went on, that face looking out at the world, bearing his dignity and his ruin.

Her eyes grew wet. Her foot ached, her chest ached.

'They'd stop me at the airport, Bankole. There's no way.'

'There are lorries, you know . . .'

'God . . .'

Bankole reached his hands towards her, palms out as if hesitating to touch something fragile.

'A woman like you should not go to prison.'

'I lied, I stabbed, I stole, Bankole.'

'Why did you do it? You drink too much. Weh you drunk?'

Another, fuller laugh burst out of her, sending the brimming tears down her cheeks, and he laughed too. Then she started to cry in earnest. 'The whole . . . damn time. It was like this . . . temporary insanity, like this . . . this . . .'

'I will be your friend, Etta. It is my turn to help you. My cousin's husband has promised me a good job in his office. No puzzles, no security guarding! Come with me!'

'I can't,' she said.

'I no fall your hand, Yoruba woman,' he said. 'I won't let you down.'

'It's just so—'

'Etta Oladipo. Please come with me.'

She once more scanned the street for a black car.

'I'm sorry. It's impossible.'

He turned and walked away, slowly; she could feel every step of the distance growing between them, her silence pushing at his back.

Etta looked down at the carving. Such an immortal gift to come of a tree hewn three thousand miles away; a straight-up solid little thing, from roots twisted but true. Radiant yet dark; it softened her. An impossible thing.

As he walked away, she pressed her thumb into the wood, so hard that it hurt.

'Bankole!' she cried.

He turned.

One soaring look. It staked everything and asked her to do the same.

We are all gamblers.

The dying day grew bright as the words flew from her depths, all-conquering, lightning fast:

'I'm coming.'

Risk VIII

LONDON – JUNE 2018

She stands on the steps of the registry office.

It feels like a mistake to have arrived first and alone. She had insisted that it would be best to meet him here, fresh from Dee at the salon. It is best, probably, as now she still has time. She can still tell him, give him the chance to walk away.

Medina looks up at the ivy framing the arched door with its variegated green gloss. Certainly more beautiful than the building up the road from their house which she had favoured: it reminds her of her primary school in Bosnia. But Ola had not wanted them to marry in Rilton itself; she had not pushed it, they were close enough.

She looks down the wide street. It is what he calls leafy. The houses are bigger, crouching further back, away from the road and from passing strangers. Maybe, one day . . . No, that had to be someone else's dream. She does not need a haven for a family. She just needs to be safe.

A taxi drives up the road; it does not stop. She fiddles with the gleaming cuff on her wrist. London silver, a gift. He will be here soon.

Her man – funny and full-feeling; strong yet nimble of head and heart; extravagantly in love with her – this man is not without his complications. He has told her about the woman he owes, that it requires slow disentanglement, for reasons of money and loyalty and, she suspects, shared roots – you don't disrespect your own, right?

They do not ask too much of each other, but they give much.

He wants her, which is why neither of them could wait to share a home, already furnished with more memories worth saving than she has ever known. It is the only way to keep her in this country and he needs her. He has already risked everything for her, digging around for information among the associates of friends of his High Desford cousins, asking for contacts who might help them with passports, papers. The woman who called herself Nadia had charged a fortune for her services, but the papers had been flawless, the service end-to-end. He got his cousin to sort out the details, and kept well away from all the goings-on, but even so, he had risked everything to get her to his home country. This is why he will be here soon.

She needs to play it straight with him from now on. He deserves it.

She will tell him, one day soon: no children.

She will tell him, once again, that England has healed her and that marriage to him would heal her further.

They will live past the lies and then truly give everything, the full works, to each other. She believes this, here and now, waiting on these white steps.

A whisper of breeze where the edge of her cream shift meets her nape makes her shiver. Turning to look back up the avenue, she sees a black man in a blue suit, peacock teal, he had called it, the colour of the eye on that fine bird's feather. The shine on his shoes is visible from where she stands; the expression on his face, she cannot see.

Out of nowhere, an almighty rattling as a million ice stones start bouncing off the pavements.

He ducks into a shop doorway; she edges under the portico. They wait, looking at each other.

Hail in June? A miracle or a curse?

Moments later the frozen downpour stops as abruptly as it began.

He walks back out onto the pavement, suit saved.

Here he comes.

Acknowledgements

To my editor, the brilliant Anna Kelly: your belief spurs me on, your standards raise me up, you are beyond wonderful. Thank you.

Joanna, my dear agent and friend, you have shown faith in this novel as it has evolved from ever-burgeoning ideas to the printed page. I am grateful every day for you, Thérèse, and the whole Hardman & Swainson team, and I look forward to enjoying many more literary adventures together.

Michelle Kane, you suggested that the days after my debut, *Darling*, might be a rollercoaster experience – sure enough, it has been quite a ride! Looking forward to our *Lucky* trip. Very many thanks and let's book in those post-Covid cocktails, as soon as.

Most sincere thanks to David Roth-Ey, Matt Clacher, Liv Marsden, Paul Erdpresser, Malissa Mistry, Bethan Moore, Tara Hiatt and Lucy Vanderbilt. Your support means the world.

I adore the cover, Jo Thomson, thank you for wholly capturing the *Lucky* spirit.

Many thanks also to Essie Cousins, Eve Hutchings and Katy Archer; thank you to Anne O'Brien for copy-editing; thank you to Martin Bryant for proofreading. My deepest gratitude to the rest of the 4th Estate team and HarperCollins

– with a special shout-out to Elevate! You have all been fantastic.

To Robert Peett, thank you for your reassurance that my early attempts to write my 'gambling novel' mattered.

The Private Life of the Brain, by Baroness Professor Susan Greenfield, particularly the passages about addiction, made for fascinating and fruitful holiday reading circa 2011, and is as brilliant a neuroscientific page-turner as I am ever likely to come across.

Thanks to the College of Policing for the help on being arrested and other aspects of detention I hope never to experience.

To Professor Chris Jones of The Institute of Cancer Research. The tour of the lab where you do your work inspired well beyond research; what I learned lingered more in my mind than on the page. Your scientific endeavour is a force for good, and profoundly humbling.

To the exceptional authors, too many to mention, who I have met since publishing *Darling*. I appreciate the huge support and thank you for welcoming this relative newcomer into the fold. Special thanks to the Ant to my erstwhile BBC Berkshire Book Club Dec (or vice versa), Jenny Quintana, and to the wonderful #Ladykillers.

To all my closest friends: thank you for your continued support and enthusiasm for me and for my writing; for telling the world about my novels; for your love, laughter, wit and wisdom, and for giving me the most memorable souvenirs from this mad journey that is life – you know who you are.

To Emma and Charlie, thanks for your ongoing patience and love for this stepmother who has always preferred writing to almost any useful endeavour (at least until lockdown lured her into baking bread). She loves you to distraction.

To my husband, Peter, thank you for everything, forever. That does not quite cover it, but I hope my love always will.

To my mother and my late father. Mum and Dad: you rolled the die and landed here in England, a doctor from Nigeria and a nurse from Negril, a beauty of the Windrush Generation. A lot happened. I happened. At the end of it all, this book, which goes back to the beginning.

Here's to the best and bravest gambles that we take.